Juniper's Christmas

ALSO BY EOIN COLFER

Juniper's Christmas

EOIN COLFER

Roaring Brook Press

New York

Published by Roaring Brook Press
Roaring Brook Press is a division of Holtzbrinck Publishing Holdings
Limited Partnership
120 Broadway, New York, NY 10271 • mackids.com

Our books may be purchased in bulk for promotional, educational,
or business use. Please contact your local bookseller or the Macmillan
Corporate and Premium Sales Department at (800) 221-7945 ext. 5442 or
by email at MacmillanSpecialMarkets@macmillan.com.

Library of Congress Cataloging-in-Publication Data is available.

First edition, 2023
Printed in the United States of America by Lakeside Book Company,
Harrisonburg, Virginia

ISBN 978-1-250-32194-7 (hardcover)
1   3   5   7   9   10   8   6   4   2

For Christmas babies everywhere

Prologue

I'm sure you know Santa's story. Everyone knows it, but since it's one of the greatest tragedies of all time I shall summarize here before we move on to the story of a girl from London who would track down Santa Claus when he hid himself away from the world.

It all started one Christmas past when young Nicholas Claus was getting a feel for his future job by working as a postman in North London. One lunchtime, Nicholas met a university student in Cedar Park who was volunteering at a local shelter and spoke so passionately about helping the people experiencing homelessness that Nicholas was utterly and immediately besotted. The young woman, Sarika, may not have been quite so quickly smitten, but she agreed to a first date, and then another, and then a third, by which time Sarika realized that she had found her true love.

And so Nicholas Claus confessed his family secret, and when Sarika had finished her degree they moved to the North Pole. There they tied the knot under what all the wedding guests agreed was the most magnificent aurora borealis in years. Young Nicholas eventually inherited his father's magical work sack and took over the family business.

And they lived happily ever after.

Not exactly ever after.

But for a time.

Nicholas made a most excellent Santa. He was a list man by nature, was as strong as a horse, had a way with animals, and liked cookies a little too much. He grew into the job with the support of his wife, Sarika. But the mantle of Father Christmas weighs heavily on a soul, and after forty years or so Nicholas found himself growing disheartened with his job. Even though Christmas Eve flashes by in a single night for most people, for Nicholas, inside a bubble of Santa Slow Time, it went on for more than a year. So that made forty years in all during which he did not see his beloved wife and put on several kilos thanks to a diet of mince pies and cookies. His frustration was only increased by elf reports showing that more and more North Pole presents were being dumped every season while still in their wrapping paper.

And then one year Sarika fell ill. Very ill, in fact, and there was nothing elfin doctors could do to save her with either tools or magic. Santa could not bear to let his beloved wife go, and so he broke one of the rules of the North Pole and took his wife along on the Christmas Eve trip.

Sarika and Nicholas lived in Santa Slow Time for over a year, and that time changed Niko forever. He watched his wonderful wife struggle bravely with her illness, and with every present delivered he resented more and more the demands of children who took him from Sarika's side. Finally, when the last gift was tucked under the last tree, Niko realized that he was keeping Sarika with him for his own benefit, although she never complained and hardly ever let the pain show in her eyes.

He knew it was time to let her go.

And so, when Niko landed the sleigh at the North Pole, he wrapped Sarika up in her favorite blanket, and they watched the aurora borealis one last time. When Niko felt Sarika's spirit leave her body, he cried bitter tears, and he thought: *That's it for me, dearest. I have given enough to this job.*

Niko buried the love of his life in glacier ice and flew

the sleigh out of the North Pole, resolving to honor his wife's nature by helping those who really needed his talents just as Sarika had always tried to do.

This all happened some years ago, and Santa Claus hasn't officially delivered any presents since then.

1

Juniper

When Juniper Lane's father died, one of the more thoughtless children in her class, a boy by the name of Rusty Johannes, commented that she was halfway to being an orphan. A remark that he'd felt certain would make eight-year-old Juniper cry in front of the other children on the playground. However, Juniper had fixed him with quite a piercing gaze and said, "I think you must be very unhappy to say that, Rusty. Is everything all right at home?"

Her father had often said, "Mean words are the fruit of a sad tree," so Juniper couldn't help wondering what sad thing was making Rusty so mean. After a few days' surveillance, Juniper deduced that the main reason for Rusty's meanness was that he didn't seem to have any lunch most days. And so Juniper asked her mother for an extra sandwich in her own lunchbox, which she slipped to Rusty in the cloakroom before assembly every morning. This secret sandwich drastically improved Rusty's mood and, because the sandwich was made with high-fiber bread, it improved his bathroom regularity too.

That little episode should tell you quite a lot about Juniper Lane and what a special person she was.

Before we get swept into Juniper's adventures with Santa Claus, we should deal with the name Juniper Lane, which seems to refer to a place rather than a person. There's a simple explanation for this. Juniper's father, Briar Lane, had been the park-keeper for London's Cedar Park and so, when Juniper was born on Christmas morning, it seemed only fitting that the Lanes should name their beautiful daughter for the *Juniperus virginiana* or red cedar Christmas trees after which the park was also named.

When the smitten parents brought baby Juniper back to their cottage in Cedar Mews on Boxing Day, after only a single night in the Portland Hospital's maternity ward, it seemed as though all three would live happily ever after.

And they did.

Not exactly ever after.

But for a time.

Eight years and nine months to be exact.

Then Briar Lane died from an undiagnosed heart condition, and Juniper cried every night for over two years.

Let's pick up the story from there.

2

Jennifer Juniper

That year was to be the tenth Christmas since Santa Claus had stepped down from his position, which meant there was an entire generation of children who knew nothing about him apart from the facts that he never showed up when he was supposed to and their teenage siblings never stopped going on about how amazing he'd been. And, truth be told, this generation of Santa-Claus-free kids were getting a little fed up of Santa stories anyway. Many of them were inclined not to really believe in an oversized elf who rode a magical reindeer carriage around the entire globe in a single night.

The idea that children would forget about Santa Claus horrified Briar Lane, a man who had come to London from Ghana via the Mediterranean, and who'd spent his youth in children's homes. He often told Juniper how the yearly

Christmas gift had been one of the beacons of hope in his tough childhood.

"Santa Claus found me every year. So I always knew that someone cared enough to choose a gift especially for me."

And then he would show Juniper his most treasured gift from Santa Claus. It was a worn book entitled *Tomescu's Complete Guide to Flora*, and they would pore over the beautiful illustrations together.

"I never knew there was a love of plants inside me, but Santa did," Briar would say every time. "This book gave me a direction. It kept me going until I met your mother, which saved my life."

And so, after Santa had been gone for four whole years, Briar initiated what he hoped would become a new Cedar Park custom: the Santa Vigil. This gathering of Christmas carolers would take place in the park on Red-Letter Day, which as everybody knew was 18 December, the absolute last chance for children to write their Christmas lists.

The vigil started off as a small gathering of Christmas enthusiasts who simply sang carols to the stars in the hope that Santa would somehow hear and have a change of heart, but over the years it morphed into something more. Cedar Park had become a haven for people who were forced, or chose, to live outdoors, and so it was natural that the Santa Vigilers, being full of the Christmas spirit, would start to bring donations for them. After a couple of years, there were so many donations that Briar had to set up a registered charity just to deal with them all, and Juniper's mum, Jennifer, spent December and January handing out the gifts.

And now, on the second year after Briar had passed away, Juniper and Jennifer Lane were preparing for the park's annual vigil. It was not *strictly* speaking annual, as Jennifer and Juniper had let it slide the year before. They had been too overcome with grief to even think about putting together an event that took more organizing than a person might realize.

"But it will be annual again from now on," Jennifer had told Juniper. "Your dad started the Santa Vigil so we're going to keep it going. His legacy is kindness to our fellow humans."

After her husband died, Jennifer became, at first, a sort of unpaid park-keeper. About a month after that most terrible of days, Jennifer had tugged on Briar's work boots and ventured out into the park, doing any little jobs that needed tackling just to distract herself. Then, after a bit, when the council realized they needed a new park-keeper, they also realized that they already had one, and since there were no other applicants for the job, Jennifer was hired.

✷ ✷ ✷

Earlier that day, Jennifer sent Juniper out into Cedar Park with a stack of Santa Vigil flyers and a backpack full of woolen socks.

"I'd like everyone to turn up this year, Junie," she told Juniper. "And bring Duchess in. The forecast is subzero, and her chest is bad. I've sent her a text asking her to watch you as a cover. Once I get her in here, I'll dust off the nursing degree and have a listen to her chest."

This was excellent news for three reasons:

1. Mum had called Juniper "Junie," which she hadn't for almost two years. Junie had been her father's pet name for her and even saying it made Jennifer Lane cry. It had the opposite effect on Juniper because hearing it reminded her of her father, which made her smile.

2. Duchess was coming to hang out, and that was great because Juniper loved Duchess, and . . .

3. The fact that Mum was bringing in Duchess meant that the Mews' spare room was once again open to homeless visitors, which in turn meant that Mum was on the road to being her old self.

And, after this excellent news, Juniper's mum bent down and wiggled her nose. Juniper's heart lifted because she knew what to do. She placed her index finger on her mum's nose and sang, "Jennifer."

Mum placed her own index finger on Juniper's nose and sang the response: "Juniper." It was something Dad used to do on his way out to work every morning. It had been the Lane family version of a high five. There had been three people involved in the greeting, and in a way there still were three, even though one was only present in the hearts of his family.

But the positive thing about this was that before today Mum hadn't responded to any of Juniper's attempts to perform the Jennifer-Juniper routine since Briar's death, and now she had been the one to start it off with a nose wiggle.

"It's time the Lane girls made a comeback," said Mum. "Your father used to say that even on a cloudy day the sun is always in the sky."

"But it's okay to be sad too?" said Juniper. "At night sometimes. Or when I walk past Dad's shed? Or when I sit on his bench?"

When Briar had passed away, the council had installed a new bench in Cedar Park's amphitheater with a brass plaque that read:

BRIAR LANE. HUSBAND OF JENNIFER, FATHER OF JUNIPER, KEEPER OF CEDAR PARK AND ALL ITS RESIDENTS.

It was such a lovely dedication that Juniper had done a brass rubbing of the plaque and kept it framed on her bedroom wall.

"Of course it's okay to be sad," said Jennifer. "As a matter of fact, it's healthy. Your dad was a great guy and a fantastic hugger."

"And a top-class piggyback-giver," said Juniper seriously.

"I'll have to take your word for that, sweetie," said Jennifer. "You were his only passenger."

Juniper remembered something. "Dad charged two Smarties per piggyback. I owe him twenty Smarties."

This kind of thing was usually enough to set Mum

crying, and Juniper regretted saying it as soon as it was out, but today Jennifer just smiled. "I'm sure the Bank of Briar will waive your debt if you keep his brass plaque nice and shiny."

"Deal," said Juniper, and they shook on it.

Juniper left the cottage in a bit of a happy daze.

Could things actually all work out? Was it possible to keep going in life even when one of the two people you loved most in the universe was gone?

She didn't know for sure just yet, but the signs were positive. Mum had been in a good mood. Not brilliant but good. And what's more she had promised Juniper a big surprise later.

"I need to nip over to Sandra's, and when I get back there'll be a big surprise for you, my girl. The Lane girls are turning a corner."

This is all good stuff, Juniper thought. *Very positive. We're turning a corner today.*

She was right about the turning a corner, but wrong about the positive.

Juniper summarized all her news in a text and shot it off to her best friend, Jade, who had been taken out of school a week early to spend December with relatives in Jamaica. It was a trip her family had been planning for over two years, and originally Juniper was supposed to go along.

Maybe next time, thought Juniper. *When Mum can do without me for a while.*

She went out the back door directly into the park with her mum's command to stay on the path ringing in her ears. Not that Juniper would be going anywhere on her own. She could actually see Duchess over by the main gate.

The upswing in Jennifer's mood put a little extra pep in Juniper's step, and she sang on her way through the small patch of back garden and across the mulch border to the park's cobble path.

"Jennifer Juniper."

She was into her third repeat when Duchess heard her coming.

"Jennifer Juniper? I haven't heard you singing that in a long time."

Duchess was somewhere in her fifties and from the British Isles with an accent that roamed across the region just as much as Duchess herself must have. There was Scottish in there, but also Welsh and even Cockney. And if Duchess got very emotional it seemed she was mostly Irish.

Juniper had managed to winkle some nuggets of

history from Duchess over the years and found out that maybe-possibly her ancestors had been some kind of royalty who had been forced to flee their estate at the beginning of the last century for a mysterious reason. Duchess certainly cut a regal figure in her flowing midnight-blue opera cloak, which had been patched around the hem with various offcuts that Duchess had trimmed into star shapes and stitched onto the velvet material.

For the past ten years, she had been calling Cedar Park her home, and she often declared that she wouldn't leave even if Pavarotti himself came to serenade her. Juniper googled Pavarotti at the first opportunity and found out that he was a famous singer. From this, she deduced that Duchess was a romantic at heart.

"It is so good to hear you singing, Juniper," Duchess said now. "With that sound coming to my ears every morning, I would never leave this park even—"

"Even if Pavarotti came to serenade you."

"Yes," said Duchess. "Cheeky."

Duchess opened her arms for a hug, and as they embraced Juniper noticed she could touch her own elbows round the back.

"I'm glad you're looking after me today," Juniper said.

"So am I, child," said Duchess. "But we both know your mum is worried about my chest."

"I'm measuring your waist with my arms," said Juniper. "I can touch my elbows, Duchess. That's not good."

Duchess didn't like to speak of her health because she didn't like hospitals. In fact, she had a terror of all institutions, and Juniper knew from occasional comments that Duchess must have spent time in one.

"Where's Jade?" Duchess said. "You two usually come as a package deal."

"Changing the subject," said Juniper. "Classic Duchess. And you know very well Jade is in Jamaica for December."

Duchess mock-frowned. "Oh yes. I remember now. But I do have a rather spectacular change of subject for you. First, I'll show you, and then we can go to the Mews so you can put your mother's mind at rest: This magnificent thing is good for my chest."

Juniper looked up into her friend's face and was worried. Duchess's mane of hair was mostly gray now when less than a year ago it had been almost completely copper red. That was okay, she supposed. Duchess had explained that it was entirely natural for the pigment cells in hair follicles to die as a person got older, and there was nothing sinister about it. But while Juniper always appreciated a scientific explanation, she couldn't help worrying. Now it seemed that Duchess was also losing weight at an alarming rate, and her eyes had lost their usual sparkle.

"So, if I look at this magnificent thing, whatever it is, then you'll accompany me to the Mews?"

Juniper had used a posh accent to say "accompany me" because she knew it would make Duchess smile, which it did. She placed a hand on her heart and declared: "I shall indeed accompany you, Lady Juniper. You have the word of a duchess."

This was good enough for Juniper because she guessed that her mother would take one look at Duchess and organize a house call with a doctor, ignoring any of their guest's objections.

A bargain struck, the pair strolled arm in arm across the park toward Duchess's bodega, which is what she called her living quarters because she'd lived in Spain for a while.

There were many homeless dwellings dotted around the periphery of the park, but the bodega was the oldest and by far the oddest, as it was constructed round the trunk of an oak tree, using the tree itself as its main support. Duchess had often explained that a bodega was actually a cellar, but it could also be a market, and she did a brisk trade in watch repairs from her front hatch. Duchess was so technically minded that she could even fix smartwatches.

To get to the bodega, Duchess and Juniper passed the

bandstand with its brightly painted panels, tiled steps, and wrought iron trimmings shaped like creeping ivy. From there, they crested the amphitheater, and then it was less than five minutes down the slope to the majestic oak tree that seemed out of place among so many red cedars.

"Well, Lady Juniper, what do you think? Fantastic, isn't it?"

"Yes," Juniper said. "It is fantastic. But what exactly am I looking at?"

"Look closer," said Duchess. "At the trunk."

Juniper stepped closer. There was the trunk. As usual. A big oak trunk in the shade of the canopy, with a curved bulge a few meters off the ground.

That was unusual. Juniper didn't remember that being there before.

"The bulge is new," she said, but how could a suitcase-sized lump be new? Did they just appear overnight on trees? Surely not.

"Is it a bulge?" said Duchess.

"You could just tell me . . ."

"That's no fun," said Duchess. "Use that big brain of yours."

Juniper walked right up to the tree and put her hand on the protruding section. Then she realized. "It's not part of the tree," she said.

"No," said Duchess. "It's new."

Juniper was intrigued now. The bulge was actually clamped onto the trunk somehow and had been stained to be so perfectly camouflaged that Juniper had not seen it from six meters away when she was looking right at it.

It was a wooden structure, which curved upward round the trunk. Juniper knew a little about carpentry because her dad had been a very talented woodworker, but the construction of this thing was off-the-charts amazing.

Dad would love this.

The bulge was made from dozens of curved laths that fitted together without any obvious joints, nails, or even glue.

It looks like an armadillo, Juniper thought. *Narrow at the ends and with some volume in the middle.*

"What is it?" she asked Duchess. "An armadillo sculpture? Storage?"

"Armadillo," said Duchess. "That's what I'll call it, and yes, it is storage, but not the way you think. Reach in behind."

Juniper did what she was told, and her fingers found a handle that was connected to a crank.

"There's a crank," she said to Duchess.

"Well, child, what do we do with a crank?"

We crank, thought Juniper, so she did.

With each turn of the handle, the armadillo plates slid

upward, folding over one another to reveal a space inside padded with a net of woven bark.

"It's a bed," said Juniper. "This is amazing!"

"Keep cranking," said Duchess. "There's more."

Juniper gave the handle a few more turns, and when the plates were completely retracted the action switched to the bottom of the Armadillo, and a beautiful mini-staircase dropped down.

"No way," said Juniper. "My dad would have loved this."

"Yes, this is exactly the sort of thing Briar was always building."

"Except like a billion times more advanced than any wooden stuff I've ever seen. Can I try it?"

"Of course, my lady," said Duchess.

Juniper climbed inside and relaxed in the netting.

"This is great," she said. "Really comfy."

"There's even more," said Duchess, leaning into the Armadillo. "Niko has lined the walls of the shelter with bark from the tree that's still growing, so you are right now, for all intents and purposes, inside a tree. Can you feel how warm it is?"

"I felt the temperature go up as soon as I got in," said Juniper. "And who's Niko?"

Duchess ignored the question by pulling a light bulb from the folds of her cloak. "Ready for the ta-da moment?

The pins on this bulb have been coated in sap. So go ahead and twist it in."

Juniper couldn't believe this. "Twist it in? Into a tree?"

Duchess jabbed the light bulb at a hole bored in the trunk. "Try it."

Juniper screwed the light bulb in, thinking that maybe Duchess was kidding, but no. After half a dozen rotations, the light came on.

Juniper was flabbergasted but played it cool. "No toilet?" she said. "And I still don't know who this Niko guy is."

All Duchess would say on that subject was: "I can't talk about him. I promised."

Two short sentences that made Juniper, who we've already learned was a very curious person, absolutely determined to find out everything she could about the mysterious Niko.

Duchess did, however, share a few more nuggets of information about the Armadillo over a cup of tea when they arrived back in the Mews.

"I'm not supposed to be telling you this," she said, "but the Armadillo—I love that name so I'm keeping it—the

Armadillo has even more tricks up its sleeve. The tree sap is good for my asthma so Niko assures me that sleeping in there will be like sleeping in a spa. Isn't that amazing? I could do with a spa day."

"That's brilliant, Duchess," said Juniper.

"Niko said that the Armadillo should work fine whatever the English winter throws at it. Even if something does go wrong, he somehow seems to know and sorts it out during his nightly patrols. There are eight Armadillos in Cedar Park."

"That's all great, Duchess, but you're still too thin. And your breathing isn't clear, even if you pretend it is."

"The Armadillo is waterproof but not airtight," continued Duchess, who had the ability not to hear what she didn't want to. "It has built-in heating and is elevated," she said, sounding more Irish now that she was excited. "So I really don't need to sleep in your spare room at all. I'm actually totally fine, and Niko said he'll check in on me later just to make sure there are still no teething problems. Wait until I tell him how you christened the Armadillo. I bet he'll get a big laugh out of that, even though . . ."

"Even though what?" asked Juniper, but Duchess avoided this Niko-related question by checking her vintage iPhone for texts.

"Oh, look, honey. Something from your mum. She'll be a few more hours, and do I mind staying on? There's a vegan stew in it for me. As if I need paying to look after you, Junie." Duchess turned off the phone. "You're looking after me, really. But your mother's a natural chef, and I do love her stews. Jennifer has the magic touch. She never needs a recipe book—she just knows what a dish needs."

Juniper knew exactly what Duchess meant. Her mum could concoct a meal from ingredients that did not seem to go together. She'd once mixed French mustard with vanilla ice cream, and it had been revolting for the first two spoon-fuls, but then fantastic.

"And I know she's going to give me the once-over. You can take the girl out of nursing, but you can't take the nurse out of the girl. But she'll see—you'll both see—that I'm fine."

And then Duchess coughed for about a minute, which ruined her whole argument.

"You are not fine," said Juniper, really concerned. "You're too thin, and your voice sounds different, and tree sap and magic bulbs aren't going to fix things. You need a hospital."

Duchess went a shade whiter than she already was. "A hospital's the last thing I need and the last place I will ever go," she said quietly, focusing on her fingers. "So please don't bring it up again, Junie, or I won't be able to look after you anymore."

Juniper decided to stop badgering her friend for now.

Duchess may be able to get round me, but Mum will sort this out as soon as she comes home.

The only problem with that logic was that Mum did not, in fact, come home.

3

Missing

It was only a few hours initially. And while Juniper waited she read her favorite book, which was *The Science of Christmas* by Professor Josephine Spangles. Her favorite chapter was the one where Irish professor Josephine Spangles claimed to have identified the unit for measuring Santa Claus's Christmas magic. A unit that she named a Spangle, after herself. Spangles were, she theorized, basically a measurement of hope. And concentrated hope could be harnessed as magic.

But what the book didn't say was that, even though Professor Spangles's discovery was a significant scientific breakthrough, not a single person believed her, and she became something of a laughingstock in the scientific community. Josephine was fired from her job, and her very name became a cruel jibe. Whenever a scientist made an outlandish claim, they were said to have "a bad case of the Spangles."

No one knew what happened to Josephine Spangles as she had disappeared nearly twenty years ago, but there were rumors of dangerous experiments and a generator meltdown.

Duchess saw what Juniper was absorbed in and gently closed the book.

"Perhaps now is not the best time to worry about Josephine Spangles," she said.

Juniper nodded. "I heard her colleagues were mean to her and no one's seen her for years. It's not fair."

Juniper wasn't really worried about Professor Spangles going missing. In fact, she wasn't initially worried about her mother because Jennifer Lane was famous in the area for helping out whoever, whenever and wherever it was needed. It was why she'd become a nurse, and why she'd taken over as park-keeper, and why she'd volunteered as classroom assistant when Juniper had been in Year One.

Before Briar died, it had not been uncommon for Jennifer to return home late with an injured sparrow in a shoebox under one arm and a bag of donations for the Santa Vigil under the other. So, when she wasn't home in time to make a vegan stew, neither Duchess nor Juniper was overly concerned, especially now that Jennifer was on the road to being her old self again.

In fact, Juniper and Duchess spent a couple of hours joking about it, inventing ridiculous excuses.

"Sorry I'm late. I was collecting nuts for a squirrel with vertigo."

That was a good one from Duchess. And Juniper came up with the classic: "Sorry I'm late. I was opening invisible doors for a mime in the park."

How they chortled, but the laughter ran out when it got late.

Mum. Where are you? Juniper texted.

And a few minutes later a reply came through:

I'm having a big bag of crisps that will take me ages to finish. Just stay put and don't contact anybody. With love from your mother.

This was puzzling to say the least because Jennifer wasn't a crisp person. Juniper couldn't remember ever seeing her mother eat a single crisp.

"Maybe it's a joke?" suggested Duchess.

"Funny joke," said Juniper. "Or definitely not a funny joke."

Duchess stared at Juniper's phone and tried to stifle a cough. "I don't know, Junie. It's strange."

Juniper felt tears gathering under her eyelids. "Do you

think Mum is okay, Duchess? Do you think she's really upset about something?"

Duchess handed back the phone. "It's just a text. Call her."

So Juniper did, but it went straight to voice mail. Then she did a find-my-phone and didn't get a ping. The next obvious step was to ring Sandra, who said that Jennifer had left her place ages ago and should be home by now, but she was sure there was nothing wrong.

Juniper tried to stay calm, but half an hour later she said in a trembling voice: "Okay, Duchess, it's really late now. Mum is always worried about you staying outdoors on freezing December nights. And now I'm worried she's doing the same thing."

Duchess covered her mouth for a quick series of coughs, then said: "Me too, Juniper. Let's get busy."

The pair split up and got busy on their phones, both calling anyone they could think of who might have seen Juniper's mum. They tried all the establishments Jennifer Lane might conceivably have dropped into that were still open. The late-night pharmacy and newsagent's, the Hop Inn pub and Jaggery Indian restaurant where the Lanes used to go for a special treat. No luck with any of these. Everyone knew Jennifer, but no one had seen her.

Round two was the hospitals, doctors' surgeries, and

clinics to see if a dark-haired woman in her thirties had been admitted. All no, apart from the hospital, who did have a dark-haired woman in Accidents & Emergencies, but she was the receptionist's own cousin and could be ruled out.

Juniper wasn't on social media so she couldn't post, but Duchess was a member of a message board called Parklife where anyone who was sleeping out for whatever reason could post notices, warnings, directions, hints, and tips that might help the thousands of people sleeping rough in London.

"I'll get an alert if anyone responds," she said.

Juniper had just finished speaking to a constable at Cedar Park police station who hadn't had any reports whatsoever relating to a dark-haired Caucasian woman in her thirties.

"I don't understand," said Juniper. "How can a whole person just disappear?"

Duchess knew that people disappeared all the time. She also knew from personal experience that the people who did usually wanted to vanish for personal reasons. But that wasn't the case with Jennifer Lane. She would never, ever leave Juniper.

"Jennifer hasn't disappeared," Duchess said. "The reality is that it's only been a few hours. Your mum is going to stroll through that door any second now with a perfectly reasonable explanation. You'll see."

Somehow Juniper knew that Duchess was wrong. Her mum was missing. Something bad had happened.

★ ★ ★

The next twenty-four hours were a waking nightmare, apart from the three hours when Duchess and Juniper dozed side by side on the sofa. Those three hours were a sleeping nightmare.

Jennifer Lane didn't turn up, there were no useful comments on Parklife, and the constable on the desk of Cedar Park police station informed Juniper that, although she could report her mother missing straight away, nothing much would happen until Jennifer had been missing for twenty-four hours.

Duchess, who was very uncomfortable in a police station, had not been impressed at all by this news and said to the police officer: "Most crimes are solved within twenty-four hours or they're not solved at all. But you refuse to investigate until the twenty-four hours are up, which seems ludicrous to me, but what would I know? I'm just a . . ."

Duchess clammed up then, possibly realizing that she'd said too much, and walked out the front door, leaving Juniper to fill in the report on her own.

★ ★ ★

Duchess was all apologies outside the station.

"I'm sorry, Junie. I shouldn't have snapped at that offi-cer. She was only telling us how things are. But it's good news actually, don't you see? The police don't even consider your mum to be missing yet. And they're the professionals so there's no need for us to worry too much. We should certainly be concerned, but not overly anxious."

"Too late," said Juniper on the verge of tears for the umpteenth time. "I'm overly anxious."

"Don't be," said Duchess. "The best thing to do is stay busy. I've been through this before with friends of mine. People who live outside society go missing all the time so I know what to do. Just because the police aren't investigat-ing yet doesn't mean we can't."

So they printed MISSING flyers in Cedar Mews and stuck copies all along the high street. From there, they cut through the back gate into the park to ask Duchess's friends to keep their eyes peeled.

Duchess steered Juniper over to her bodega so she could check on her few meager belongings, which included a fold-ing bicycle that she kept winched up in the oak tree, the face cream that she made herself from avocado scrapings, and a slim travel magazine in a ziplock bag, which Juniper had seen her reading dozens of times. The bicycle she left where it was, but the cream and the magazine went into a drawstring bag that Duchess hooked over her shoulders.

Juniper was eager to get back to the cottage, but Duchess rested her hand on the Armadillo and left it there for a long moment, then seemed to make a decision.

"Okay, Junie, I'm going to tell you about Niko. I'm not supposed to. Actually, he expressly asked me not to talk about him, especially to children, but this is an emergency."

"Do you think he can find Mum?"

Duchess shrugged. "Maybe. If anyone can."

Juniper glanced over her shoulder toward Cedar Mews where her mother could be right now. Waiting.

"Can we go home and talk there? Just in case?"

Duchess clipped the string straps of her bag together. "Of course. Fingers crossed we won't even need to contact Niko."

Juniper held up two sets of crossed fingers, but she wasn't optimistic.

When they got back to the Mews, Juniper had the sudden idea that maybe her mum was hiding somewhere in the cottage. Or maybe she'd been standing on the bed, fixing the curtains, and slipped down between the wall and the bed. Or maybe she'd been in the attic, looking through some memories, and banged her head on a roof beam. Jennifer Lane could have been at home the entire time just praying for her daughter to come home and find her. And what had her daughter actually done? Wasted her time sticking up flyers in the high street.

"Mum!" she called, taking off upstairs as soon as they were through the door. "Mum, I'm coming!"

Duchess sighed and put the kettle on. She'd seen this kind of desperate grasping at straws before, and it was heartbreaking to watch someone dear fall apart, but all she could do right now was be there for Juniper. And she would be there for the Lane girls for as long as it took.

Juniper banged around upstairs for a few minutes, then traipsed down to the kitchen, took a sip of the hot chocolate waiting for her, and said, "Tell me about Niko, Duchess."

And so Duchess did.

"Niko appeared about three years ago. One day, he was just in the park, helping people out. He'd fix up shelters or arrive on your birthday with your favorite muffin, or build an ingenious drainage system on a roof. His specialty, and this might sound gross, was latrines. Nearly every shelter around here has a Niko-special outdoor toilet that ferries everything away from the shack into a vegetable patch or something. On Parklife, people started to refer to him as the Angel of Cedar Park."

"Why have I never seen him?"

"He doesn't want to be seen," said Duchess. "A lot of us don't. I think that something happened to Niko, and his heart is broken. So he stays on the edge of society and helps people who really need it."

"You said earlier that he can find anything?"

Duchess smiled. "Yes, it's amazing. Somehow he knows what people need, and he gets it. The free-food truck, which distributes leftovers that are still in date, needed a barcode scanner, and Niko found one in a fire sale and fixed it up. The local community center needed some stuff for the teen drop-in room, and Niko found a pool table and an old *Space Invaders* game that was water-damaged, but worked fine."

"How did he find them?"

"We don't know," said Duchess. "We don't even know how he knew they were needed. Or how he moved them to the center. He really is an angel."

"And you think he could find Mum?"

"Maybe," said Duchess. "But I'm betraying a trust asking him. He said no kids. Ever."

"But it's Mum, Duchess. It's Mum."

Duchess sighed. "I know. Of course. I just don't want to lose Niko. I haven't had a friend my own age in so long."

She looked into Juniper's big brown eyes and said, "Stop it with the puppy-dog eyes, Junie. I'll leave a message on Parklife right now, and Niko will find me as soon as he can. If Jennifer isn't back by tomorrow, we'll spend the day in the bodega and wait for him to show up. Does that sound like a plan?"

"Yes," said Juniper, but her mind was racing.

Tomorrow. I can't wait till tomorrow.

4

Finding Niko

Once Duchess had broken her code of silence regarding Niko, it seemed like the floodgates had opened, and she spent a couple of hours spilling all the information that she'd been holding back.

The mysterious Niko lived in the Christmas-tree forest according to Duchess, though she wasn't sure where exactly and had never personally seen him emerge from the forest or return to it. Nevertheless, she was 90 percent certain that Niko lived in there and came out to find things that people needed.

As well as the previously mentioned *Space Invaders* game, pool table, and barcode scanner, Niko had found a crate of plastic chairs for the women's shelter and even a flue for the free clinic's chimney. Juniper hadn't been quite sure what a flue even was until she'd done a search on her phone and found out it was a pipe for conveying exhaust gases. Duchess had assured her that the flue Niko had shown up with had fitted the clinic's chimney perfectly.

"That's more than good luck, Junie," she'd told Juniper. "Those things are custom-made."

With each story, Juniper had grown ever more certain that Niko might just be the person to help find Mum. After all, if Niko could find a perfectly sized flue for the clinic, surely he'd have a few ideas on how to track down an entire person. Even if Juniper wasn't 100 percent sold on this idea, she didn't have a better one at the moment.

When Juniper found herself wide awake in her bed and fretting well after midnight, it occurred to her that the mysterious Angel of Cedar Park could be doing his Armadillo rounds right at that moment, and she could corner him at the bodega and ask for help. So Juniper Lane changed into warm clothes and pulled on her reversible Puffa jacket and climbed out of her bedroom window onto the roof of the extension.

Duchess had told her that if any of Niko's Armadillos were damaged then somehow he would show up in the dead of night to replace whichever peg, panel, or pulley needed replacing. And, since Duchess was safely installed in the

Cedar Mews spare room, Juniper trotted off across the park, using the torchlight from her phone to guide her, though she probably could have found the way with her eyes closed.

It took her eight minutes to reach the bodega, and once there, she reached up into the innards of Duchess's Armadillo, feeling around with her eyes closed so she could focus on the mechanism under her fingers. She quickly realized that the clockwork operating system would be completely banjaxed if she wiggled a certain small wooden cog from the peg holding it.

Those projecting pegs are called dowels, Juniper thought as she fiddled. Her father had taught her all about dowels and cogs and dovetail joints, and so it didn't seem strange to her that an eleven-year-old girl would be able to disable a complicated system of gears without doing any permanent damage.

Juniper studied the strange carvings on the wooden cog for a long moment and then wound it onto a twig stub below the Armadillo where Niko would be sure to see it. Juniper felt heartsick that she had disabled something, even if only temporarily, that her dad would definitely have loved, but she needed to speak to Niko, and he needed to listen. She checked her work by climbing inside the pod and winding the mechanism with the second interior handle. The plates slid halfway shut, then ground to a halt. Phase one of Operation Enlist Niko's Help was a success.

Phase two of the operation—Make Contact with the Angel of Cedar Park—might take considerably longer to accomplish. Earlier, Juniper had done all the stuff she was supposed to be doing—putting up more missing person flyers, visiting the three hospitals and two police stations in the borough to make inquiries, helping Duchess with dinner and tidying up—before she could get going on the stuff she was definitely not supposed to be doing.

The park was different at night. There was noise, but it was different noise. The animals were braver, and there weren't many cars, but the main road was a trade route so there were quite a few lorries roaring by, making a sound that always reminded Juniper of a video she'd seen of a giant wave.

Lying here now in the Armadillo, Juniper noticed that she was up high enough to see the lorry drivers in their cabs over the treetops.

It looks like they're driving spaceships, she thought.

Her dad would have loved that notion. Her flights of fancy always made him smile. Briar Lane had often told the story of how three-year-old Juniper had invented a game called Cloud Babies where she would find clouds that looked like baby animals. The scoring system was:

Insect—1 point.
Mammal—2 points.

Fish—3 points.

Bird—4 points.

Octopus—whammy 10 points (because of the arms and legs).

Juniper never lost at Cloud Babies.

It was a mistake thinking about her dad while on a stakeout because it allowed Juniper's exhaustion to creep in. Determination had kept her going till now, but Juniper Lane was an eleven-year-old girl under tremendous stress, and in such conditions the human brain wants nothing more than to switch itself off. The second Juniper's mind drifted to such a comforting memory as playing Cloud Babies with her mum and dad, she went into shutdown mode.

"Hmmm," she said, remembering the time she'd spotted not one but two Cloud Baby octopuses and beat her parents outright with a double-whammy twenty points.

And then she was fast asleep in an incredibly comfortable Armadillo.

* * *

Juniper slept deeply in that elastic dreamtime where she saw her mum and dad in the night clouds. When the clouds drifted in front of the moon, its silver rays lit up their smiles.

"Mammals," she mumbled in her sleep. "Four points. But not babies so minus two."

Then Juniper felt herself waking up. With her eyes still closed, she wondered what had woken her. There hadn't been any distant doors slamming or horns beeping, and no sweeping headlight had pierced the gap in the Armadillo's plating, but something had roused her, Juniper was certain of it. A feeling maybe.

But it was more than that. A sensation like the crackle of pins and needles had spread across her forehead. The closest equivalent she could think of was the time she had blushed in assembly when Miss Dunbar praised her artwork. This feeling was like that one, but without the accompanying tummy butterflies. As the fog of sleep cleared from her senses, she understood what those pins and needles across her forehead meant.

Someone is watching me.

Juniper had always experienced this telltale tingle. Her father had the same early-warning system. He'd called it their superpower.

The best way to catch someone watching you is to surprise them, and so Juniper snapped open her eyes suddenly and saw, through a gap in the plates, a man standing not two feet in front of her, outside the Armadillo.

This was her first look at the Angel of Cedar Park,

and he didn't look much like an angel. For a start, Niko was frowning so hard that he didn't appear to have any eye sockets. Just two Sharpie eyebrows, glittering eyes, and cheekbones. He sported a thicket of gray-blond beard that roamed untended across most of his face save for the lower section, which had been gathered into a Viking-style braid that reached halfway down his belly. Any features that weren't obscured by bristles seemed to have been sculpted out of gray marble with sharp shadows cast by his own wrinkles, which just showed how deep they were.

This was not the face of a man you asked for help. This was the face of a man whose features were set in a permanent scowl so that they'd prevent people asking him for help.

Nevertheless, Juniper was desperate.

Niko didn't seem to have noticed that she was awake and was instead glaring at the tree trunk just below the Armadillo.

He's looking at the cog, Juniper realized. *And he's not happy about what I did.*

Niko twisted the cog from the branch stub and set it spinning on the tip of his little finger.

"I know you're watching me, child," he said without taking his eyes from the spinning cog. "Tell me why this cog in particular?"

That was an easy question to answer. "I didn't want to break the Armadillo."

"Armadillo?" said Niko. "You mean the nodboks. Nut box. Armadillo . . . hmmph."

Juniper wasn't sure if Niko liked his little shelters being called Armadillos or not.

"You can put that cog right back in," she said. "I can do it if you like."

Niko ignored the offer of help and tucked the cog back into the innards of the clockwork mechanism.

"So why go to the trouble?" he asked.

Juniper knew this was her chance to enlist this grumpy stranger to her cause. She had dealt with grumpy people before and knew that they usually got grumpier the longer a conversation went on. She would have to answer Niko's question and make her argument at the same time in a concise sentence.

I should have worked this out in my head, she realized, *instead of taking a nap.*

But Juniper never got to make her argument because apparently Niko had worked out that the only reason this girl would have disabled one of his Armadillos was so he would appear.

"No," he said, his brows furrowing even more severely. "Whatever it is, no."

Juniper sat up. "But . . ."

And that was as far as she got. Niko thumped a specific spot on the Armadillo's casing causing the plates to shut entirely, trapping Juniper inside.

"Wait!" she cried. "Don't go."

But Niko didn't wait, and he did go.

A lot of people would probably have given up at this point, but Juniper was not one of those people. She had learned all about determination from her mother, who had taken over as park-keeper without any training, and her father, who had come out of the immigration system with a degree in horticulture. So Juniper wasn't about to give up because this person Niko was a grump who didn't want to listen to a reasonable proposition.

He's going to go back into the Christmas-tree forest, thought Juniper. *And I'm going to follow him.*

This was not an ideal plan. The whole point of the remove-a-cog idea had been to get Niko out of the forest so she wouldn't have to go in, but "needs must," as Duchess often said.

And I need so I must, Juniper thought now.

She patted the tree trunk until her hand landed on a key and she twisted it clockwise to wind the mechanism.

"Come on," she said aloud. "Come on, he's getting away."

Earlier, she had marveled at the Armadillo's smooth clockwork action, but now it seemed infuriatingly slow, and in her mind Niko got three steps farther away with every second that passed. Juniper knew this because she'd once timed herself running flat out and calculated that she could run three steps per second.

I knew that information would come in handy, she thought, sliding herself out through the smallest possible gap in the Armadillo's plating without waiting for the wooden staircase to assemble itself.

Juniper Lane landed on her feet and set off running in the general direction of the forest. Niko would be headed for home, she was sure of that, but where exactly home was inside the forest she had no idea. The elements themselves seemed to be cooperating with her pursuit as the night was bright, and moonlight poked into any corners that might have provided shadow cover for Niko.

As Juniper ran, she looked around as much as possible, searching for any sign of the Angel of Cedar Park, but there was nothing. It was as if he'd simply disappeared. At this point, most of the people who would not have given up having been shut inside an Armadillo would have accepted defeat, but again Juniper was made of sterner stuff, and the hot flame of determination inside her neither dimmed nor wavered. She ran on toward the border line of cedars, still looking all around, hoping Niko would put even a single toe into her line of vision.

But Juniper wasn't looking in the right place.

5

Into the Forest

Juniper should have been looking up because Niko, who was, of course, Santa Claus in hiding, was also a polar craftsman. He had made sure that all his Armadillos, or nod-bokses as they were known in the elf tongue, could be accessed for repair from any angle, one of those angles being from above. So, when Niko closed the Armadillo hatch, instead of running away, he had simply climbed up the makeshift rungs embedded in the shell of the sleeping chamber and squatted on top of it, drawing his woven robe round him for camouflage, then watched to see what the girl would do.

He knew she was Briar Lane's daughter, Juniper, but even though Duchess told him that Briar had been a real friend to those in the park who were in need, Niko had had his fill of children asking for favors. His whole life had been dedicated to it, a life that could have been spent with Sarika.

So instead of Santa Clausing, Niko had wandered from place to place, helping those who needed it, and three years ago he had set up camp beside Cedar Park. Niko knew that he really should move on before someone started looking into the mysterious angel, but he found himself drawn to the place and the people in it, most especially Duchess, who had been through so much and yet had so much spirit.

I have stayed here for three years, and that's too long, he realized. *Children instinctively know to ask me for presents and favors.*

There was no danger that this Juniper person could actually find his vinterhus in the forest. Niko still had enough North Pole magic in his system to wreak some havoc with navigation and weather systems, but if children were starting to look for him then how long could it be before the elves showed up? Led, no doubt, by Tomescu.

Niko sighed. Tomescu. Christmas's greatest champion. The brain behind the North Pole operation and the elf who had already found him twice and tried to persuade him to return to work.

So why haven't I moved on? Niko asked himself for the umpteenth time.

The reason, he knew deep inside, was mostly just Duchess.

From his perch inside the tree's foliage, Niko watched

the girl run. He had excellent night vision, which had come in handy during his tenure as Santa, and it seemed the girl did too, as she navigated twists and turns in the bumpy forest path without missing a step.

She's quick and determined, he thought.

And there was something else. Juniper had known he was there outside the nodboks. She had woken up and looked straight at him. That never happened. Or hardly ever. Niko had prided himself on being the quietest Father Christmas in generations. He could count on the fingers of one hand the number of times he'd been rumbled by a child, and every time it had been his own fault, but this was different. Juniper had sensed him. Niko realized that he was grudgingly admiring the girl and squashed the feeling.

It doesn't matter how fleet-footed or alert she is, he decided.

Because, once Juniper Lane reached the edge of the forest, this entire incident would be over as the fence would stop the girl in her tracks. Then she would give up and go home.

In fact, Juniper had already reached the edge of the forest.

Goodnight, little girl, Niko thought.

And then she disappeared into the tree line.

I'll give her a few minutes, Niko decided. *Then she'll be back out, shoulders slumped in disappointment that she can't persuade the Angel of Cedar Park to find her a pony or whatever it is she wants from me.*

A few minutes passed.

And then a few more.

Juniper did not emerge from the tree line, shoulders slumped or otherwise.

Niko finger-combed his Viking-style beard thoughtfully.

I'd better check, he thought, jumping down from his perch.

Niko's mistake in this instance was to underestimate Juniper Lane. We know that Juniper was a smart and resourceful girl, but as Niko wasn't wearing his Santa hat, so to speak, he was a little hazy on his encyclopedic knowledge of children and where they were on the behavioral scales. He also had no idea just how far Juniper was prepared to go for the Angel of Cedar Park's help.

Niko stuck to the shadows as much as he could on this bright winter night, keeping his ears open for restless park residents, both human and animal. The only creature to cross his path was a large urban fox who liked to spend weekends in the forest, but was mostly to be found in his den of flowerpots behind a garden center in Bloomsbury.

The fox tapped the flash of white on his muzzle in tribute to one of the ancient people, a gesture that Niko acknowledged with a tap on the side of his own nose.

At least the foxes remember us, he thought, and continued on his mission.

If it hadn't been for the fox, Niko more than likely

would have noticed the movement in the lower branches of a cedar in the tree line and realized that Juniper, who was named for the exact type of tree she had climbed into, had accidentally turned the tables on him.

★ ★ ★

Juniper had soon realized that there was no wriggling through the fence that separated the bulk of Cedar Forest from the park to which it gave its name. The barrier had at one point been a simple chain-link affair. In fact, Juniper could remember walking along it with her parents, poking her fingers through the links. Now, however, it had been reinforced with foliage as the forest seemed to have expanded to fill any spaces in the fence. Each gap in the links was stuffed with the leaves and evergreen branches of the red cedar.

The Christmas trees had completely taken over the small forest and had a famously quick growth rate because of the shade, the moist environment, and the deep alluvial soil, which had a pH value between five and seven. All this, according to Juniper's dad, produced the ideal conditions in which the Christmas trees could flourish.

But this is nuts, thought Juniper. The tree line was so dense beyond the fence that she couldn't even see into the forest. Surely trees weren't supposed to grow this quickly?

You're supposed to be on my side, she beamed at them. *I'm named after you.*

As expected, the trees did not reply, and Juniper decided the only way she was catching up to this Niko person was if she made it happen herself.

I have two options, she thought. *I go all the way along the fence, looking for a Juniper-sized gap.*

This was not a real option. It could take her all night to walk along the entire fence, and two-thirds of that walk would be beside the main road, which had no footpath for most of a route that had supply trucks thundering along it twenty-four hours a day.

That left option two.

I go up and over.

Juniper started to climb.

It's not an easy thing to climb a Christmas tree during the day, but at night it's almost impossible.

Structurally, the red cedar is closer to a bush than a tree with tightly packed branches and a trunk that has more spikes than a prickle of hedgehogs. But Juniper was small, wriggly, and wore gloves and a padded green winter coat that protected her from the tip of her nose to her knees. But, even with her size and wriggliness, Juniper quickly found that fighting a tree in the middle of the night was hard work, and it was only her determination to leave no stone unturned in her quest to locate her mother that kept her going.

"Jennifer," she breathed, and imagined her mother singing the response: "Juniper."

This mantra helped Juniper to reach a height of about twelve feet off the ground, but then she found herself completely stuck. She could go back down, but not one inch farther up. Also she was exhausted.

"Jennifer," she said through gritted teeth, trying to force her head upward, but it was no use: The way was blocked by a lattice of branches.

I'll rest for a bit, she decided. *Then try another tree.*

And while climbing a Christmas cedar is tough, resting in one is actually quite easy. Juniper simply hung there, and the tree cradled her gently in its branches.

It was at this moment that Juniper noticed Niko making his way to the fence below her. She didn't hear him because the Angel of Cedar Park made less sound than a field mouse, and the only reason she saw him was because she'd always had excellent night vision. So good, in fact, that Duchess had once commented that Juniper would make an effective special-forces operative, but added that she wouldn't recommend it as a career.

Juniper didn't really have time to look at Niko as such. She just caught the tail end of him as he disappeared through the fence, at a spot where there didn't seem to be a break.

What? thought Juniper. And then, *How?*

But she soon stopped wondering what and how and concentrated on her descent to solid ground, trying to keep the spot where Niko had disappeared in sight.

The climb down was much easier than the climb up. Juniper adopted a technique that would have had her mother covering her eyes, unable to look. Jennifer's daughter raised her arms, pointed her toes and wiggled herself like a Slinky toy, allowing gravity to do most of the work. It was a bumpy descent, but very rapid, especially when the tree funneled Juniper to the outer branches, and she slid down the shining canopy and was deposited more or less at the exact spot where Niko had disappeared through the fence.

Thank you, tree, Juniper broadcast at the cedar. *We're friends again.*

One problem out of the way, another to solve.

The other problem was the same color as the first, but much bigger.

How do I pass through a fence blocked with trees?

Juniper pulled down her hood and stepped close to the fence. She was right at the spot where Niko had gone through, but couldn't see how he'd managed it. There was no gap. If anything, the barrier was even denser here than in other sections of the line. In fact, the cedar growth was so thick that Juniper couldn't even see the metal of the fence. She checked left and right, and there were links glinting through the greenery, but not here.

Is that weird? she wondered. *Or not weird?*

Juniper reached out her hand, expecting her fingers to tap the wire, but there were no wire links inside. Juniper was surprised, but not yet suspicious.

Maybe it's another inch or two farther in.

She thrust her hand in a bit more.

Still no wire. And no branches either, just the brush of tickling foliage.

Now Juniper was suspicious enough to forget all about her balance.

We've all done it: leaned against something that we expected to be solid only to find out that it was mobile. Usually, the result of this is an embarrassing public stumble, but for Juniper there was no public embarrassment, just a stumble. She fell forward, expecting to scrape her face along the cedar branches, but instead a flap in the fence opened. She felt a flurry of branches slapping her arms, and she tumbled through into Cedar Forest.

The branches had turned her round as she fell, so

Juniper landed on her back, looking at the barrier just in time to see the flap sweep closed.

Niko has put in a secret gate, she realized. And when you go through a secret gate you're past the point of no return.

But it didn't matter. Mum was missing. There was no return.

Juniper stood up and saw that the forest was much less dense than it had appeared from outside the fence. Nevertheless, she caught sight of the flap of Niko's coat disappearing behind a wedge of cedar branches.

Juniper took off in pursuit, thinking: *Niko finds things. He will find Mum.*

Niko was not on the other side of the wedge, but Juniper was pretty sure she saw his coat fluttering round a bend up ahead.

I've got you, she thought.

But she didn't have him. There was nothing round that bend or the next one, or the one after that.

I'm getting in too deep, Juniper thought, but she kept going, threading her way between Christmas trees that almost seemed to be growing bushier as she watched. She could hear a crunching noise. Could that possibly be the trees growing?

No.

Juniper realized the sound was coming from the ground

under her feet. And even before she looked down she knew what was happening.

Snow.

She was right. There was fresh snow compacting beneath her boots with each step.

How could the snow be so deep in here when there wasn't a single flake in the park?

Was this weird?

This was definitely weird.

Niko had disappeared, and now it had actually started snowing.

Juniper ran faster, her boots sinking ankle-deep in the powdered snow, trusting that if she kept running forward then—if nothing else—she would arrive at the far side of Cedar Forest, which was less than a mile all the way across.

But what Juniper could not know was that this particular forest had not obeyed the laws of physics or meteorology for more than three years.

On she ran, thinking: *What else can happen? Surely that's it.*

But that was not it. There was more to come. Not on the weather front, but something potentially more immediately dangerous. It could take a blizzard hours to kill a person, but a reindeer could do it in seconds.

✳ ✳ ✳

Niko had no idea where the child had gone, which was strange because, even though he'd stopped being Santa nearly a decade previously, some of the magic had traveled with him, and he could often sense people in his orbit. His father had called it the Christingle, which Niko had thought hilarious when he was six. And, of course, he still cared about children; that wasn't a quality you could just shake off, even though he hadn't spared a moment to ask what the girl wanted.

"It doesn't matter," he said to himself gruffly. "I'm an under-the-radar helper now. No missions. You help one child, and the next thing you know you're flying round the world in Santa Slow Time, delivering presents to children who barely look at them."

Niko decided he would forget all about Juniper. Let her simply go home. He slipped through the trees, feeling the refreshing polar chill settle on his shoulders. The bite of the frost calmed him, and he followed a random zigzag path, confident that his special homing abilities would lead him to his vinterhus.

Thanks to the magic that trailed round after him, Niko's surroundings could start getting a little polar if he stayed in one place too long, and the mere fact that it was snowing in the Christmas-tree forest was a red flag.

I do need to move along before this place is under six feet of powder, he told himself. *Juniper is only the first. Soon she'll tell her friends that there's a bogeyman living in here, and there'll be gangs of children trying to film me for the internet.*

This was just Niko being melodramatic.

No Claus could be filmed for the internet or anything else. His robe had a magnetic field woven into its fabric by the elf Tomescu and his crew. This meant that many types of electronics went temporarily wonky around him, including cameras, compasses, and phones, which was a nuisance as Niko would have liked to stream music as he did his rounds.

He moved swiftly through the forest, his feet picking out green patches in the snowfall so that he wouldn't leave tracks, shoulders angled so he could fit into the narrowest gaps.

It took Niko several minutes to reach the vinterhus, a traditional elfin log cabin that had been built into the crook of three large cedars with the trunks functioning as the cabin's supporting pillars. Even in full daylight, the vinterhus would be more or less invisible from over twenty feet away as, in the past two years, moss and lichen had spread over the walls and most of the roof, apart from a large skylight, which allowed dappled sunrays in during the day. It needed a lot of scraping, but it was worth it, and Niko knew that he would be up on the roof later with his snow brush, carefully clearing the skylight that he had fashioned from the bay window of a broken-down caravan.

He stopped thinking about skylights when he noticed a smear of blood on the top beam of a small pen beside the cabin.

Blixxen was out.

Blixxen was Niko's eldest reindeer and normally one of the most placid in the team, but a couple of days ago he'd got hold of a stick of rhubarb that someone must have thrown over the fence. Rhubarb was toxic to reindeer, and Blixxen should have known better, but he wolfed the whole thing down and was now enduring the consequences. These included painful abdominal cramps and a form of caribou paranoia that meant he saw everything as a threat for a couple of days, which was why Niko had penned him in.

A paranoid reindeer may seem like a figure of fun, but it is worth remembering that when a reindeer feels threatened it can be a dangerous animal. For example, it can take half a dozen wolves to bring down a young reindeer in the wild, but only a single adult reindeer to decimate an entire pack of wolves.

Niko examined the fence now. It seemed as though Blixxen had butted his way out and perhaps gashed his forehead in doing so.

"I'd better find old Blixxen in case he tramples a fox," said Niko to the other reindeer he knew were watching. "Sometimes I think I should have left you fellows in the North Pole."

This was not a thought that Niko had ever actually seriously entertained. Reindeer have a very special magical bond with their own Santa Claus. Niko could no more leave them behind than he could leave one of his own limbs.

But then Niko had a thought that he did entertain.

The girl.

Could she have followed him into the magical forest?

Niko shrugged off his robe and ran toward the vinterhus.

The forest could be dangerous at night, especially during a blizzard with a confused reindeer on the loose.

He needed his work boots.

Juniper didn't usually feel the cold. As a toddler, it had given her immense pleasure to scandalize her parents by rolling around in any available snow, dressed in not very much. But now in Cedar Forest it seemed as though somehow the temperature had plummeted to far below anything she had ever experienced.

Juniper remembered a phrase her dad had used about

the park: "Sometimes I think this place has its own micro-climate when it comes to weather."

Briar Lane had been half joking, but Juniper felt the phrase actually applied in this case. Looking up at the snow-covered Christmas trees, she felt almost like she was inside one of the Scandinavian postcards from her mother's fridge collection.

Something thumped to her left. More than one thump. Several. A flurry.

Juniper stopped in her literal tracks.

What was that noise?

It sounded like there was someone playing the drums in the trees. The same beats over and over. Louder each time.

That's an animal, she realized. *A big one.*

Soon the drumbeats were accompanied by something else: a breathy huffing.

The big animal is running this way.

And suddenly Juniper was afraid. There weren't supposed to be big animals in here. But then again there weren't supposed to be blizzards either. Even if the snow got worse, she was only ten minutes from her house, but big thundering animals didn't care how far she was from home.

Juniper felt a ball of fear in her tummy. She just knew she was in danger. She should never have come into a park alone at night. Something was after her.

Don't be silly, Junie, she heard her father say. *It's probably a fox or a badger.*

Usually, just thinking about her father was enough to calm Juniper down, but not this time.

"That's not a fox, Dad," she whispered. "It sounds like a bear."

It probably wasn't a bear either, but it was something much bigger than a fox.

How she wished her father was with her now to hold her hand and tell her that Mum was waiting for them both at the Mews.

What is that, Dad?

In the time it took her to ask the memory of her father this question, the question was answered by the animal itself, which burst from the tree line perhaps forty feet in front of her and proceeded to charge directly toward Juniper.

Juniper was so scared of the hulking gray beast that her shaking legs were actually deepening her footprints in the snow.

Run, she told herself. *Run.*

And, *That's a reindeer.*

As a Christmas baby, Juniper knew quite a lot of facts about reindeer, but the one that popped into her head right now was that a reindeer's branching bone antlers had been known to disembowel a polar bear.

But reindeer are peaceful, thought Juniper. *Usually.*

Usually, maybe, but nothing about this night was usual. She was standing ankle-deep in snow that shouldn't be there, looking for her mother who should be. There was nothing *usual* about any of that. And, if she was in any doubt that this particular reindeer was not his usual peaceful self, the creature had lowered its head for battle and was blowing out a jet trail of steam through its nostrils.

Move, thought Juniper, but she couldn't, even though the reindeer was less than thirty feet away.

Move, she ordered herself again, and this time she did, but only her hands, which she put over her nose and mouth to prevent herself from screaming.

Twenty feet away now and coming so fast that it had to right itself by bashing its flanks into tree trunks.

Clumps of snow are plopping to the ground, Juniper thought, and usually she'd consider *plopping* a comical word, but she never would again.

Ten feet.

She could see the reindeer's black eyes glittering behind the curve of its lowered antlers, and it was the sight of those rolling marbles that loosened her joints.

Juniper suddenly flashbacked to a time when her five-year-old self had been marooned at low tide on a small beach rock besieged by tiny crawly crabs. She had been petrified by their beady eyes and bubbling mouths.

"I can't move!" she'd wailed to her mother. "They'll pinch me."

Her mother leaned in and held out a hand. "You can move, darling," she'd said. "Just step into my arms."

Mum, Juniper thought. *That's why I'm here, and that's why I have to get out of here.*

You can move, darling.

I can move, Juniper realized.

She squinted her eyes so she might see a little better, and bent her knees for a good spring . . .

✳ ✳ ✳

Apart from Professor Josephine Spangles, who we mentioned earlier, people usually get it wrong when it comes to interpreting magic. For example, in the countless versions of the King Arthur legend, people always assume the magic came from the sword in the stone, when in fact the magic resided in the stone, and Excalibur had just absorbed a few Spangles.

Another example of this is Santa Claus. The common belief is that most of the magic is in the suit, and that whosoever wears the suit becomes Father Christmas. This isn't true. Most of the magic is in the bones of the family, and the rest is in the sack, which we shall explore later. But the boots were mechanical marvels that were powered by a spark of Santa's magic.

Niko hadn't worn the boots in a while because putting them on completed a magical circuit that was as good as a beacon for Tomescu and the polar elves. The circuit was mostly in his head, but there was something about donning the boots that turned him from being Niko into being Santa Claus.

But in these circumstances, he had no choice. In all probability, the child was not even in the forest, but he couldn't take that chance with Blixxen roaming around in a paranoid state.

Thanks very much, rhubarb, thought Niko as he ripped the lock right off the carved wooden chest by the vinterhus's back door without even bothering with the key. Inside was his gray work suit, folded and tidy, and his boots were standing beside the suit, the shafts wilting under the weight of the fur cuffs.

"Upa-uda," he said to the boots, which was an old elvish phrase usually used to urge sleepy children from their beds, or sleepy reindeer from the stables. The phrase basically meant "up and at 'em," and even though Niko was speaking to the boots, he was really talking to himself.

Niko kicked off his walking shoes and dragged on the boots, which seemed too big for him at first, but then shrank to grip his calves and feet, sending a tingle through his toes as they did so.

Niko was out the door and running before the boots had even finished adjusting to their wearer.

He had no trouble picking up Juniper's presence now that he was in full Santa mode. The magic buzzed from his heart right out to his fingers and toes like a low-level electric charge. He could see more clearly, hear bugs under the snow, and see scents ripple in the air.

The girl was a few hundred feet to the southwest, and Blixxen was bearing down on her. Niko felt his heartbeat accelerate. A child was in danger. It was one thing to step away from giving gifts to children, but quite another to stop caring about their well-being. Niko had never stopped caring. The happiness of children was the Claus Code, and Niko could no more abandon that than he could his reindeer.

His priority was the girl's safety, and anyway it seemed pretty obvious from the sound of the reindeer's hoovklappen that he and Blixxen were headed toward the same destination: the girl.

Heaven only knows what Blixxen thinks he's looking at. Some kind of demon?

It was incredible what a single stick of rhubarb could do to a reindeer's mind, especially if it had been sprayed with pesticides.

Niko ran as fast as he could, and the ingenious layered insoles designed by Tomescu, the chief Christmas elf, multiplied the length of his stride by a factor of five so that he could cover several meters with each step. His square teeth glinted through the bushy mustache, and a person would be forgiven for thinking that Niko was smiling, but this was actually his determined face.

He could not, though, deny that it did feel good to use the magic.

I'm enjoying it now, Niko thought. *But this will cost me later if one of the techy elves picks up a blip on the scanner.*

He knew Tomescu and his crew of Christmas elves would be watching, and they had nearly got him back before.

The noise of Blixxen galloping seemed to be shaking the trees, and Niko couldn't help but be reminded of that scene in the classic dinosaur movie where the T. rex was hunting a human, but he tried to banish that particular set of images because it hadn't ended well for the human.

Blixxen would never bite someone's head off, he thought. *No matter how rhubarb-crazed he is.*

That was probably true, but if he was confused enough to barge out of a pen, then the aging Blixxen could easily plow straight over little Juniper.

Nevertheless, Niko picked up the pace to such an

extent that if he didn't time this perfectly then he was going to flash right by Juniper and Blixxen, which would be of zero use to anybody.

Please don't let me have lost my touch, he prayed silently to the ghost of his dad, who had been the finest Santa ever to wear the boots and could jump between rooftops on tiptoe without disturbing so much as a dry leaf.

Niko hadn't lost his touch. It had been years since he'd last pulled the boots on, but it didn't feel that way.

It seems like yesterday, he realized. *Like this morning*.

And it was just as well that he hadn't lost his touch because he was cutting it really fine.

* * *

As the trees began to thin out toward the edge of the forest, Niko caught a glimpse of Blixxen flashing through the slats of moonlight between trunks at his five o'clock. Juniper was dead ahead and seemingly rooted to the spot, which wasn't actually surprising.

I need to get between the reindeer and the little girl, thought Niko.

And that's what he did, sliding in like a baseball player onto the mound.

And then the girl moved.

Juniper dodged right, leaving it to the last split second so the reindeer wouldn't have time to follow.

Out of the corner of his eye, Niko just barely saw her go and knew that she had underestimated Blixxen's course-correcting ability. Maybe an almost two-hundred-kilo moose couldn't pivot at the last possible moment, but reindeer were a little more agile, and Blixxen threw his head sideways, scything the deadly bone antlers toward Juniper. The antlers certainly wouldn't skewer the girl now, but they could still take off a limb.

Niko knew he would have to do something he'd hoped to avoid. If putting on the boots sent a blip to the North Pole elves, this would be like planting a neon flag. But there was nothing for it. He twisted his head, clicking a bone in his neck, which activated the full flow of his magic, and the world slowed down. The plumes of his own breath curled slowly away from him, and individual snowflakes hovered before his eyes. Niko felt the magic crackling in his eyeballs and heard the beat of his own heart's bass drum.

Blixxen pivoted on his hindquarters and sent the entirety of his bulk after Juniper, whose forest-green coat was streaming behind her like a superhero's cape. Close on the girl's tail, Niko could see Blixxen's massive head, the red pennant of his tongue flapping along his jaw, and the individual spiky hairs of gray on the reindeer's nose bristling like magnetized pins. Blixxen made a final lunge for the girl, his head down, haunches raised, like a sprinter going for the tape. The tip of one antler snagged the tail of Juniper's Puffa, releasing a snowfall of padding.

I'm too late, thought Niko, but he tried anyway.

Everybody knows that Santa's reindeer can fly, but they're not magical creatures themselves, just especially receptive to polar magic, and Niko hadn't given Blixxen a boost in over a year. Niko concentrated a burst in his palm and touched Blixxen's underbelly as the reindeer barreled by.

Upa-uda, old fellow, he said, and hoped for the best.

From Niko's point of view, what happened was this: Gravity lost most of its power over Blixxen, and he rose like a reindeer-shaped balloon, passing over Juniper's person completely, but pulling the tail of her coat upward until the girl was forced to lift her arms, allowing the coat to be dragged off.

Blixxen kicked around in the air, uncertain as to what was happening. Eyes that had been clouded were now clear, as a secondary effect of polar magic is healing, so Niko's burst had effectively driven the toxins from Blixxen's bloodstream.

The elderly reindeer knew he was flying, but his last memory was snacking on a delicious red stick, and the next thing he knew he was in the air. If he could have spoken, he might have said: "Master Niko, I'm flying. Is it Christmas?"

Blixxen drifted higher and would probably have cleared the forest and floated off over Greater

London had he not become entangled in one of the upper branches of a cedar and got himself good and wedged in there like an ornament.

It was at this point that the polar magic worked its way through the reindeer's limbs and into the tree itself, casting an orange glow over the entire cedar. And, to complete the seasonal picture, Blixxen's internal thermometer decided that the reindeer was overheating and opted to release heat through the extremely dense array of blood vessels in the reindeer's nose, a release that caused the nose to glow red.

From Juniper's point of view, what happened was this: She dodged the reindeer, then her coat was tugged off, then she pitched forward into the snow and saw with one eye the reindeer fly into the tree, which then lit up like a . . . Christmas tree.

Niko, for his part, took several deep breaths and thought that, boots or no boots, he definitely needed to do some cardio more regularly as his heart was rattling his ribs with every beat. He took a minute to do a yoga breathing exercise that he'd learned at one of Duchess's sessions, then assessed the situation as calmly as he could.

Firstly, I hope my rope is long enough to wrangle Blixxen out of the tree before the magic wears off. And then I'm going to have to think of a story to tell the girl, which explains how a forest hermit who makes reindeer fly is definitely not Santa Claus.

Niko glanced down at the girl, who had rolled onto her back. Juniper appeared unhurt, but her eyes were closed. Shock often put people to sleep, especially if they'd been exposed to magic. For a moment, Niko's dislike of children softened. Duchess said that this girl Juniper was one of the special ones, and indeed she must be to even make it this far into the forest.

"What am I going to tell you?" he said softly.

Juniper's eyes flickered open. Not asleep after all.

"You can tell me what you're doing hiding in Cedar Forest," she said, and then added, "Mr. Santa Claus."

6

Extorting Santa

Two minutes before Niko clicked his neck to flood his system with magic, there were six elves huddled in a camper van at an autobahn service station outside Frankfurt in Germany. This was the Christmas support crew, and they were feeling quite frustrated that a recent blip on their ectoplasm scanner had turned out to be a false alarm.

Tomescu, the head honcho, was taking out his infuriation on his team.

"Tell me again," he said to Nord, who had reported the blip, "why we traveled all the way to Germany?"

Nord pointed to the array of scanning equipment jammed into the camper van. "The satellite picked up an ecto-bloom."

"Which you interpreted as a Santa sighting?" said Tomescu, his piercing eyes boring into the unfortunate Nord.

Nord nodded, and the bell on his pointy red hat tinkled.

"That's what it looked like to me," he said.

"But what did it actually turn out to be?" Tomescu pressed.

"Cats," said Nord.

"Say that again," said Tomescu mercilessly.

"Cats!" Nord wailed.

"Because sometimes cats can set off the scanner," Tomescu explained, twisting the pointed tips of his waxed white pencil mustache. "Sometimes, when enough cats find enough fish, their pheromones can cause what looks like an ecto-bloom to the satellite. But it's not, because a real ecto-bloom is purest orange, whereas that one has a blue tinge. What do we call that, Nord?"

"A False Feline," said Nord, looking at the curly toes of his red shoes.

"Exactly," said Tomescu. "And we don't have time for False Felines because . . . ?"

"Because it's almost Red-Letter Day when the sack gives up its Christmas letters."

Nord was correct. The following day was indeed Red-Letter Day when the magical Christmas sack surrendered the Santa letters it had gathered from around the world.

This sack was by far the most magical manufactured item on the planet, and it came from a time when elfin warlocks could bend the elements to their will. The sack's proper title was the FørsGyff, or First Gift, because the warlocks had presented it, along with its bearer, Santa Claus, to the humans when the fairy people had decided to leave the surface world for good. The FørsGyff would remind them once a year that the fairies were their friends; even the one who wielded the sack, being half human and half fairy, would be a symbol of the many alliances between humans and fairies.

Everyone at the North Pole knew what the sack was capable of, but the warlocks took the secrets of its workings to their graves. Tomescu had studied the FørsGyff for over half a century, and although he didn't fully understand its quantum aspects he did conclude that it was more of an interdimensional portal than merely a sack. In fact, he had tested the sack's material and found that it was possibly from another world. As far as he could tell, letters intended for Santa Claus were whisked from fireplace grates and stored in an in-between place where they existed out of time and space until Santa Claus called for them by simply putting his hand into the bag.

The FørsGyff had many laws and quirks, but there were three main rules that were so important they were embroidered in pictographs on the sack itself.

RULE THE FIRST:
No Claus may dive inside the sack.
Who knows if he shall e'er come back?

That one was self-explanatory. No one inside the sack. *Ever.*

RULE THE SECOND:
Should Yuletide not go right to plan,
Who draws the note becomes the man.

This meant that, should Santa be unwell or indisposed somehow, then whoever pulled out the first letter after sunrise on Red-Letter Day was crowned the Gift Giver. The Gift Giver would be able to stand in for Santa Claus and give presents that year. Usually, the sack only interacted with magical folk, but this was a one-day-only loophole where literally any creature on the planet could pull out a letter.

And finally, most important:

RULE THE THIRD:
If Claus should shirk a decagon,
The magic in the sack is done.

This meant that if no Christmas letters were pulled out by midnight on ten consecutive Red-Letter Days, then the sack would simply lose its magic and become a regular sack. Which would spell, for all intents and purposes, the end of Christmas forever.

Letters had not been pulled out for nine years. Red-Letter Day this year would be the tenth. Red-Letter Day was tomorrow.

Why did Nicholas take the sack with him? Tomescu wondered for the umpteenth time.

For ten years, they had been chasing Niko, and one way or another that chase ended tomorrow.

As he worried about the consequences of not finding Santa Claus, Tomescu noticed that a monitor registered a pure orange bloom for the briefest second.

"Where is that?" snapped the head elf.

Nord took a seat at the monitor, eager to make amends for his cat blunder.

"Southern England," he said. "We're too far away to say where exactly."

Tomescu calculated the times and distances in his head. They could still make it to England before Red-Letter Day. If they could find Nicholas Claus by tomorrow night and persuade him to come back, there might still be a Christmas, and there might still be a Santa Claus. And, if not, perhaps Nicholas would at the very least hand over the sack.

"Turn the camper round," he said to Vible the driver. "Destination UK."

Juniper may not have been fully asleep, but as she had been super stressed, and touched by one or two magical sparks, she drifted in and out of a state that could have been described as dopey. It seemed to her that Niko unwound a vine rope from around his belt and then lassoed the glowing reindeer, who was wedged into the also glowing cedar, and dragged it out of the branches.

Maybe that's how Christmas lights were invented, she thought dreamily, although *invented* was the wrong word.

Inspired, Juniper thought, correcting herself. *Maybe that's how Christmas lights were inspired.*

The reindeer stopped glowing when it was still six feet from the ground and fell with a heavy thump into a snowbank.

Juniper thought she heard Niko say "Serves you right, Blixxen," as he unwrapped his rope from the reindeer's antlers.

He's talking to the reindeer, she thought.

Juniper's perspective shifted as she was hoisted from the snow and slung over the reindeer's broad back and, in spite of the fact that Blixxen had been trying to run her over only minutes earlier, she knew that he posed no threat now. Indeed, the animal swung his shaggy head round and seemed to be wearing a guilty expression as he rose gently to his hooves.

Ha, thought Juniper. *A reindeer is trying to apologize to me.*

"That's okay, Blixxen," she said.

She would not, she decided, hold a grudge. For some reason, the reindeer had not been himself and, after all, everyone has off days.

I need to stay awake, she thought. *There is magic happening here, and I don't want to miss a moment of it.*

But she couldn't stay awake, not fully. Blixxen's hindquarters began to sway rhythmically as he walked, and Juniper, who was up way past anyone's bedtime, began to nod off.

Niko heard Juniper's breathing become slow and regular and reckoned she was fully asleep.

"Finally, I have a minute to think," he said to Blixxen, leading the odd little troupe back toward the vinterhus. "No thanks to you. How many times have I warned you about rhubarb?"

The reindeer's nose dipped, and he closed one eye. It was the expression of a deer who knew how much trouble he'd caused.

"I know it tastes nice, but it affects your senses. Your forehead is all bloody, and more importantly you nearly ran over a girl."

Blixxen's nose sunk even farther.

"I'll tell you one thing," Niko continued, "if we were doing the Christmas Eve deliveries this year, you would not be leading the team."

That was quite a harsh thing to say, so Niko relented and added in a gentler tone: "The others look up to you, Blixxen. Especially the younger ones. Skära follows you around like a puppy. What's he going to think? The great Blixxen chasing a child through the forest and all because he couldn't resist a stick of rhubarb. You need to stay near the vinterhus where civilians won't happen across you."

From somewhere in the gloaming mist between waking and sleep, Juniper eavesdropped on Blixxen's scolding and really hoped she'd remember it when she woke up. But then the swaying and exhaustion overpowered her, and her mind shut down for a power nap.

Maybe an hour later, Niko was pacing in front of the vinterhus fireplace, running over his cover story.

"You didn't see anything," he said to Juniper, who was asleep on the small bed, covered by a plush blanket woven from shaggy molted reindeer winter coats. "You bumped your head and imagined Blixxen was flying."

Irritated with his own weak excuse, Niko kicked the

hearth and immediately regretted it when the pain in his toe reminded him he'd left his work boots by the door.

"What were you doing following me anyway?" he asked. "At three in the morning. Whoever's looking after you will be worried sick."

"No one's looking after me," said Juniper. "That's why I'm here."

Niko glanced sharply at her. So the girl wasn't asleep. His Christingle must really be on the blink if Juniper had fooled him twice. All he could think to do was launch into his cover story.

"Ah, Juniper. You're awake. Good, excellent in fact. I was worried because you bumped your head, and that could cause you to hallucinate and see all sorts of things, and draw all kinds of mistaken conclusions."

Juniper opened her eyes. "Keep talking, Mr. Santa Claus. You're not fooling anyone."

Niko was momentarily flummoxed, but only momentarily because there was actually an in-service workshop in the North Pole that dealt with precisely this situation, i.e. when a Santa is accused of being Santa. The steps to deal with this are the three Ds:

De-escalate.

Deny.

Distract.

Which Niko proceeded to do.

"Take it easy," he said. "I'm not this Santa Claus fellow. Why don't I make you a mug of my famous cocoa? You could use it after the wild night you've had."

Juniper sat up. "I would like the cocoa because I have had a wild night, but you're still Santa Claus."

Niko rolled up the sleeves of his *Star Wars* sweatshirt and clattered around in the cabin's small kitchen. "Why would you even say that? A lot of people don't even believe in Santa Claus."

Juniper noticed a tattoo on Niko's right forearm. The word *CHANGE* was in stylized capitals and then leading down to it in smaller letters were the words: *Don't wait for*, and then from the left and slightly underneath was: *be the*. It therefore read: *Don't wait for CHANGE, be the CHANGE.*

Interesting.

Juniper filed this away to think about later.

"I believe in Santa Claus," she said. "I was born on Christmas Day."

Niko busied himself with a jar of cocoa and a wooden jug of milk. "So you're a Christmas fanatic. I've run into people like you before. It's all about the presents, right?"

"Yes," said Juniper. "It is all about the presents. Giving them."

Niko wasn't expecting this and slopped half of the milk intended for a tankard onto the worktop.

He added several spoonfuls of cocoa powder while he thought about how to get rid of this child.

"Here," he said, thrusting the tankard into her hands.

"It's cold," said Juniper, unimpressed. "And you didn't blend."

"I don't blend!" Niko shouted. "I don't blend cocoa or anything else. So drink it and go."

Juniper took a defiant slug of the cocoa. "I'm not going until you help me, Santa."

Niko closed his eyes. "Don't call me that, girl. My name is Niko."

"I don't believe you," said Juniper. "There's too much evidence. Santa goes missing, and you show up here, giving people presents. You live in a Christmas-tree forest with actual snow and reindeer. And you have a big beard."

"Big beards are in," countered Niko.

Juniper was well-known for never backing down from an argument, so she retorted, "The beard is not my primary evidence. My slam dunk is that you made a reindeer fly."

"You imagined that," said Niko.

Juniper took another sip of cold cocoa, which she realized was quite nice. She wondered absently if the milk was reindeer milk, but that was a conversation for another time.

"I might believe that," she said, thrusting out her lower jaw belligerently. "Except I heard you telling me what I imagined before I told you what I'd imagined. So either you can read minds or Blixxen did fly. Unless you're saying I imagined hearing you say that too. There's a lot of imagination going around."

Niko rubbed his forehead. "*What?*"

Juniper finished the cocoa in three massive glugs. "You know what."

Niko sank into a wooden armchair padded with a cushion of the same woven reindeer hair that covered Juniper.

"All this jabber," he sighed. "Your screeching makes my skull ache. What do you even want, child? Let me guess. A new phone?"

That was a cold thing to say, and Juniper felt tears spring up out of nowhere. She could not believe that this Niko man, who was most probably Santa Claus, believed she had risked her life for something like that.

"Do you really think I would do all this for a phone? You think I'd sneak out on Duchess and follow you into the forest for a *phone*? I need actual help, and I thought you might give it since your job is supposed to be helping people."

Niko's eyebrow twitched. "Duchess?"

"Yes, Duchess. Duchess is looking after me."

"Staying with you. You mean staying with you and your mother?"

Juniper stood for her big speech. "No. I mean looking

after me. Because that's why I'm here. Mum went missing and I thought Niko, the great, super, big-time Angel of Cedar Park, might be able to find her. And then I thought: Wow, he's actually Santa Claus! He'll definitely be able to help, even if he is on a break. But now I know the truth . . ."

Niko knew he shouldn't ask, but he couldn't help it.

"What truth?"

"The truth is that you hate children. That's why you quit. If you think I came here for a stupid phone . . ."

This caught Niko off guard. He didn't hate children. That wasn't it at all.

"If I hate children so much, how come I just saved you by making . . ."

"By making a reindeer fly," said Juniper triumphantly. "Checkmate, Santa." Which was pretty patronizing.

Niko's beard visibly bristled. Which was pretty scary to watch.

"I see, and if I don't help you then I bet you go and tell everyone that Santa Claus is living in Cedar Forest. Well, go ahead, child. Take a photo if you can because I'm not going to be extorted."

Juniper looked down at her shoes. "Don't worry. I would never tell on you, Mr. Niko, because you help Duchess, and I love Duchess. All I wanted to do was ask for a little bit of that help, and I thought asking would be enough. If you don't want to help, then I'll do it myself."

Niko was a little conflicted. The girl wasn't even going to threaten him with exposure. Should he simply help her? But how could he? There was nothing he could do that the police wouldn't.

I give help to people sleeping rough, he thought. *That was Sarika's mission, and now it's mine. I try in my own small way to make society a little fairer. And I can't break my cover to be the third wheel in a police matter.*

So he said, "Child, you must be tired. Would you like to hear my famous lullaby?"

Juniper was incredulous. "Lullaby? How old do you think I am? Three?"

It infuriated her that most adults couldn't tell the difference between a toddler and an eleven-year-old.

For one thing, we don't wear nappies.

Having said that, she did love a lullaby, but now was not the time, and she was about to tell Niko/Santa that in no uncertain terms when he sang the first line:

"It's growing late around the world . . ."

Niko's voice was rich and warm, and it somehow seemed like there was a whole choir singing instead of just one person.

"For every boy and every girl . . ."

Juniper realized her left eye was closing. The left lid always went first.

"Goodbye to sun, hello to moon . . ."

Juniper felt the cotton wool of dreamtime expand in her skull. *Stay awake, silly*, she told herself. *This is a magic trick.*

"Santa Claus is coming soon."

Juniper's right eye closed, and she was gone, lost in warm and wonderful dreams.

Niko sang another verse to be sure that the girl was asleep, and then began to plan. If there had been any doubt before, it was gone now.

I must leave this place.

The signs had all been there. The increasingly polar conditions. Being given a nickname: the Angel of Cedar Park, for goodness' sake. That was like wearing a novelty hat with the words I AM SANTA! stitched into it. Blixxen becoming increasingly relaxed around the rules. And now this girl showing up in the forest.

It could have been worse. She could have been seriously injured, and Juniper was nice enough, he supposed. At least she wasn't one of those obnoxious children who had driven him out of the family business. But nevertheless she was a child and could expose him whether she meant to or not.

Time to fly, he decided. But first he'd drop the girl home.

Niko felt a little guilty for using the lullaby trick on Juniper. He wasn't precisely sure of the mechanics of how the song worked, but it was something to do with the sequence of certain vowel sounds in the lyrics combined with a sprinkling of polar magic. Together, this meant that whoever heard the song would have lovely dreams and wake up reinvigorated and optimistic and, most importantly, with a very fuzzy recollection of the moments before sleep.

The lullaby was generally used to get children to nod off who might be lying in wait on the stairs for Santa to come down the chimney, as if any self-respecting Santa would squeeze down the tiny chimneys they had these days. It wasn't really recommended for use outside Santa Slow Time, but Niko had been feeling cornered by the little girl. It occurred to him now that as soon as he dropped Juniper off he would conjure himself up a little tïmboble and dismantle the vinterhus so that, by the time a puzzled Juniper made her way back to the forest for reasons she couldn't understand, he'd be reassembling the structure on another continent.

On the plus side, he would be safer anywhere but here. On the minus side, however, was the single stark fact that Duchess was on this continent, and Niko suspected that his heart had softened just enough to feel something for her.

He rubbed the CHANGE tattoo on his arm.

Another reason I must go, Sarika, he thought.

* * *

Our story would be just about over at this point had it not been for the fact that Juniper was a restless sleeper who thrashed in her sleep.

Niko settled her into the sleigh, making sure that the girl was comfortable, even though he was understandably annoyed by her, and taking special care that she faced away from the section of forest behind Blixxen's pen. But he should have taken more care. Although, in fairness to Niko, the chances of what was about to happen actually happening were a billion to one against, and he was preoccupied.

It happened because of the reindeer calf Skära who was

being trained for any sleigh duties that might pop up, even though the Christmas Eve run was off the table.

Polar reindeer are a very special breed who are compatible with magic because they share the same magnetic-field frequency as the magic itself.

One of the final stages in a reindeer's training is the imprinting. This is when a reindeer is paired with its Santa. When a calf is old enough, its magic receptors activate, and at that point the current Santa will visit the enclosure and look deep into the calf's eyes. There then follows an exchange of magic that bonds both parties forever, and that calf will work with that Santa until one of them can't work anymore.

Here's what happened: Skära was sniffing around the cedar line to the southwest of Niko's vinterhus, trying to find the source of the magic that was making him sneeze. Usually, Blixxen would keep any calf with the rest of the team until the current Santa was ready for him, but Blixxen was snoring behind the vinterhus.

So picture the scene: Skära was being drawn to Niko's magical aura, which shrouded both him and Juniper. Niko was busy hitching himself up to the sled for the short haul to Cedar Mews, and Juniper was turned away from the calf, nose down in the sleigh, eyes tightly shut.

But then Juniper rolled over so that her head was facing

Skära. She was still not awake, still not looking at anything, but her left eyelid popped open as her head bumped the rail, and—for a good five seconds—Skära stared deep into that one brown eye.

Even then, the imprinting should not have worked because nature had provided a further safeguard. Imprinting usually takes place in arctic summer before the mirrored layer in the reindeer's eye turns blue for winter vision. But, because Skära had been born under London's skyglow, he'd never known the darkness of the Arctic, and the mirrored layer behind both the reindeer's retinas, or to put it in scientific terms the tapetum lucidum, never changed from gold to blue.

Juniper only opened one eye, and that eye was unfocused, but it was enough for magical contact to be established. The imprinting itself was barely visible, hardly more than a heat blur between girl and calf, but the effect it had on both participants was electric.

Skära was blasted bodily back into the trees and landed with a heavy thump in a snowdrift, which immediately melted all around him. Juniper performed a reverse flip with a twist, landing on Niko's back as he was securing the sled reins across his chest.

"Be calm, child," said Niko. "All is well."

But all was not well.

Since Juniper had latched on to his back, Niko decided to abandon the sled idea and take the girl home on foot.

She's very jittery, he thought as he trudged through the snow, *and hadn't Duchess mentioned something about the girl being a restless sleeper?*

But this spasming was more than just Juniper's nightly gymnastics.

Her very DNA was undergoing fundamental change. The imprinting had baked the polar magic into Juniper's very bones and created a brand-new being. In effect, Juniper Victoria Lane had potentially become the world's first non-Claus Santa.

7

These Boots Were Made for Walking

Juniper woke up smiling. This was unusual, for although she was a very positive child by nature she usually did her worrying subconsciously and awoke with the faint imprint of an anxiety dream bothering her mind. It never took her long to dispel the gloom, usually tugging back the curtains did the trick, but this morning there was no bad mood. She felt great.

Juniper lay in bed, enjoying the unexpected happiness, until guilt crept in and ruined the feeling. She shouldn't really feel so cheerful, not with her mother still missing. At the very least, she should use this mysterious positivity to search for Mum with renewed vigor.

I should make a chart, she thought as the realization hit her.

Juniper's teacher Mrs. Mebrouk was a great believer in to-do charts, and each student had their personal charts taped to the classroom wall.

I can color-code it, Juniper thought, flinging off the quilt. She was surprised to find that she was still wearing her clothes from earlier.

I must have been stressed out with everything that's going on and just collapsed into bed.

But hadn't she left her clothes on for some other reason? Juniper felt certain that she had, but couldn't quite recall. Juniper was even more surprised when she pulled back the curtains to find that the park was bright and green without so much as a snowflake on the spiky winter grass.

Why did I expect snow? she wondered as there hadn't been December snow in London since her seventh birthday.

Juniper lost herself in thought for a moment, looking out over Cedar Park. Something was nagging at her memory like a woodpecker pecking at her skull, making the sound *think . . . think . . . think*.

What couldn't she remember? It was something important, she was sure of that, but for now she couldn't pin the memory down.

It'll come to me when my mind's on something else.

The woodpecker sound changed. It wasn't *think-think-think* anymore, it was *knock-knock-knock*.

Someone was at the door.

"Mum!" blurted Juniper, and she raced from her room and down the stairs.

She opened the sky-blue front door wearing what her dad had always called her high-beam smile. This particular smile was so wide that Juniper knew from experience that her cheeks would ache if she had to hold it for more than a minute.

As it happened, she didn't have to maintain the smile because when she opened the door, her heart pounding with hope and anticipation, she found that it wasn't her dear mum standing there.

Of course it's not Mum, she told herself. *Mum wouldn't knock on her own front door.*

Her mum had been gone now for more than thirty-six hours, which meant her missing-persons file had been active for over twelve hours.

And what have I been doing? Juniper thought. *Nothing but sleeping and waking up happy.*

How could she? How could she simply snuggle up in bed when her mother was missing and needed to be found?

The man at the door was speaking to her. "Has your mother come home, child?"

Juniper didn't answer immediately, taking a moment to drag her mind away from the fear of what might be happening to her mum and focus on the man in front of her.

It was the regional park director, Dafydd Carnegie.

Mr. Carnegie was wearing the regulation green park-keeper overalls, but Mum had once confided in Juniper that he'd definitely had them altered. One of Jennifer Lane's many talents was dressmaking, and she sewed all the costumes for the local Christmas pageant, so she knew what could be done with a garment. It seemed that Mr. Carnegie must have spent quite a few pounds on turning casual overalls into a smart suit.

He'd separated the overalls into a jacket and trousers and replaced the zip with brass buttons embossed with a crossed shovels logo. The park-keeper had also added gold piping to his new trousers and, if Juniper was not mistaken, the jacket shoulders had been severely padded and decorated with military epaulettes. The uniform was topped off with a green beret, which also bore a twinkling embossed brass button.

Carnegie did not appreciate being kept waiting and so repeated: "Has your mother come home, child?"

Juniper scowled. Child? Mr. Carnegie was the second person in the last twenty-four hours to refer to her as a child. She couldn't quite remember who the first one had been at the moment, but in Juniper's opinion she was definitely not a child.

"My name is Juniper," she said. "Not *child*."

Carnegie's eyes narrowed. "There's no need for your life story, child. Please announce my arrival to your mother."

Juniper didn't move from the door, and Carnegie jumped to the correct conclusion.

"Your mother has not come home," he said. "Therefore you are unsupervised. And if you are unsupervised then you must stay with a relative or, as a last resort, be placed in the system."

The phrase "in the system" flicked a switch in Juniper's mind as she flashed back to all the times she'd heard it growing up. Her dad had spent a decade in the system when he'd literally washed up on Europe's shores more than twenty years ago, and the experience had traumatized him for the rest of his life. Briar Lane had been a sunny individual by nature, but sometimes, when he was especially tired after a long day's work, he would tell Juniper that no matter what happened she must never, on any account, let herself be put into the system.

"The system is a cruel labyrinth, Junie," he'd told her.

Jennifer Lane would argue that things were better now, but Briar was insistent: "People get lost in the system, Jen," he'd said. "They get separated from their families and sometimes never find them again."

And, if Juniper had any lingering doubts about the evils of the system, Duchess soon dispelled them. She'd spent years in one somewhere and wouldn't say too much about it.

"They told me I was choosing not to work," she said. "And that if I wanted help I had to go into a residential program. So I did, and I was stuck in it for years. Never go in the system, Juniper."

In the end, Juniper's mother had to ban system talk in the Mews because it could go on all night and would put everyone in a sour mood.

So, when Carnegie used the phrase "in the system," it chilled Juniper to her core, even though she wasn't entirely sure which system the head park-keeper was referring to.

"So tell me, young lady," said Carnegie now, "when will your mother return?"

Juniper opened her mouth to respond, but nothing came out. She couldn't muster a denial because it was true that her mother had not come back. Carnegie saw the look on her face, and that gave him all the information he needed.

"I'm guessing that you don't know," he said. "You must have a relative somewhere. Preferably away from here. I need you out of the way before the Santa Vigil. I mean, I need you safely looked after before the vigil."

Juniper was on the verge of panic and could visualize her mother returning to an empty house while she was shipped off somewhere, lost in the system, never to be seen in Cedar Park again. Her situation had suddenly become desperate, and the idea struck her that perhaps she should just give up and accept whatever the grown-ups had in store for her.

And then a voice came from behind her in the cottage.

"Who is this gentleman, darling? Won't you introduce us?"

It was Duchess's voice, but with a posh English accent.

Why would Duchess be doing one of her accents? wondered Juniper, turning round. When she saw her, she asked
herself another Duchess-related question. *And why is she
wearing clothes from the donations box?* For Duchess was not
dressed in her usual oversized, flowing layers, but instead
was very smartly turned out in a tweed jacket gathered in
at the waist, matching skirt, and red leather walking shoes.
Her mane of red and gray hair was gathered on top of her
head like a sleeping cat.

"Erm, this is Mr. Carnegie."

Duchess stepped onto the porch and offered Carnegie
her hand. "Mr. Carnegie," she said, "it's such a treat to meet
you. You've come to report, I expect."

Carnegie was visibly disarmed by this woman. "Report,
madam? And to whom would I have the pleasure of reporting?"

"Why, to Jennifer's mother, Juniper's grandmother. I
rushed over to look after the dear girl."

This was an audacious lie, and surely Carnegie wouldn't
fall for it, but then again how would he know that Jennifer's
parents had passed away some years before within six
months of each other. Duchess knew because she babysat
toddler Juniper on several occasions during both illnesses.

"Delighted," said Carnegie, shaking Duchess's hand. "But I simply have to tell you . . ."

Duchess decided that whatever Carnegie simply had to tell her could be watered down with a little flattery.

"Mr. Carnegie, I can see from your marvelous uniform that you're from the Parks Office, and I wonder if you are, in fact, Director Dafydd Carnegie as featured in the newspaper?"

Carnegie blushed with pleasure. "In fact, I am. It is I, as they say. Surely you didn't bother reading that little piece?"

Duchess held on to Carnegie's hand. "Little piece? No false modesty here, sir. I agreed with every syllable you said. My daughter and I disagree on many issues, one being the mismanagement of this park. Clear them all out, I say. The park is for visitors not residents."

By now, Carnegie was thoroughly charmed. "Well, that is a turnup for the books. I'd thought that Jennifer must have come from one of those shiftless liberal families, but I see that you . . ."

Juniper filled in her grandmother's name without thinking. "Duchess . . ."

Carnegie straightened. "Duchess?"

"It's a very minor estate," said Duchess, her eyes flitting to Juniper's green scarf with its tartan trim, which hung on a coat hook. "Benbarty in Scotland. Purely ceremonial. Honestly, I never bother with the title."

Carnegie curtsied. "Nevertheless, I am honored to meet you. I cannot believe Jennifer kept you a secret, Duchess."

"I prefer to keep a low profile," confided Duchess. "So I'd appreciate it, Mr. Carnegie, if the press were not aware that I'm here. I don't have to tell you how they like to prattle on."

"It's an outrage. Line those journalists up and fire 'em. The scandalmongers, I mean, of course."

"Not the ones who report on real news like the efforts of the Parks Office," said Duchess.

"Precisely."

Duchess steered the conversation in another direction. "And so, Dafydd, if I may call you Dafydd? I feel I know you, having read that article . . ."

Carnegie confirmed with a theatrical bow that the duchess was indeed free to refer to him as Dafydd.

"I wonder if you had any news of my daughter, the future duchess. We're quite beside ourselves with worry. I feel certain that's why you came, out of compassion for my granddaughter."

Carnegie's forehead blushed slightly, and he stammered an answer. "Oh . . . of course, Duchess. Sadly, I have come to report that there is no news. None whatsoever. But the Met do inform me that most missing persons turn up within forty-eight hours."

Duchess sighed. "It's so unlike her. She dotes on little Juniper, who, I'm sure you agree, brightens up the entire park."

"Of course," said Carnegie through gritted teeth. "She's a gem."

Duchess placed four fingers on the doorknob, obviously intending to close the door, when Carnegie actually doffed his cap and decided to confide in this marvelous lady.

"But between us, Duchess, and I think you'll approve of these dispatches from the Parks Office, my orders are to step into the vacuum, temporarily, and make a few changes around here."

Both Duchess and Juniper felt an almost identical sinking in their tummies.

"What kind of changes?" asked Juniper, and there was more than a touch of belligerence in her tone.

"Now, now, dear," said Duchess, in character. "The grown-ups are talking."

"Yes, Juniper," said Carnegie. "This is adult business."

Duchess nodded as if approving of Carnegie's stern tone. "Go on, dear Dafydd."

Carnegie went on. "The thing is that Cedar Park has gone downhill in recent years. Not the park itself, which it must be said looks more magnificent than ever, but the culture of accommodating the indigents and vagabonds. My mission from head office is to clear these people out."

If Carnegie had been paying close attention, he would have noticed Duchess's body language change quite dramatically. Her entire person tensed as she struggled to maintain her cover.

"Clear them out? In what way?"

"It's tricky," admitted Carnegie. "People do have basic human rights, even those people. But I can make things less drifter-friendly. Break up those shelters that resemble armadillos . . ."

"Nodbokses," mumbled Juniper, not exactly sure where the word had come from. Luckily, Carnegie was not paying her much attention and went on with his report.

". . . and, of course, put an end to this ridiculous Santa Vigil."

Santa, thought Juniper. Wasn't there something about Santa that she should remember?

Duchess was so stunned that it was all she could do to repeat what Carnegie had said. "Break up the Armadillos and put an end to the Santa Vigil."

"Precisely. Can you believe that some people on the council want to extend the vigil citywide? It's already operating in half a dozen parks. No, this needs to be nipped in the bud."

"Heaven forbid people should be safe and comfortable in a public park," said Juniper.

Carnegie did not register the sarcasm. "Precisely. Parks

are a business and should be run as such. With military precision. Obviously, we would never dismiss your daughter after everything she's been through. Not immediately. But my orders are to have the new regime up and running before she gets back. And, if Jennifer doesn't like the new Cedar Park or living in Cedar Mews, then we'll need to have a conversation." Carnegie leaned in close to Duchess. "I've heard rumors that your daughter is actually inviting these homeless people into the Mews."

"No!" said Duchess.

"Yes," confirmed Carnegie. "Can you imagine? Those people in here?"

"I can't even bear to think of it," said Duchess, squeezing the doorknob till it squeaked.

"Homeless people sleeping in the same bed as a duchess," said Carnegie, wiggling his fingers like ten little worms. "Horrible. What has this country come to?"

"It's come to its senses," blurted Juniper.

"My granddaughter has a lot to learn, Dafydd," said Duchess, gripping Juniper's shoulder. "And I am here to teach her."

Dafydd chanced a compliment. "And there can be no finer teacher, Duchess. The girl is in splendid hands."

Duchess plumped up her pile of hair, and it teetered dangerously.

"So the second reason I have come is for the key to the lockup," continued Carnegie. "I need to get the ball rolling while . . ."

"While what?" Juniper demanded. "While Mum is missing?"

"No, no, dear child," said Carnegie as though Juniper was three instead of eleven. "While the weather is good."

"The ball rolling, you say?" asked Duchess.

Carnegie puffed out his chest. "I'm on a mission today, Duchess. We are continuing our clear-out of all the vigil donations."

"The Santa Vigil?" said Juniper. "My dad started that tradition. It's the biggest part of him that's still with us."

This was true. Jennifer and Juniper could always feel Briar around them, but most especially at Christmas. The previous year, when they'd let the vigil slide, it had seemed like Briar had moved a little further away from them, so this year they were determined to resurrect it in style.

The Santa Vigil had started off modestly enough with the Lanes and half a dozen friends gathered by candlelight to sing Christmas carols to the heavens on 18 December in an attempt to show Santa Claus just how much he was missed and maybe tempt him back to work. As a side note, the candles were solar-battery-powered as it's not a great idea to have bunches of people waving naked flames in a forest-adjacent park.

But the number of villagers soon increased as it seemed as though the vigil struck a chord with people in general and, by year two, there were hundreds of people crowded round the Cedar Park bandstand, adding their voices to the core group of Lanes and unofficial park residents. This year there were six school choirs registered to turn up, including Juniper's own, three cheerleading squads, and a brass band. Even more exciting was the fact that Briar Lane's Santa Vigil had spread to several other parks in the Greater London area, and there were plans for vigils in Edinburgh and Cardiff too. It seemed that there would be more every year unless park-keepers like Dafydd Carnegie succeeded in shutting them down.

Carnegie put on a sad face. "Ah, yes. Poor dear departed Briar. We've already disposed of the donations from our first park, and tonight it's Cedar Park's turn. So I will need the key."

Duchess handed Carnegie the big brass key that hung behind the door. "And what exactly will you do with all the donations?"

"The official story is re-donate them to local charities," said Carnegie, then winked. "But unofficially we'll probably burn them. The mayor wants this stuff gone ASAP."

Juniper felt Duchess lean heavily on her shoulder. The donations of food parcels, blankets, and clothing were a lifeline during the cold winter, and this so-called public servant planned to burn the lot?

Juniper knew she should simply stay quiet so this vile man would leave, but she couldn't help herself.

"You can't just burn the donations!" she said.

"You're right, of course. No burning, I promise," said Carnegie, winking broadly at Duchess.

Juniper called him on it. "You winked!"

"I most certainly did not," said Carnegie, and winked again.

Duchess could feel the tremors running across Juniper's shoulders, and she knew the girl was about to explode so she put together a sentence laced with trigger words.

"Now, Juniper. Mr. Carnegie has a system. A big system that can seem quite cold, but really we should let him be about his official business or else we'd be interfering in that business and might get tangled up in the system."

Juniper glanced up at Duchess and nodded. She got the message: *Don't interfere right now or you might end up tangled in the big cold system.*

Carnegie seemed quite touched. "Thank you, Duchess. I can't tell you how much I appreciate the support. You wouldn't believe how many people harbor sympathies for the undesirables who squat in our parks."

"Really?" said Duchess, who was such a good actress that even the word *undesirables* couldn't shake her.

"Oh yes. And these are the very same people who write letters to the *Guardian* when they find a chocolate wrapper in the bushes. They want it both ways, you see?"

"I see," said Duchess, and now her fingers clamped on Juniper's shoulder. Tight with tension. "We really should let you get on, dear Dafydd. You have a busy day ahead smashing Armadillos."

"I do, Duchess," confirmed Carnegie. "Obviously, I won't be doing the smashing personally. I have outsourced that labor."

"They've already started, one supposes?" said Duchess innocently.

"No. Not a single hammer swings until I say so, but rest assured that this afternoon the sound of illegal shelters being smashed will ring through the forest. And late tonight we will clear out the lockup when there's no one around to object. I've already disposed of one load of donations from another park, and it went off without a hitch."

Juniper filed that information away: this afternoon.

Duchess spoke as she closed the front door. "I wish you the very best with your endeavors, and rest assured that there will be no interference from my granddaughter. If news of Jennifer, future duchess of Benbarty, should happen to come your way, please don't hesitate to call. No appointment necessary for you, dear Dafydd."

"Of course, Duchess," said Carnegie. "You may count on me."

And, with that false promise, the park director bowed and scraped his way backward down the short paved path.

Once they were absolutely certain that Carnegie had gone, Duchess and Juniper sat at the kitchen table and put a plan together.

"One," said Juniper, "we keep on looking for Mum."

"Agreed," said Duchess. "That is our main mission and our priority."

"Two, we save the Armadillos by this afternoon."

Duchess took out her phone. "I've got that one covered. One post from me and Mr. Carnegie will find his outsourced hammer-swingers are met with serious opposition."

"And three," said Juniper, "the donations. They've got to be saved. How are we going to do that?"

"That depends on how saving the Armadillos goes," said Duchess, but she didn't seem so sure about step three.

Juniper didn't have anything to add. The clock was ticking, and she did not want to let her father's legacy go up in smoke, but uppermost in her mind was step one: *Look for Mum.*

8

Be the Change

Duchess was as good as her word and not a single Armadillo was smashed that afternoon because she posted a call for help on Parklife, and an army of decent folk turned up to form human shields round the eight Armadillos dotted about Cedar Park. Duchess and Juniper stayed away because they didn't want to blow their cover story about Duchess being Juniper's grandmother. It would only take a bit of digging to tear that fiction apart, especially the Duchess-being-an-actual-duchess bit, and then Juniper would be put into the system that almost broke her dad's spirit. So their hope was that Jennifer would come back before any investigation was needed.

Duchess kept tabs on the whole showdown online and nearly cried with relief when a red-faced Carnegie was forced by the arrival of local TV cameras to pretend that his team were actually there to do a safety check on the Armadillos.

The rest of the day was spent looking for Jennifer Lane. Juniper made two trips to a local police station to make sure that there was no news. There was no news, and the constable at the front desk assured her that no news was good news. This didn't seem right to Juniper, who felt that no news made her feel like bad news was coming. Only good news would be good news. And good news would be great news.

After several more hours of no news, Juniper lay on her bed with her green scarf draped over her and tears running from the corners of her eyes into her ears. She could have easily adjusted her pillow so that the tears would miss her ears entirely, but even that seemed like way too much effort at the moment. She knew that important things were going on in the park, and she knew that on any other day she would have been the middle link in that human chain round Duchess's Armadillo shelter, but right now the stress was pummeling her like a tsunami.

How could everything go so wrong so quickly?

It seemed as though the Lanes had finally been on the way back to some kind of normality and now all of this: Mum was missing, the Santa Vigil donations were being incinerated in a matter of hours, and the Armadillos were still on Carnegie's hit list.

Not Armadillos, said her inner voice. *Nodbokses.*

Juniper barely heard the little voice. It was just her imagination making things up. After all, what did the word *nodboks* even mean?

It means, said her inner voice patiently, *nut box—like a bigger version of a squirrel feeder.*

Juniper thought that maybe her imagination was running riot, and she should concentrate on the main problem of finding her mother.

But really there was nothing to do till morning. There were flyers up all along the high street and round the general Cedar Park area. The hospitals had been checked. Duchess's friends who also lived in the park combed the area and sent word out across the city. Of course this could mean she'd be put into some kind of temporary care, but that was a risk she would have to take. And it would be temporary because Mum was coming back. There was an explanation for this that might not be simple—it might even be convoluted—but there would be one because Juniper could not even contemplate that something terrible might have happened.

Mum is fine, she told herself. *Completely fine. Someday we'll look back on this and have a good old laugh.*

But today was not that that day. Today was for crying.

"Mum," she said softly, her voice warbling a little. "Come home, Mum."

★ ★ ★

Juniper might have stayed like that all night, lying on the bed, crying, had someone not told her that if you wanted things to change then you had to make that change happen.

"Who told me that?" she asked the ceiling.

And this question set her thinking and slowed her tears from a flood to a trickle.

Change. Change. What was the exact phrase?

Juniper woke her phone and typed in the phrase: Don't wait for change, be the change.

Where had that come from?

"I must have read it somewhere," she muttered while the search wheel spun.

There were several million hits. Juniper scrolled with a thumb until she hit an exact match.

"Don't Wait for Change, Be the Change. How We Can Solve the Housing Problem," a doctoral thesis by Sarika Khatri.

Underneath the heading was a headshot of a young Indian woman smiling into the camera. Juniper smiled back; she couldn't help it. In spite of all that she had on her mind, she just knew instinctively that she would like this person.

Or I would have liked her, she thought with some dismay as she noticed the dates under Sarika's photo, which in cold black and white told the story of a woman who had died far too young.

Why is the world such a horrible place?

Juniper noticed something in the photo. There was an arm round Sarika's shoulder. The rest of the person had been cropped out, but Juniper could see the rolled-up cuff of a flannel shirt and a forearm wrapped in clingfilm, and under the clingfilm was a fresh tattoo: Don't wait for CHANGE, be the CHANGE.

Interesting, thought Juniper. *That must be her boyfriend.*

And being inquisitive by nature she decided to investigate further.

In the dark ages, maybe five years ago, it would have been impossible to find out more about the cropped photo unless you worked for MI6, but now a two-year-old could do it in a few swipes. Juniper copied the photo and ran another search with an app called *Put Me in the Picture* and in less than a minute had the original photo on her screen, sourced from Sarika's sister's Facebook page.

Why am I even looking at this? Juniper wondered, then went on to scrutinize the picture.

She could see now that Sarika wore a red sari underneath her graduation robes, and that the man embracing her had a wide smile, a blond beard tinged with gray, and blue eyes so piercing they looked like they'd been passed through a filter. The shaggy man's hand rested on Sarika's neck and on the third finger gleamed a wedding ring.

That man lost his wife, she realized.

All that happiness pulled out from under him like a rug.

Why am I thinking about his problems when I have so many of my own?

What I should do is follow his advice.

Be the change.

Maybe there was nothing she could do about finding Mum till the morning, but she could certainly keep an eye on the donations in case Carnegie tried to sneak into the park after the protest had disbanded. Duchess had not specifically forbidden her from mounting a very early-morning stakeout of the donations shed so Juniper dressed warmly, winding her green scarf round her neck.

Before Juniper could put on her coat, she heard a noise from outside the window. There were plenty of sounds drifting up from the park and the motorway beyond, but this was new, halfway between a goose honk and a trombone.

Juniper laughed at herself that her first thought had been: *My reindeer has arrived*, but when she opened the curtains a crack she saw in the moonlight that there was indeed a young reindeer waiting in the garden. He was maybe five feet high and colored like a Labrador with starter antlers that looked like two fuzzy boomerangs stuck onto his head.

Juniper opened the curtains wide and let the reindeer see her. He raised his head, exposing a ruffle of chocolate fur along the underside of his neck, and then their eyes met and a ripple of magic flowed between them like a concentrated jet of glowing orange plasma. It barely lasted a second, but in it was contained an exchange of information big enough to fill an entire data center.

Now Skära knew everything about Juniper, and she knew everything about him, becoming lifelong friends in a single moment. It was a funny feeling to be utterly and completely at ease with someone you had barely met, but that's what it was like. Skära and Juniper knew in that split second that they would die for each other.

Suddenly Juniper remembered everything from the night before. She remembered falling asleep in the nodboks. She remembered the magical forest snowfall. She remembered the extremely grumpy Blixxen, and of course she remembered the equally grumpy Niko, who she now realized had been married to Sarika and was, in fact, the absentee Santa Claus that the world was looking for.

In short, everything Niko's lullaby had made her forget now came rushing back.

Juniper sat on the edge of her homework desk for a moment just to process all that was happening, and then she grabbed her coat and opened the window. She climbed onto the flat roof of the extension and from there down the rose trellis so that she might introduce herself properly to her new best friend, who just happened to be one of Santa's reindeer.

She beamed a thought to Jade in Jamaica: *You're still my best human friend, Jade, but we have someone new for the group. He's called Skära and you'll love him.*

The elf squad were three hours from Paris in their camper van, on the A2 motorway outside Brussels. It was 2 a.m. Red-Letter Day. The satellite picked up another magical bloom. It was faint, barely enough to register on the scanners, but it was enough to give Nord the confidence to announce: "I've got something!"

"Meow," said Vible, snickering over her shoulder.

"Keep your eyes on the road, navigator," ordered Tomescu.

"I don't know why she gets a title. She's not even navigating," Nord grumbled. "The GPS is."

Tomescu sighed. He wasn't surprised that his elves were bickering. The Central Elf Council had given them till the end of Red-Letter Day to find Santa and bring him back, because after that Nicholas Claus would have passed a full decade without a soaking in the liveflud, and his magic would disappear forever. If that happened, there

was a strong majority in the council who wanted to shut the Santa program down for good. After all, it had never directly benefited the elfin community and, if anything, it had drawn attention to their existence.

The polar elves were the only fairies left living above-ground, if inside a glacier could be counted as such, and, for as long as Santa flew, humans would be trying to find his base. There had been a notable decrease in the number of probes, drones, and satellites passing over since Nicholas Claus had stepped down, and a lot of elves liked it that way.

But Tomescu and his team believed in Christmas with all their hearts, and not just because their jobs were at stake.

Tomescu was a statistics guy, and his numbers didn't lie: Christmas made people nicer to one another. There were more complicated ways to say it, but what it boiled down to was that for the months of December and January hostilities dwindled and kindness went up. And the elves knew this was due to Santa Claus, because now that he wasn't delivering, those positive-action figures were crumbling, and international meanness was on the rise. There was more corporate greed, pollution, war, and loneliness.

The world needs Santa Claus back, thought Tomescu for the millionth time in the past ten years. *And we need to find him before midnight.*

He swung his chair toward Nord and the instruments. "What have you got?" he asked.

Nord tapped the screen, and there was an orange bloom captured over North London.

"There. Very faint—almost transparent—and I've never seen this configuration before."

Tomescu had, but only in simulations. "That's a pairing. Nicholas must have a young reindeer calf in the herd."

Tomescu tapped a quick search into his tablet. They could still make it to London in time if they caught the Eurostar from Paris. But North London was bigger than most European cities, and unless there was a major magical bloom they would never find Nicholas by midnight. But Tomescu wouldn't give up hope even with the council deadline looming.

"Step on it," he ordered Vible. "The Eurostar leaves in three hours."

★ ★ ★

Meanwhile, in Cedar Park, North London, there was, of course, a magical reindeer outside Juniper Lane's house. But how did that happen?

When we left Skära, he'd just imprinted with Juniper

outside the vinterhus, and had been sent tumbling into a snowdrift by the Spangle exchange. And, by the time Niko returned from dragging Juniper home in the sleigh, Skära was up and about, shaking away the sparks in his vision and wondering where his new best friend had gone.

Before the calf could investigate this, Niko magicked up a time-containment membrane, or tïmboble, so he would have enough time to disassemble the log cabin. Using magic like this didn't worry him because the tïmboble was the only spell that wouldn't show up even on Tomescu's radar. This was ironic because it had been Tomescu who came up with the final filters and probably Tomescu who was searching for him right now.

It suddenly occurred to Niko that maybe Tomescu had found a way to detect his own spell so he quickly set everyone to work stripping the vinterhus down to the floorboards and assembling the sleigh from the timber. In fairness, Niko did most of the stripping and assembling himself as reindeer, no offense, are better suited to grunt work.

Niko seemed to grow more morose as he labored, and you might think it was because he'd had a close brush with being discovered. It was partly down to that, but the main reason was something that had happened earlier at Cedar Mews when he dropped off Juniper.

It was after Niko had plopped Juniper into her own bed and was back on the Mews extension roof, mentally patting himself on the back for being so super sneaky, that he made a mistake.

Niko looked in a window.

This was a mistake because he knew who was staying in the cottage, and the last thing his sensible side told him he needed was to see that person one last time.

Duchess was sitting at a table, doing her best to get a brush through her wild head of gray-streaked red hair. It was no easy task. Duchess had the sort of thick, wiry locks that could tangle in seconds. At one time, hair like this had been stylish, and people had paid a lot of money to get their hair crimped, but Duchess's was all natural. It grew at a forty-five-degree angle from her scalp in waves that grew looser the farther they traveled from her head. At the moment, her hair was too long for Duchess to reach the ends, even with her arms straightened, so she had to brush it in sections with one hand while she draped it over the other arm. It was tough going, and Niko noticed her glancing at a pair of scissors on the dresser.

"No, darling," he whispered. "Don't do that."

And, as if she could hear the thought, Duchess turned her face toward him, but Niko was an old hand at making himself scarce and jumped from the roof to the garden bushes below before Duchess's gaze even landed on the window.

Niko was halfway back to the vinterhus before he realized what he'd called Duchess.

Darling. He'd said: "No, darling. Don't do that." Out loud.

He'd only ever called one other person darling.

Niko tried to kid himself that it was just a slip of the tongue, but he wasn't fooling anyone.

Duchess is why I've stayed too long, he admitted to himself finally. *And Duchess is why I don't want to leave.*

But I must go, his guilt told him. *There are so many more people to help.*

And so now Niko had conjured up a time bubble and was dismantling the vinterhus with perhaps more determination than was absolutely necessary. No one understood completely how the bubble worked, although Tomescu claimed to. It either slowed time down for anyone inside the bubble or speeded up the contained reality considerably so that, if someone was looking at it from the outside, Niko and the reindeer would appear as blurs.

At any rate, Niko labored mightily inside the bubble. He ripped apart the vinterhus and used the ingenious elfin carpentry known as wüd-drøm, which literally meant "wooden dreams," to reassemble it as the sleigh, or gifslaad.

Then he slung on the reindeers' saddlebags and harnessed them for takeoff.

There were currently six reindeer in the flight crew plus Skära, who needed to be imprinted before departure so he could fly alongside. Actually, Niko had been expecting Skära to wander over at some point as he must be ready to pair by now, but there was no sign of the scallywag.

I should have checked him earlier when I packed his saddlebag, Niko thought. *Probably off somewhere looking for a nice fern to chew on.*

There was no need to worry though. Skära couldn't wander too far. It took polar magic to enter or leave the tïmboble, and Skära hadn't been activated yet.

He's here somewhere, thought Niko, and then forgot about it and got back to finishing off the sleigh. There were a few rough joints to be sanded down or the wind would sneak in and rip the thing apart.

"Stop moaning," he told Blixxen, who was huffing loudly in protest at being back in a harness. "We're not going too far. North Africa maybe for now. You keep complaining like that and maybe I'll decide to relocate all the way to New Zealand."

Eventually, everything was done and dusted. Niko's possessions were piled high on the gifslaad, and the only loose end was Skära, who had managed to hide himself inside a bubble with a radius of twenty meters.

Niko whistled. "Skära, come here, fellow. Come to the gifslaad."

Blixxen raised his nose and snuffled. It was a three-part snuffle that Niko interpreted as: *He's not here.*

"You must still have rhubarb in your system," said Niko. "Of course he's here. Nothing living can leave the tïmboble unless it's magical, and Skära is not yet . . ."

Niko stopped speaking, and he froze in his heroic pose on the sleigh's bench, his eyes losing their focus as he ran through a possible sequence of events.

Was Skära really gone?

If he was, he must be magical now.

The only way to become magical was to imprint with a magical human.

The only other human Skära could ever have met was Juniper.

Juniper wasn't magic; he was certain of it.

She'd only had a few sparks in her during the lullaby.

Those would have worn off unless . . .

"Oh, Christmas bells," said Niko. "We need to find that calf."

And not just because he was one of the gang, but because of what was in his saddlebags.

★ ★ ★

Juniper did not approach Skära tentatively as she might a horse, leading with her fingers so the animal could get a good sniff of her; she ran up to the reindeer calf and flung her arms round his neck.

"Hey, fella," she said. "It's me, Juniper. We're partners now, right? Forever."

Skära answered her with a nuzzle, and the short hairs on his face scratched along Juniper's coat.

"I can't believe all of this," said Juniper mostly to Skära but also to herself. "I've met Santa. He's magical, and I'm full of magic too. It feels like I drank too much fizzy cola, except in my brain and not in my tummy."

That didn't make much sense, but Skära seemed to accept it.

"Maybe you feel the same way, Skära," said Juniper, scratching the brown fur under the calf's chin. It never even crossed her mind to be afraid of a reindeer who was certainly big enough to knock her over at the very least. After all, they'd been imprinted on each other, and Skära would no more harm her than she would him.

"What are we supposed to do?" she asked the reindeer. "A girl and a reindeer."

Skära pulled away from Juniper and presented his hindquarters.

"Charming," said Juniper. Mum often said that when something was just the opposite.

But then Skära wiggled his rump, and Juniper realized that he was drawing her attention to his saddlebags.

"What's in there?" she asked.

Juniper was perfectly aware that those saddlebags were most certainly not her property, but she was very tempted to take a peek inside.

I shouldn't look, she thought.

But, if there's a child alive who can resist a magical reindeer inviting her to look in Santa's saddlebags, Juniper was not that child.

She opened the leather straps on the left saddlebag and peered in. Inside was a sack with some strange little cartoons stitched into it. The right saddlebag contained a pair of black boots.

Juniper thought about these items for a moment, and then the penny dropped.

"Are those what I think they are?" she asked her reindeer partner.

Skära looked back over his shoulder and nodded. He knew what they were.

Juniper thought about the sack and the boots and wondered if she should use them. She was thinking that maybe she shouldn't when the headlights of a large truck went by on the road. Nothing unusual about that, but these headlights swung in a tight arc, slicing through the shadows inside the park itself.

The truck's destination was confirmed when Director Carnegie climbed down from the cab and unlocked the main gate. Carnegie had found a window of opportunity after the protestors went to bed and before they came back, and he would use that time to steal away the vigil donations.

"I know what that truck has come to collect," Juniper told Skära, and suddenly her doubts about using the saddlebag items vanished. She knew exactly what the first mission with her reindeer partner should be.

After all, this is the kind of thing Christmas should be all about. I bet Niko would do it if he was thinking straight.

Skära ducked down and poked Juniper's coat with one of his fuzzy antlers. Juniper checked the point the antler had touched, and saw that the repair tape she'd used to fix up her coat was like an arrow and was glowing bright yellow in the dark. A glowing yellow arrow that was pointing at her head.

"You're right," she said, tugging off her green coat. "This will lead them right to us." She left her right arm in the sleeve and then whipped the coat like a skipping rope so that it turned inside out.

"But don't worry, Skära. This coat is reversible."

The Puffa coat was indeed reversible, and the inside that became the outside was fire-engine red.

9

Intrude

Director Dafydd Carnegie wasn't a bad man, but over the years he had become rather a mean person, which occasionally led to him doing bad things like threatening Juniper Lane with the system. People are not born mean, and usually the journey from kind to mean is a long and tortuous one filled with harsh life lessons, but Dafydd Carnegie had completed most of that transformative journey in a single Christmas Day.

Dafydd had been a gifted boy soprano, and his dream was to sing the lead in a musical-theater show. He didn't care about money or fame. All young Dafydd cared about was the song and the singing of it. In many ways, he was a pure artist, and this was why he was so devastated when a boy called Cabby Bellows was given the Santa role in the school society's production of *Rudolph the Red-Nosed*

Reindeer. First of all, what kind of name was Cabby? But secondly, Dafydd himself was clearly the better performer in every possible way.

The nine-year-old Carnegie was so peeved that he tore up his unsent Santa letter and burned a new one in the grate asking Santa to fix it so that he himself could take over the role for the final week of the run after Christmas Day. He didn't ask for anything to happen to Cabby, but it was certainly implied.

When Cabby broke his wrist on Christmas Day, having fallen off the skates that he'd received from Santa, Dafydd felt responsible.

The guilt was awful for a few hours, but then Dafydd was given the Santa role, and he buried the guilt down deep and enjoyed the magical experience.

But guilt never really disappears, and over the years it curdled in his heart, and his initial vow to never do something like that again was replaced by the maxim to do whatever was necessary to achieve his goal. Which was how he continued to operate long after his soprano voice disappeared.

Now that his dream was dead through no one's fault but his own, Dafydd's subconscious decided that he might as well just do as he pleased and get what he could, which eventually led him to this dark mischief of collecting goodwill donations to be incinerated in the dead of night.

As he watched the men he had hired load up the bags of blankets, clothing, food parcels, and non-perishables from a shipping container that Briar Lane had repurposed as a secure shed, Dafydd thought: *Did I not once love Christmas above all seasons? Was Dafydd Carnegie not, in fact, a champion of Christmas?*

He shrugged. Maybe forty years ago in Cardiff he had been, as a boy who didn't know how the world worked, but time could crush anybody's beliefs. Even Santa had lost faith in Christmas so why shouldn't he?

Every man for himself, Daff, he thought now. *One does what one must.*

But, even as he repeated his mottos to himself, Dafydd Carnegie's mind flashed on little Juniper Lane, and he realized that she was Christmas's new champion. Dafydd could not avoid the cold, hard fact that he himself was most likely the one crushing her dreams, and if that was indeed the case then he was to her what Cabby Bellows had been to him.

I have become one of life's Cabbys.

This thought made his skin crawl, but only for a moment because then Carnegie did what he always did: He focused on the positives for him and shut away the objections of young Dafydd the boy soprano.

In this particular situation, the advantages of clearing out the park were obvious to him. The mayor had assured him that if Cedar Park became undesirable-free by Christmas then Dafydd would become director of parks for the entire city.

Since Santa is not delivering presents anymore, I'll just have to give this one to myself, Dafydd thought, walking toward the container to hurry the men along before that pesky Juniper Lane woke up and caused a fuss. *I have one week to clear out this park, and no do-gooder child will stand in my way.*

The men Carnegie had hired from Miss Trude Madden certainly were efficient, but Carnegie knew that local businesswoman Trude Madden and everyone connected with her had a shady side, and it occurred to him that now he had a shady side too.

I should never have contacted that woman, he thought.

There was a rumor going around that Trude Madden's full name was not Trudy Madden, as one might think, but Intrude Madden.

Intrude?

What kind of name was that for a child? And what would it do to that child's personality?

Apparently, it was the Madden custom to name their children after the crimes they would probably commit.

Carnegie shuddered.

I've made a mistake, he realized. *I've crossed a line, and it might be tricky to cross back.*

But, even so, he had to admit that Trude's men were very professional and very sneaky, making barely a sound as they stripped the container of everything except cobwebs within minutes. It also gave Dafydd great satisfaction to lock the unit behind them with a big brass key that he had no intention of ever giving back.

The driver, Miss Trude's own son, Lar, took the third exit off the roundabout opposite the tube station and then drove along a minor road lined with restaurants, pubs, and shuttered food trucks. From this street, they took a left onto Crumbly Lane, and Carnegie noticed that the granite cornerstones had been roughly rounded by the scrapes of a thousand vehicles that had failed to make the sharp turn. Miss Trude's darling boy was familiar with the route and made no such error, in spite of the fact that he was hauling seventeen meters of container behind the cab.

But even though Lar took the turn accurately, he did forget to pull in his wing mirror. This particular wing mirror was known as a smuggler's glass because it was illegally extended so that the driver could get a good look at anything coming up behind him to make sure he wasn't being followed. They had been popular in the last century, but had more or less been superseded by bumper cams. However, this was a very old truck.

Carnegie jumped when the mirror was bashed flat by something close to the cab.

"Not again," said Lar, panic written all over his face. "Not another one."

He stomped on the foot brake and jumped out, disappearing round the back of the truck only to reappear less than a minute later.

"It was just a windowsill—no need to panic," he said to Carnegie, who hadn't asked and wasn't panicking.

Carnegie might have wondered what Lar had meant by the comment "not another one," but he decided that the less he knew about the Maddens' activities outside their mutual dealings the better.

In spite of the fact that the incinerator plant was less than a mile from Cedar Park, Carnegie had never been down Crumbly Lane before. No one would come down here unless they had some desperate business as there were no lights and the tarmac was pitted and treacherous. The shadows seemed a shade darker than regular shadows, and sharp, suspicious faces glared out from behind net curtains in upstairs windows.

Finally, after a hundred pothole bounces, the truck emerged into a large floodlit yard half the size of a football field. At the front of the yard, there was a wholesome-looking

Junior Jockeys riding school, complete with stables and paddock, but behind that was a second yard where the Madden gang did their off-the-books business. Old car husks were piled in teetering towers round the fence, and at the far end squatted a huge metal machine bristling with pipes and pistons and a steel chimney belching smoke from its cowl. This was the incinerator that only ran at night because it was illegal.

The incinerator's twin loading doors were open, and Carnegie could see the fire within. It was like something out of a dystopian movie where leather-clad mutants had taken over the earth. But that wasn't a leather-clad mutant standing sentry by the doors. It was something far more sinister: Miss Trude Madden, backlit by the dragon breath of incinerator flames.

She cut an odd figure: a tiny Irishwoman with sharp, stretched features, she was dressed in a frilled white blouse and high-waisted black trousers, her short hair styled high in a quiff. Around her tiny waist hung her notorious bum bag, which local legend said was plump with cash and various weapons.

Lar pulled over, and Carnegie climbed down from the cab.

"Good evening to you, Mademoiselle Trude," he said.

"It's Miss Trude, Carnegie," she snapped. "It's short for Intrude, if you didn't know. My old dad's little joke. The family business, you might say."

"I did know that, actually," said Carnegie.

"That's why I'm called Lar," said her son. "Short for Larceny."

Dafydd flashed the Carnegie smile and waited for this madness to sink in.

"As you say, Miss Trude," he said after a silence that was very close to being uncomfortable. "At any rate, greetings to you and young Larceny."

Miss Trude had no time for pleasantries.

"Can we get this beast loaded with offerings? Time is money, council money that you're misdirecting to burn donations that are meant to help the lives of local people who are struggling . . . isn't that it?"

Carnegie nodded, thinking that what he was doing sounded dreadful coming out of the Irishwoman's mouth.

"Precisely, Miss Trude," he said. "Time is indeed money."

Miss Trude circled a finger over her head. "Fill her up, buckos," she said to her men. "I'm feeling the chill."

The four men sprang into action, unloading the donations into a large trolley.

"Are you certain it all has to go, Carnegie?" Miss Trude asked. "I'd wager there's fine pickings in there."

"It all has to go," insisted Carnegie. "Every last bag."

Trude sighed. "Very well, fella. You're the boss."

Once the trolley was piled high, the men took a corner

each and wheeled it to within six feet of the incinerator doors. Miss Trude's boys formed a chain and began passing bags along the line.

The first bag was flung neatly into the incinerator and immediately exploded into a hissing blue flame.

Miss Trude nodded. "Some fizzy drinks in that one, judging by the color." She sniffed the air. "Cola, I'd wager."

Carnegie did not care to play this game—guessing the contents of each bag—but he couldn't leave until the job was done so he'd be certain of his promotion.

"Park-keeper for the whole borough," he said under his breath, reminding himself why he was stooping to associate with the criminal Maddens.

And once he was borough head park-keeper Carnegie silently vowed that he would never associate with them again.

"Cuddly toys," said Trude as another bag went up. "You can hear the synthetic stuffing crackle. It's my favorite sound."

It didn't take long for the crew to empty the trolley, then it was back to the truck for the second load. But there appeared to be a problem because the men stopped suddenly, then bounced back a step as though they'd encountered a force field.

Miss Trude called to her son. "What's the problem, darlin'?"

"It's empty, Ma!" Lar called back. "The rest of the bags

have disappeared." And to drive this point home he mimed a hand explosion and said: "*Poof.*"

"The bags have disappeared?" Carnegie shrieked. "What do you mean, *poof*? Check, man. Check again!"

Miss Trude agreed. "The director's right, Lar, love. Bags only go poof inside the incinerator so be a dear and check again."

"Check again, is it?" said Lar. "Check again? I can see when a truck is empty, Ma. You don't have to be a brain surgeon with X-ray eyes." He shone his phone light into the shadows at the back of the trailer.

"Having said that," he added, squinting, "there does seem to be something in there . . ."

And Lar moved closer to the truck and saw a little person wearing a red coat and high black boots, holding a sack.

It looks like a mini-Santa, he thought. But that was ridiculous, so he said: "It might be an elf."

This was so unexpected that Miss Trude actually snorted, while Carnegie responded with a plosive "*Pah!*"

He followed this up with, "*It might be an elf?* Miss Trude, I don't wish to insult your son—"

Trude cut him off. "Don't bother. I'll do it." She swiveled her eye lasers to Lar.

"Listen now, you pure eejit. Get yourself up in that

trailer and ask the elf or whatever it is a few hard questions. Do you hear me?"

Lar nodded sullenly. "I hear you, Ma. There's no need for a jeering. You're undermining me in front of the lads."

Nevertheless, Lar did as he was told and stepped up on the loading lift, talking as he went.

"This wasn't my idea," he said. "In case anyone's listening, who cares about who's naughty and who's nice, if you know what I mean."

"Is he talking to Santa?" Carnegie said incredulously.

Miss Trude was running out of patience. "Lar!" she barked, striding toward the truck. "You're embarrassing me. Get in there."

Carnegie followed, eager now to get to the bottom of this. He didn't want to approach the truck, but his curious feet trumped his anxious brain.

Stay back, he told himself, even as he crossed the compacted mud yard. *Something's going on here.*

He was right. Something was going on, and everybody knew it. The night chill seemed to suddenly have edges to it, and every person outside that truck felt goosebumps break out in places they'd never had goosebumps before. Ominous night birdsong permeated the air like the moment had a soundtrack. Carnegie felt a flush rise in his cheeks as if he'd been caught doing something wrong.

It's finally happening, Daff, he told himself. *I'm about to get my comeuppance.*

He stepped onto the platform beside Miss Trude, and Lar pressed the red button. The platform began to rise slowly, and the three passengers peered into the black depths of the trailer.

There were a few lonely bags of donations littered on the container bed, but the rest were undeniably gone. Trude added her torchlight to her son's, and the twin beams reached to the very depths of the container.

Two things were immediately obvious. Firstly, there was a large hole in the canvas roof.

"Hole," said Lar.

But it was perhaps the second thing that was so surprising as to be almost incredible. Everyone on the platform took a step backward because there was a girl in a red coat, green scarf, and high black boots stuffing the last of the donation bags into a sack that should not have been able to fit more than one of those bags, but yet somehow they kept going in.

Carnegie blinked. Could they be seeing what they were seeing? Who was this girl? What was she? How come she had a magical sack?

It's happening, his inner voice screamed at him. *You knew that someday your bad deeds would catch up with you. Today's the day.*

It seemed to him that the night fell silent then. Even the frosted breath of the Maddens drifted silently through the torch beams.

We're all thinking the same thing, Carnegie realized. *Is this person Santa Claus or one of his elves?*

"Who are you?" he blurted suddenly. "*Who are you?*"

It was impossible to tell as the bag stealer's face was half covered by her scarf.

"I asked you a question!" said Carnegie with an authority that he definitely did not have in this situation.

The mystery girl turned his way and seemed to realize for the first time that she was trapped. She held out a palm and said: "Wait."

But Miss Trude was not in the mood for waiting. She elbowed past Lar, and then took a hairnet from her pocket, carefully arranging it over her quiff so that it would not get disturbed should there be a scuffle.

"Now, girleen," she said, pulling a pair of knitting needles from her bum bag, "let's see if we can't stuff you in that magic sack."

10

Mystery Girl

Juniper hadn't put together a plan as such when she and Skära began tailing Carnegie, but as soon as the truck turned into Trude Madden's yard it was clear that urgent action was called for. Juniper knew all about the incinerator because her mum had actually campaigned against that environmental nightmare at council meetings and even managed to get the machine shut down officially. But it was an open secret that Miss Trude fired it up at night when the thick column of noxious smoke was less visible over the city.

A few minutes earlier, in the wild back garden of Cedar Mews, Juniper had acted instinctively, taking Niko's work boots from one of the saddlebags and pulling them on over her own shoes. The boots reacted to the magic in Juniper's system and shrank to fit as Juniper had somehow known they would. She then, without a second thought or awkwardness, smoothly climbed onto Skära's back, locking her knees tight against his flanks.

The reindeer, for his part, allowed her weight to arch his back slightly to give the girl a kind of seat and resisted the urge to kick up his hindquarters while he ran, which would dislodge his passenger. Neither of them had ever been part of a rider-ridden partnership before, but they remembered how to do it from the dream memories, or yuledrøm, of all the Santas that had gone before. For Juniper and Skära had been fundamentally changed by the imprinting and were now members of two very select clubs: Team Santa Claus and, even more exclusive, Team Juniper and Skära, flying duo and best friends forever.

Juniper had leaned forward and whispered in the reindeer's ear, "Upa-uda," which was, she remembered, what Niko had said when he'd floated Blixxen into the tree. And now she knew what it meant: up and at 'em.

Skära knew too because he shook himself once, then took off down the garden path and across the grass toward the natural bowl where concerts, including the Santa Vigil, were often held.

Juniper lay flat along Skära's neck to decrease wind resistance, and she stretched her hands down round the reindeer's barrel chest.

I can feel Skära's heartbeat, she thought, and that was

a wonderful moment, which more than anything on this magical night drove home to Juniper that her life had changed forever.

Changed forever, she thought. *Changed forever*.

And it seemed as though her very thoughts were in time with Skära's hoofbeats.

"We're synchronized," she said into the reindeer calf's ear, and he replied with a huff and picked up the pace.

Skära ran down the slope into the natural bowl and up the other side, his heart thumping ever faster, and just as he reached the uppermost edge every guard hair on his outer coat stiffened suddenly and stood out at various angles to trap the wind that gave him the lift he needed to take off, because reindeers flying wasn't just magical, it was scientific too.

Skära jumped off the lip of the bowl and didn't come back down, his leap simply going on for ages.

We're up, thought Juniper. *Good boy*.

And they were. As simple as that. Both of them flying like aces as though this flight team had notched up a thousand missions. Juniper wiggled her feet into the saddlebags and tucked her fingers inside the front straps to give herself a little stability. She shifted her head so her cheek was just under Skära's jaw, and he could see her out of the corner of his side-mounted golden eye.

"Follow the truck," Juniper had said, confident that the reindeer would understand. They were bonded now, and she could communicate her wishes in a dozen ways including nods, whistles, finger taps on his neck, and even the rudimentary sign language she'd learned in Year Three from her deaf dance teacher who could feel music through the gym floorboards.

Skära altered his fur spikes for altitude and direction and followed the truck.

And because they were so bonded, Juniper could almost feel what Skära was feeling, pumped full of fizzing Christmas magic as he was: amazed, excited, and super confident all at the same time. She rubbed her palms against the grain of his fur and let his pure joy seep into her. She remembered in a series of shutter snaps all the Santas who had flown before her and saw their faces.

I am the first girl to fly with a reindeer, she realized. *And only the second child. And the first with African heritage.*

Not only could she see the faces of the Santas, but also what they had seen on their Christmas Eve trips. She saw the endless foaming waves of the world's oceans flash by below. She swerved round alpine peaks and New York skyscrapers. She smelled the ash clouds from volcanic craters in Iceland and followed the ethereal glint of the northern lights. For the first time in their lives, Juniper and Skära were more than living on the earth; they were connected to it.

Juniper felt more herself than she ever had in her life, if that made any sense. She felt as though she'd always been fuzzy, but now she was in sharp focus. She tried to compare the feeling to something, and the closest she could come to it was that split second at the seaside after you jumped off a rock, but before you were submerged in the bracing ocean. That moment if it was stretched out to last for ages.

"We're flying!" Juniper said as her mind returned to the present, and she watched the familiar streets of Cedarwood flash by below.

Skära honked and let his tongue loll from the corner of his mouth like a wind sock, which was his version of a deliriously happy tail wag. Juniper followed suit, and soon both were honking around, flapping their tongues.

And who could blame either of them? They were young and on an adventure. For Skära, this was the realization of the yearning that he'd felt for as long as he could remember. For Juniper, it was a diversion from her worries, and there was also the bright spark of hope that these new magics could actually help her find her mum.

But right now Juniper was protecting her father's legacy, and she would not let Carnegie dispose of those donations. She remembered that the regional park director had said they would be regifted (wink wink).

He'd meant burned, thought Juniper. *What kind of monster incinerates charitable donations?*

She could not and would not let that happen.

Skära stayed low, hugging rooftops where he could, actually touching down a few times as they tailed the truck from above, and with every contact of the reindeer's hard winter hooves on a flat rooftop Skära bought himself an extra spurt of kinetic energy, or corrected his course by a few degrees as it's much easier to navigate on solid ground than in the air.

The ride was a lot smoother than a person might think, mainly because of the low altitude, but also because reindeer have incredible vision that allows them to see not only ultraviolet light, which is very handy when a calf wants to avoid stepping in a patch of widdle in the snow, but also turbulence. So, although it might seem to an onlooker that Skära was swerving unnecessarily, he was actually avoiding little patches of air disturbance or hitching a ride on the ones that suited him.

Luckily, there weren't any onlookers as Juniper wasn't wearing the Santa suit that would have given the pair some measure of camouflage and foxed any cameras completely. At any rate, they weren't airborne for long as Trude Madden's yard was quite close to Cedar Park, especially as the deer flies. It was only a matter of minutes before Skära pulled up his head and brought them in for a textbook hind-legs-first landing on the roof of Carnegie's parked truck.

All that happened in a couple of minutes, thought Juniper, dismounting. *The whole world changed.*

She decided she would replay everything later. Now it was time to concentrate on this particular problem, i.e. saving the donations, and when the first trolley full of bags were fed into the incinerator, Juniper felt her blood boil. People had made sacrifices to give stuff to the park's residents. Stuff that would see them through till spring. And she vowed to her dad up above that not another single tin of food or warm blanket would go up in smoke.

She knelt on the cab roof and patted Skära's flank.

"We need to get into that container," she told the reindeer. "Any ideas?"

Skära did have an idea. He jumped onto the container's

canvas roof, sliding around for a scrabbling moment until his winter hooves dug in.

Winter hooves, thought Juniper. *Of course.*

Reindeer hooves are amazingly versatile tools, which is something that hardly anyone realizes. In summer, they expand to provide traction on the soft earth, and in winter they tighten and expose ice-cutter rims.

Ice-cutter rims, thought Juniper. *Perfect.*

Skära ran in a small circle, angling his inside hooves to score the canvas. After a few revolutions, a perfect circle of material drifted down into the container.

We have our way in, Juniper realized.

She pulled up her fake-fur-lined hood and zipped up the parka and pulled the scarf over her nose in case someone got close enough to see her face, and suddenly she looked much more like the mysterious figure whom Lar and co. would shortly mistake for an elf.

Then Juniper took advantage of Santa's work boots to jump down into the belly of the trailer, landing neatly behind a stack of bags.

Well done, Juniper, she thought, and then remembered that she'd left the Santa sack in the second saddlebag.

Well done, genius.

But she needn't have worried because Skära saw the problem and managed to bend himself in half to rummage in the saddlebag. He snagged the sack with the tip of one boomerang antler, and then sent it floating down to Juniper.

"Thanks," she whispered, and began putting the bags in the sack as quietly as she could.

The trick she remembered from her Santa predecessors was to let the sack touch the cargo and then it became weightless, which allowed her to easily roll the bags inside. Using this method, she moved quickly through the container, working from the center outward until most of the bags were inside the sack, taking up hardly any room and weighing her down not a bit.

Juniper couldn't glean from her dream memory exactly how the sack worked. As usual with Santa stuff, it was a combination of magic and science. She remembered vaguely that inside the sack was a different dimension, and that the donations were actually being beamed to an inter-dimensional space until they were needed.

Don't go in the sack, she ordered herself as she worked, because she also remembered that this was one of the prime Santa rules, but she wasn't sure why exactly, just that one of her predecessors had been warned that the sack was not for puppies or even goldfish. Inanimate gifts only.

Juniper was so involved with the job that she didn't notice Lar, Carnegie, and Miss Trude approach in spite of

Skära pawing a heads-up at the roof. And even when it did register Juniper kept on bagging the donations.

Ten more bags, she told herself. *Nine . . .*

Skära poked his nose through the hole and honked. *More people coming.*

Five bags, four.

Juniper was desperate to save every last one. Carnegie would not have any of these donations.

A motor whirred at the entrance to the trailer. Juniper had heard that sound before from a distance not twenty minutes ago when the men had been cleaning out her father's storage shed.

The loading lift.

They're coming in.

She'd left it too late to make a clean getaway.

My first assignment and I get spotted.

She may have had the Claus dream memories, but she had no training.

Niko is going to blow his top.

She giggled because that was a funny image, but she stopped giggling when a voice said: "Now, girleen, let's see if we can't stuff you in that magic sack."

Juniper knew that voice. Everyone around Cedarwood did and knew to steer clear when they heard it. Miss Trude Madden.

Juniper's heart sank. Of all the people to be spotted by.

You're in her yard so what did you expect? said Juniper's inner voice. But the truth was that Juniper had been trying not to think about getting caught. She had been hoping that her beginner's luck would hold.

But it hadn't. Now she was in Miss Trude's sights. And it was as if, for just a moment, time stopped.

People said that Trude was short for Intrude, which was what the Irish rockabilly lady had been christened. Apparently, intruding into other people's affairs, residences and personal space was the family business.

Intrude? Juniper had often thought. *What kind of family gives their little girl a name like Intrude?*

Juniper checked her hood was zipped up all the way and then glanced at Trude Madden, who was brandishing knitting needles. Knitting needles were usually the least threatening members of the spike family, but not today. In Miss Trude's hands, they flashed like lethal weapons.

Juniper held out a flat palm. "Wait," she said. "Give me a minute."

"No waiting," said Trude. "And no minutes nor seconds for that matter. You're stealing from me. Taking the bread out of the mouths of the Madden family, and I won't be having that. So dump the lot out on the floor and hand over the sack while you're at it."

"Well, I won't be having that," said Juniper, and bent at the knees slightly as though preparing to fight.

Trude clicked the needles together and obviously this was a signal to Lar, as they tumbled together into the trailer, leaving Carnegie solo on the platform.

"You'll not win this fight, girleen," said Trude, who was apparently fond of the word *girleen*.

And perhaps Juniper would indeed have lost the fight had the bent knees signified she was committing to a fight, but they didn't; Juniper Lane was committing to a jump.

"Upa-uda," she whispered to herself, and swung one arm over her head, her entire body following it, and swished out through the hole ten feet overhead.

"Jump," said Lar.

Miss Trude was caught by surprise because what she had witnessed didn't look like a jump. It looked like a dive, but dives weren't supposed to go up; they were supposed to go down.

"Well, if that don't bate all," she said, lapsing into bad grammar.

Carnegie backed off the platform, falling the three feet and landing hard on his behind.

My plan! he thought. *My beautiful plan.*

For him, this strange jumping creature may as well have had Cedar Mews inside her cavernous sack, because if those donations did not get incinerated he could kiss his scheme to occupy the cottage au revoir.

I must find those missing bags, thought the prone Dafydd Carnegie. *And save my plan.*

However, his current plan was pushed way down his list of priorities when the director saw what happened next.

"My goodness, Daff," he said. "It ain't an elf—it's a little female Santa Claus."

And it was a mark of how shocked and surprised Carnegie was that he used the term "ain't" for the first time since moving out of the East End nearly thirty years earlier.

From her perspective, Miss Trude Madden saw the same event from a different angle. And she quickly realized that this could be the opportunity she needed to move up in the world, financially if not legally. But there was more going on in her mind that she was trying to compute. For the previous couple of decades, every decision Trude had made was based on cold, hard cash: how much could she make or steal. But, as soon as Carnegie breathed the term "female Santa Claus," a childhood's worth of submerged Christmas hurt came back to wound her again.

Santa Claus, she thought. *I hate Santa Claus.*

The reason for this was very simple. Trude had committed her first robbery (a Pretty Pony toy saddle set) at age six, and on Christmas morning that year the little girl had found an elaborately wrapped lump of coal in her stocking.

"Learn from this," her father told her.

"Learn not to steal?" little Trude had asked.

Her father laughed. "Not to steal? You're adorable. No, pet. Learn that this fella Santy is against you. And if he's against you he's not with you. And what do Maddens do with people who aren't with them?"

"We go against them," replied Trude.

"Exactly," said Pa Madden. "Crush Santy, pet. And his silly season."

So now, when Trude set eyes on this elf person, her father's advice seemed to echo round the inside of her skull.

Crush Santy, pet. And his silly season.

I will, Pa, she thought now. But, while crushing Christmas would have been enough for the child Trude used to be, the adult businesswoman Trude realized instinctively that there was money to be made here too.

Juniper underestimated the power of her own magic coupled with the Christmas boots and shot up through the roof hole like a rocket. She only needed maybe ten feet to reach Skära but achieved nearly twice that altitude with hardly any effort.

Maybe I can actually fly, she thought as she hung in the sky for about as long as it took a star to twinkle. Then gravity took hold and began dragging Juniper down, but that was all right because Skära swooped up underneath for a pickup. Juniper sensed him coming and relaxed as much as she could to avoid breaking any bones. Skära turned his head sideways so that his partner wouldn't get skewered by his antlers and intercepted Juniper with barely a bump.

Juniper rubbed his neck. "Thanks, pal," she said. "Now take us to the park."

The reindeer did as he was bid, showing off a little by flying low over Cedarwood, tracing the streets and roundabouts, and once even stopping playfully at a traffic light.

It was all very jolly. Their first mission had been a complete success.

"No one will believe that Miss Trude or Carnegie saw anything," said Juniper into the wind.

But that didn't matter because Miss Trude and Carnegie believed themselves.

And . . .

. . . because one of Lar's mates had filmed the getaway.

★ ★ ★

Once the reindeer calf was off the ground, he used his extremities to cut the air and carve a path through the sky. His tail was too small to be an effective rudder for sharp turns, but it did help with looping swoops. However, it was by using a combination of unnatural-looking leg contortions that he controlled the skies, and when he was on a steady flight path Skära simply tucked his legs tight underneath and pointed his snout forward for maximum aerodynamics.

Juniper lay flat against the reindeer's neck, doing her bit to decrease drag, and felt Skära's blood pulse to the rhythm of his heartbeat. It washed over her again how unbelievable all of this was. How fundamentally amazing the night had been. And then, of course, she felt guilty because Mum was still missing. But she remembered something her father had said to her when she was upset about people dumping litter in the park.

"Don't feel bad, Junie. Do something good."

And back then she had. And it had worked. Doing cleanup patrols with a few school friends.

That advice applied here too. *Don't feel bad. Do something good.*

"Let's do something good," she told Skära. "You and I will use this Santa magic to find my mum."

Her Santa dream memories pitched up a useful fact.

Polar reindeer had an excellent sense of smell, and when their magic was activated it was even keener.

The scarf. Mum often wore Juniper's green scarf.

"Skära!" she said excitedly. "Would you follow a scent for me?"

Skära shrugged. Of course he would. Easy peasy.

"Why didn't I think of this before?" Juniper asked the night sky. The post-magic fatigue lifted like a morning mist, and suddenly her thoughts were crystal clear.

"We should do it now when it's still dark. We could have Mum back for breakfast. You're not too tired?"

Skära snorted and then pawed the sky. Tired? He was bright as a brass button.

"Good boy," said Juniper. She wadded a handful of her green scarf and held it under the reindeer's nose.

"There are two scents on this!" she shouted into the wind. "Find the one that's not me! Find Mum!"

Skära took three deep sniffs to get the smell into his scent membranes and then ducked into a thermal corridor that would take them directly into the heart of Cedar Park. For the first time since her mum disappeared into thin air, Juniper felt the shadows of anxiety that lurked in the corners of her vision being illuminated by a spark of hope.

✳ ✳ ✳

Three hours later, that spark of hope was all but extinguished. Skära and Juniper had searched the entire suburb, but the reindeer had failed to pick up a single hit. No sign of Mum anywhere. Not in Cedar Park, not on the high street, and not even outside Sandra's where Juniper knew for a fact she had been.

Their last stop was the tube station. Juniper could hardly bear to even think it, but she supposed there must be a chance that her mum had simply left town for some reason.

Skära had a quick sniff round the entrance to Cedarwood Underground but found nothing. He snuffled in frustration and danced in a puddle to show Juniper that the previous day's rain had muddled any trail that he might have picked up.

Juniper scratched his brown fur and said: "It's okay. The rain washed Mum away. It's not your fault."

And, in fact, Juniper was actually relieved that they hadn't found a trace of her mother here. At least she could rule out the possibility that her mum had voluntarily left her.

"Come on, partner," she told Skära. "Time to go before we're seen."

Because even at four in the morning there were always people hanging round a tube station.

Skära executed his trademark standing takeoff simply

because he was young and he could do it, and soon they were backlit by stars once again.

It occurred to Juniper that there was another way for a person to leave town. In fact, several other ways.

"We're not done yet," she told Skära. "A few more places to check."

Skära got a hit at the third bus stop they tried. Mum's scent on the scarf may not have seemed very strong to a human, or even to the average reindeer, but a Christmas reindeer has over four hundred million scent receptors and can follow a scent as easily as humans can follow a footpath. So when Skära picked up Mum's scent he simply thrust his nose forward and allowed the odorants to reel him in.

He landed on the Perspex roof of the bus shelter and honked delightedly because he'd succeeded in his task.

Juniper was not in a honking mood because, even though they seemed to have found a clue, things weren't any better just yet.

She swung herself down to the ground and sat on the shelter's only unbroken seat, which had been protected from the rain. She knew this stop. It was where the early-morning Heathrow Airport bus stopped. The last time she was here was on a joyous occasion when the entire Lane family had flown to Ireland for a holiday. Their last holiday.

"Maybe I'm not the only Lane flying," she said.

Could Mum have had enough of looking after her? It wasn't possible, surely.

"You'll never leave me, Mum," Juniper said into the night.

And her memory of her mother was so strong that she almost heard Jennifer say: "No, sweetie, I'll never leave you."

Skära gave a warning honk, but Juniper didn't pick up on it, consumed as she was by worry.

Skära tapped on the bus-stop roof with his front hooves. *Come on. Let's go. We'll be seen.*

But it was too late.

A small lady and her slightly taller child stepped out through a gap in the hedge behind the shelter, lugging a heavy woven luggage bag between them, one handle each. A second ago, their faces were creased with effort and the straps dug into their small hands. But now all that was forgotten because there was a reindeer on top of the bus shelter and a figure in a red coat and high black boots inside.

The child, a boy of sevenish, was the first to jump to a conclusion.

"Santa," he said, pointing to Juniper. "And Rudolph."

The mother was far from convinced. "No, Nikesh. That is perhaps a climbing goat. And everyone knows that Santa Claus is a bearded man. That is clearly the shape of a girl."

Juniper found herself on the boy's side. "That's only a stereotype. Santa could be a girl."

The boy dropped his side of the bag, running round to the front of the shelter. "It is Santa Claus. You've come back." Then his face fell. "But I won't be home by Christmas. How will you find me?"

Juniper felt the weight of massive expectation settle on her, and she got an inkling of the importance of Niko's job. She felt that this boy and his mother were undergoing massive upheaval in their lives. Perhaps they were journeying to a distant country or maybe to a new home in another borough. Whatever it was, Juniper could tell by the stress lines round the mother's eyes that all was not well in their lives.

Juniper knew she should leave. She could do a little damage limitation and use the boots to leap high in the air, and Skära would do his swoopy thing and pick her up. Nobody would believe the woman in the red sari. And certainly nobody would believe the boy.

Red sari. Like Sarika.

But the boy's face was so hopeful now. His mood had shifted from way down to way up. He was hopeful and maybe desperate.

For a gift, Juniper knew.

And it would not be just a gift. It would be a talisman, a parcel of human kindness tied up in a bow, a reminder that there were people who cared and who would help.

Juniper was struck by an irresistible urge to give

something to this boy. The exact thing that would carry him through his journey.

But what?

She had no idea. But the sack would know.

"Why don't I give you your present now?" she said.

The boy didn't speak, but his clenched fists punching the air was answer enough.

His mother was understandably nervous. After all, there was a deer with horns looking down from above.

"Have a care. Step away now."

Juniper took down her hood so the woman in the red sari could see her face.

"Don't worry, Mother," she said. "Just a little gift from Santa."

Juniper whistled, and Skära stepped off the roof, floating slowly to ground level.

"*Ohhhh*," said the boy Nikesh. "He flies. It is Rudolph."

"Rudolph retired a long time ago," said Juniper. "This young buck is Skära. And he wants to know if he can pet you, Nikesh?"

Nikesh, who was a good boy, asked his mother for permission. "Can he pet me, Momma?"

The mother wanted to say no, but she could not refuse such big imploring eyes.

"Very well, jaata, go. But quickly."

Skära stepped close to the boy and placed his head on top of the boy's crown, giving him a gentle pet. Nikesh closed his eyes and concentrated completely on the moment, storing it forever.

"You can give him a hug if you like," said Juniper while she took the sack from Skära's saddlebag.

Nikesh hugged Skära's neck tightly, and after a moment his mother joined in from the other side, and it seemed like a weight of woe lifted off them, and Juniper understood. This was the magic of animals.

That's it, she thought. *From now on, I'm vegan.*

Juniper shook out the sack and stuck her arm inside.

Something will come. She knew this from her Santa yuledrøm. *All I need to do is concentrate.*

There were no elf-made presents in the sack, but somewhere among the donations was a suitable gift for young Nikesh.

For a moment, it felt like her arm was inside the suction pipe of a vacuum cleaner, but then something solid landed in her hand. It was flat and about the size of a skateboard.

Juniper withdrew her hand to find she was, in fact, holding a scooter-skateboard, which she knew was called a scootboard. At first, she was puzzled as to what the sack had in mind, but then she noticed a hybrid skate-scooter, and the penny dropped.

Ohhhh, she thought. *I see how this works.*

"Here you are, Nikesh," she said. "Sorry it's not wrapped, but that's better for the environment."

Nikesh disentangled himself from Skära and took the scootboard like it was the Holy Grail and said, "Look, Momma, a scootboard!"

"That's wonderful, Nikki," she said, but it was clear she was wondering how they would carry a scootboard too.

Juniper knelt to the boy's level. "I bet a smart fellow like you can figure out how to use this to help your mother."

Nikesh chewed this over, then folded out the handle until it clicked. Meanwhile, Skära trotted round to the bag and hoisted its handles in his mouth.

"Here!" said Nikesh, pointing to the scootboard's deck. "Put it here, Skära."

Skära did as he was told, and the bag sat balanced on the board.

"You see, Momma," said Nikesh, almost hopping with excitement. "It's like a trolley and a toy. Am I useful, Momma?"

Nikesh's mother smiled, and her day got a little brighter.

"You are a very useful boy," she said, and turned to Juniper. "Thank you, Santa Claus."

Juniper almost looked around for Santa Claus, then realized that for this mother and her boy she was Santa Claus.

She pulled up her hood. "You're welcome," she said. "And good luck."

Nikesh was rolling the scootboard forward and backward experimentally.

"Thanks, Santa," he said. "And Happy Christmas."

Juniper hopped up on Skära's back and replied: "Happy Christmas to you both."

Then Skära reared up on his hind legs and leaped into the sky. It was undeniably a melodramatic exit, but Nikesh would never forget it, and neither would Juniper.

For the next hour, Juniper lived according to her dad's saying: "Don't feel bad, Junie. Do something good," and while she was doing this it occurred to her that there was a bright side to finding Mum's trail at the bus shelter.

"If Mum did leave town," she said into the reindeer's flattened ear, "that means she's alive. There's an emergency somewhere, and she's sorting it out. After that, she'll come home."

This theory sounded pretty logical to Juniper, and she convinced herself that it was true. It had to be.

So, armed with this new theory and buoyed by the look on young Nikesh's face, Juniper set about doing the kind of thing Niko did for the people experiencing homelessness in Cedar Park, but on a flashier scale.

Unfortunately, since she had neither Niko's camouflage suit to hide inside nor enough magic in her bones to interfere with cameras, Juniper's streak of getting spotted by people continued, and within the hour several reports had popped up on social media.

@walkiewalkie said on her channel:
> OMG. Just spotted Santa. I kid thee not. Landed in #cedarpark right beside @therealmisterbones when I was walking him. Left a bag of blankets at a bonfire for cold park sleepers. #literallyshaking

@boomshaketheroom wrote:
> Heeeeeeeee's back. Or maybe he's a she. Anyway, Santa has returned, flying reindeer and all. This is a photo of the mountain of toys left by the mysterious Yuletider outside the children's hospital. Remember to send your letters to the North Pole today because it's Red-Letter Day. Only seven sleeps till Christmas.

> Ho-ho-hope you haven't been naughty.

On the Parklife website, there was a blurred video of what looked like a reindeer doing a vertical takeoff along with the paragraph:

Is it a bird? Is it a plane? No, it's a reindeer. Is it possible that Santa has made Cedar Park his first pit stop in nearly ten years? It certainly looks like it. We already have an angel and now we have Father (or perhaps Mother) Christmas. Check back for updates.

A local stargazer @allinthegutter posted on her accounts:

Was filming Orion from my rooftop so expecting to see stars. Not superstars. Ladies and gentlemen, for your viewing pleasure, a hi-def movie of the new Santa Claus riding an honest-to-goodness reindeer. Is that a red nose I see? I'd love to hear your comments.

Comments that were mostly negative, as internet comments often are. Including:

Are you kidding me? Total fake.

And:

That's no reindeer. That's a flying gerbil.

Not to mention:

> Is there a Christmas blockbuster coming out?
> #publicitystunt

Harsh though these comments were, they probably saved Juniper from being pursued by a legion of television trucks, so she managed to drop off a large part of the hijacked donations where they were supposed to go, getting slicker with her delivery each time, stopping herself from feeling bad by doing something good.

Juniper was almost feverish in her efforts to deliver as many gifts as possible before the sun rose above the trees in Cedar Park because, while she was busy being Santa, she didn't have time to be Juniper-whose-mum-was-missing. But eventually, when the city glow was replaced by the first watery rays of gray London light, Juniper called it a night and directed Skära to land behind the Mews.

Juniper stuffed the magical sack into the reindeer's saddlebags then stashed Skära in the mini garden shed. It was ideal really because her father had often fostered shelter dogs in there until they could be matched up with suitable humans, so the little shed was insulated and comfortable with several large doggy beds to choose from.

"The door's not locked," she said. "And I've filled the water bucket."

Skära clanged the steel bucket with a hind leg to show that he understood this.

"Of course you understand, buddy," said Juniper. She walked out of the door, yawning as she went, then turned and ran back. "I forgot to hug you," she said, throwing her arms round Skära's neck. "Thanks for choosing me. Together forever, right?"

The reindeer nickered.

Together forever.

Juniper forced herself to slow down before entering the cottage. She didn't want to wake Duchess because explaining everything would take too long, and possibly get her sent to bed, which wouldn't be too bad since she'd been up all night.

How many days have gone past? Juniper knew that Duchess believed passionately in Santa Claus and Christmas, but she wasn't ready to hear that her eleven-year-old-pal Juniper had a magic reindeer in the shed and was possibly the new Santa herself. Oh, and also that she had used the old Santa's sack, which was stashed in the shed too, and she'd been flying round Cedarwood with her green scarf, using the reindeer calf like a tracker dog.

It sounded far-fetched even to Juniper. But it was true.

Every word. So, all things considered, it was better to simply sneak in and out without having to simplify the whole Santa thing for an adult.

At any rate, none of Juniper's creeping and sneaking mattered because Duchess was awake when Juniper climbed in through her own bedroom window.

"Okay," said Juniper. "You're not going to believe this . . ."

"Juniper, listen to me now," said Duchess, her cheeks pale and wet with tears. "The police have found something. I think it's your mother's."

11

He Knows If You've Been Bad or Good

Dafydd Carnegie had the feeling that he was in over his head. He had hired Miss Trude and the Trudettes to do a little midnight burning, but now the Irishwoman was talking like they were partners in crime.

You're not exactly blameless in all of this, Daff, his inner voice said. *So please don't cast yourself as the hero. Didn't you recently threaten a young girl with going into the system?*

The memory made Dafydd wince. What had he become?

"Let's run through it again, Mr. Carnegie," Miss Trude was saying now. "What we have here is a golden opportunity."

"I don't understand."

"What we saw was magic," Miss Trude insisted. "That was Santa Claus out there."

"Surely not," said Dafydd. "Santa Claus is a plump gentleman. That was a young girl."

"Yes, yes, but see, the details don't matter, fella. What matters is the sack. And the reindeer. Don't you get it, Carnegie? Don't you see what the future could be?" Trude closed her eyes and placed her fingers on her temples. "Because I see a future where Santa Claus returns, maybe just to London for the first year, but then worldwide, because with that flying reindeer and that magic sack we could be Santa Claus."

Dafydd blinked. *We could be Santa Claus?*

Then the penny dropped.

"Ooooh," he said.

Miss Trude spelled it out. "If the real Santa doesn't want to deliver gifts, then we do it, for a fee of course. And anyone who doesn't feel like paying the subscription gets a lump of coal."

Trude's eyes were as bright as embers from those lumps. "We use the sack to steal the gifts, and then we use the reindeer to deliver them. It's foolproof."

"But . . ." said Dafydd.

"But what?" said Trude, slamming her palms on the desk. "But what, Carnegie? Tell me."

"But nothing," he stammered.

"That's right, fella," said Miss Trude. "But nothing. This is our chance. Christmas is going corporate, so long as we all work together."

"I will certainly do what I can," said Dafydd, who at this

point would promise anything to get out of the cramped office. "But what exactly can a park-keeper do?"

Miss Trude smiled. "You can help me find that girl."

He laughed. "Find Miss Santa? And where should we look? The North Pole?"

"I don't think so, Carnegie. That girleen knew all about our incinerations tonight."

"But she would know," Dafydd pointed out. "Santa knows if you've been bad or good and so on."

"No, no," said Miss Trude. "I think this particular version of Santa is not the real deal. She was seen, wasn't she? And not just by us: There are reports all over social media. And getting spotted is not Santa's style. So I think this young lady got hold of Santa's tools, and if she took them from the man himself we can take them from her. So my question to you, fella, is who did you tell about our midnight bonfire?"

Dafydd knew immediately because he'd been obsessing about the duchess of Benbarty since meeting her earlier that day, and she'd been with a little girl.

"I didn't tell anyone," he said, playing his cards close to his chest.

"Oh, don't be trying to kid a kidder, fella," said Miss Trude. "The Maddens are Irish so obviously we never squealed, but you are a spineless jelly of a man so it stands to reason that you told someone. So who was it? Take a look at this photograph."

Miss Trude thrust her phone in his face. On it was an enlarged image of the girl who was clearly wearing a green scarf. Dafydd knew that scarf. He'd seen one just like it on a hook in the Lanes' hallway.

"Tell me who this is," said Miss Trude, "and leave the rest to my lads."

"And no one will get hurt?" asked Dafydd.

"No one will get hurt," said Miss Trude. "You have my word."

So he told her, regretting the words even as they tumbled out of his mouth.

12

The Lowlands Low

Duchess did not want to get into the police car.

"That's how they get you," she confided to Juniper. "Just climb into the car, they say. Or the ambulance. Or any official vehicle. The next thing you know, ten years have gone by and you've forgotten why you got in the back seat in the first place."

Juniper did not have the brain space for this at the moment. She knew that they needed a long talk soon about Duchess's past, but not right now. All she could think about was what Duchess had said before: "The police have found something."

Juniper and Duchess were outside the Mews' gate, hesitating by the Met police car that had come to take them to the police station.

"I have to go," said Juniper, squeezing Duchess's hand. "You know I do."

Duchess squeezed back. "Of course you do. We both do."

And she ducked into the back seat like she was entering a deep, dark tunnel, and Juniper could feel her shaking for the whole of the short drive.

There was so much going through Juniper's mind that her thoughts swirled like a swarm of angry bees round the truth of whatever the police had found less than a mile away. Could it really be something of her mum's? Of course it could. Anything was possible. She should know that after flying round the city with Skära last night. Had that actually happened? Surely not. It was just a flight of fancy. Could it all have been a dream?

Juniper caught her breath suddenly at the notion that everything that had happened over the past few days had simply been a fever dream.

"Maybe I'm actually dreaming in bed," she told Duchess, wishing it to be so. "Maybe all of this is just me with a temperature. It makes sense. I have been out in the cold and the rain."

Duchess squeezed her hand. "Maybe, sweetie."

But they both knew it wasn't.

★ ★ ★

Duchess experienced a moment of panic when she realized that the police car's rear doors were locked, but the constable stepped smartly round to the back of the car and let them out.

Duchess exhaled the huge breath she'd been holding and was suddenly dizzy.

"Are you okay?" Juniper asked her, and Duchess felt immediately ashamed.

"I'm fine, sweetie. Here you are looking after me when it should be the other way round. Shall we go in?"

"You don't have to," said Juniper. "It's my job."

Duchess gripped Juniper's shoulder, to support them both. "You're eleven, sweetie. You don't have a job."

So they went into the station together, following the officer who had introduced herself as Constable Sarah Carol and made Juniper half smile earlier by saying she had a first name second name like Elton John. Duchess had not half smiled; she had not even quarter smiled.

"Okay, Juniper, it's just through here. I know this is a stressful time for you both so if there's anything I can do to make things easier let me know."

Duchess glared at Constable Sarah like every word out of the young woman's mouth was a brazen lie. Including her name.

"Don't worry, Constable Sarah, we won't be asking you for anything."

The constable was accustomed to people shooting the messenger and didn't miss a step. "I'm sorry I couldn't bring it to your house, but it's potential evidence so it can't leave the station."

"Evidence of what?" Juniper asked, her heart suddenly in her throat.

Constable Sarah avoided answering that question. "Let's just have a look first, Juniper, then we can talk about it."

It was dark at the back of the police station beyond reception, past the open-plan offices, and the corridors were painted olive green. Gloss paint on the bottom so marks would wipe off and matte paint on top, which was cheaper. Duchess knew the detail about the gloss paint because the system she'd been in for several years had exactly the same color scheme, which was unfortunate because it made the short walk to the waiting room almost unbearable for her.

But in the end it was just a room with a very simple table and chairs that might be found in any office around London.

"Sit down for a sec," said Constable Sarah. "Let me get the envelope. Try not to stress; it could be nothing."

"I'll look," said Duchess to the constable. "That's okay, isn't it? I'm her grandmother."

"That's fine," said Sarah. "But you'll have to sign. And Juniper will probably have to look anyway."

Signing was a big deal as Duchess's grandmother fib could be rumbled, but for now it didn't seem important.

"I'll do it, sweetie," Duchess said to Juniper. "Cover your eyes until I tell you."

Duchess's effort to be kind was stymied by the simple fact that there were two chairs. One didn't have a cushion and the other did. Juniper chose the padded chair, but as she stepped closer she realized it wasn't a cushion. It was a plastic envelope with one thing inside. A green scarf with a tartan border that Juniper recognized instantly.

"Mum's scarf," she said, ripping it from the envelope. "Her favorite. Dad bought two in Scotland. I have a matching one."

Duchess felt her heart speed up in her chest. Panic was flapping round her head like a ravenous seabird.

"That doesn't mean anything," she said. "It's just a scarf."

Constable Sarah was flustered. "That's not supposed to be in here yet," she said. "They're supposed to wait."

But whoever was supposed to wait hadn't waited, and now the cat was out of the bag, or rather the scarf was out of the envelope.

"Where did you find this?" Juniper asked, frantic.

"It was handed in. Someone saw it hanging out of a

clothes bank in the park, and they thought it looked suspicious because . . ."

Constable Sarah didn't finish her sentence, but she didn't have to because Juniper saw that she was looking at a red stain on the scarf.

"Because there's blood on it," she said. "There's blood on Mum's scarf."

"We don't know that's blood until the test results come back," said the constable. "For now, it's a red stain, nothing more. It could be anything from strawberry juice to red wine."

"Mum doesn't like strawberries or wine," said Juniper, even though she knew that wasn't the point. "And why was Mum's favorite scarf in the clothes bank? She left the house wearing it."

"Those are questions we can investigate if that is blood," said Constable Sarah. "All I need for now is confirmation that it's your mother's scarf. So are you sure, Juniper?"

Juniper nodded dully. "The tartan is clan Brodie. Mum's grandparents were from the lowlands of Scotland. And Mum sewed the receipt into the hem because Dad had written a note on it. It's her scarf, and she would never have thrown it away."

Juniper squeezed a spot on the hem and it crackled. There was paper in there.

"That's good enough for me," said the constable. "Let me take you home."

Duchess steered Juniper out of the room. "No, thank you very much," she said. "We'll walk."

✳ ✳ ✳

Juniper and Duchess simply walked out of the station and back toward Cedar Mews. They walked most of the way silently, holding hands like toddlers.

Juniper was so distracted that she would have stepped onto a pedestrian crossing against the light if Duchess hadn't held her back. This seemed to snap her back to reality a little.

"I thought things would get better," she said. "But everything just gets worse."

"Not always," said Duchess. "Good things happen. Your mum will come back. I'll find Niko and make him help. I should have tried harder yesterday instead of waiting for him to come to me."

Juniper flushed. She'd forgotten all about Niko and the Santa-related adventures. But that wasn't why she was flushing. She was flushing because it could be argued that she'd stolen one of Santa's reindeer.

"You do what you can, Duchess. No one does more than you."

Perhaps it was the chill in the December morning air or perhaps it was the stress of looking after a missing friend's daughter, but something started Duchess coughing. She had always coughed so far as Juniper could remember, but this was worse. This fit grew so intense that the effort curved Duchess's spine, and she had to lean on the Cedar Mews gatepost.

"I think we both need an hour's sleep," said Juniper when Duchess had recovered.

"Agreed," said Duchess. "But we keep our phones on."

"Full volume," said Juniper. "In case there's news."

Juniper and Duchess were physically and emotionally exhausted so the one-hour nap turned into three, and when Juniper awoke with a start she realized that she had wasted most of the day when she could have been out looking for her mum. She jumped from her bed and ran downstairs without pausing even to twist her hair into a scrunchie. From the bottom half of the staircase, she could see Duchess sitting at the kitchen table, but Juniper didn't launch into her planned moan about oversleeping because Niko was sitting opposite her, wearing an angry expression that Mum would call a face like thunder.

Juniper was instinctively thrilled to see Niko. She wanted to run to him and tell him everything.

I know now. I understand. I'm magical too, and I flew over the city. And today is Red-Letter Day.

She felt her heart race at the memory and was on the verge of racing down the hall, but Niko's look when he saw Juniper stopped her in her tracks.

Duchess spotted Juniper on the stairs. "Is it all right that I invited Niko inside for tea when he called? I can vouch for him."

Juniper nodded. Historically, it wasn't easy to keep Santa Claus out of a house.

"Good," said Duchess, and to Niko, "and you behave, mister. Or I'll have to lock you in the closet." She laughed to show she was joking, but the laugh turned into a cough.

Niko was instantly concerned. "I worry about you, Duchess. Your breathing is worse. I can hear it rattle."

"Rattle," said Duchess, smiling. "How romantic."

There was a spark between Duchess and Niko, Juniper realized.

I'm only eleven and I can see it.

And, in spite of everything that was going on, the smile on Duchess's face made Juniper's heart sing.

"Duchess, I'm serious," said Niko. "You need to get checked out."

"It's nothing," Duchess insisted. "Just pollen allergies."

"In December?" said Juniper.

Niko pointed at Juniper. "Exactly. In December?"

Duchess did her old trick of changing the subject. "Anyway, Niko, why are you here? Surely not to interrogate me over a tickle in my throat."

"Classic Duchess," said Juniper and Niko in unison, which seemed to annoy Niko.

"I'm here to see Juniper actually," he said. "I think she found something of mine in the park. I'm just here to pick it up, and then I have to fly."

"Fly," said Juniper. "Ha."

Duchess didn't see the joke. "Fly, Niko? Are you leaving?"

Niko dropped his eyes. "I have to. Not forever but for a while at least."

Juniper waggled a finger between the two adults. "And what about all of this?"

"All of what?" asked Duchess.

"Oh, come on," said Juniper. "I'm eleven not five."

Niko slapped his forehead. "She's doing your thing, Dutch. Changing the subject."

"Maybe I am, but I can tell when something's going on. He called you Dutch. No one calls you that."

"Nothing's going on," insisted Duchess. "Is it, Niko?"

"I don't know," said Niko.

Juniper blurted out something then that she probably shouldn't have. "He still misses Sarika, Duchess. That's why he won't say."

Niko stood up so fast he spilled his tea. "How do you know that name?"

"I looked up your tattoo," said Juniper, not in the least cowed by the towering man. "You should hide that if you don't want people to find out."

"I do hide it when I'm out and about!" Niko thundered. "I was at home. And anyway how do you even remember my tattoo? I put a . . ."

Spell on you was what Niko was about to say before he stopped himself, because he knew with absolute certainty that his suspicions had been correct. The girl had imprinted with Skära.

She has felt the magic, Niko realized. There was no feeling to come close to a magical imprinting. Elf scientists had been trying to explain it for years. Tomescu had often theorized that it was a level of blissful awareness that yoga experts and meditation gurus searched for but could never quite reach. Niko's own father, who had imprinted with over twenty reindeers in his time, memorably compared the experience to jumping out of the sleigh over a volcano into a universe of clarity.

Once a person had imprinted, there was no going back.

This is a disaster, Niko thought, then realized that Duchess was talking to him.

"What did you say?"

"Just answer the question, Niko. Did you put a spell of some kind on Juniper?"

Juniper finished my sentence, he realized, but all was not lost because Duchess was smiling. She wasn't going for it.

"Of course I put a spell on her," he said, loading the words with sarcasm and wiggling his fingers for effect. "I am a wizard, here to recruit her for magic school."

"He is not a wizard!" said Duchess. "That's silly."

Niko sat down. "Exactly. Silly at the very least. The child has something of mine and doesn't wish to return it, Dutch. Simple as that."

"Well, that's true, I suppose," said Juniper. "But it's not the whole story."

Duchess took Niko's hand, and the effect of that simple gesture was extraordinary. All the bluster left his body, and he grew tranquil as though sedated.

"Now, Niko, I know in my heart that both of you are wonderful, kind, gentle people. I would go so far as to say you are the best people I have ever known. So I need you both to look each other in the eye, see the goodness in there, and then take a breath and tell me what's going on here."

What could Niko and Juniper do but look each other in the eye? Because of the polar magic in their systems, they shared a high level of empathy so Juniper could read Niko's glare and it said: *You are forcing me to lie to this wonderful woman.*

But Juniper didn't see it like that. She believed that if Niko would only come clean about everything then they could all team up and find her mum together.

We would be unstoppable.

Niko knew what Juniper was asking, but he had to stay true to his mission to help people in need as Sarika had always tried to do. He would not be able to complete this mission if he was outed as Santa Claus, so he lied to Duchess.

"It's like this, Duchess. You know I have projects? Well, one of them is animal welfare."

Duchess smiled. "Just when I thought I couldn't like you any more than I already do."

Niko smiled back, but his insides were churning. "Specifically, deer. They live wild in the forest, and I've turned the place into a kind of unofficial sanctuary. People think that poaching is a thing of the past, but times are hard so people will shoot the animals for meat."

Duchess checked in with Juniper. "All true so far, sweetie?"

"So far," said Juniper. "But since we're using the word *specifically*, can I ask *specifically* what kind of deer?"

And that's where the lying started. "I don't know really. I'm not an expert. Red deer maybe."

"It's reindeer!" said Juniper. "He knows very well it's reindeer."

Niko smiled in a patronizing manner.

"The little girl is mistaken, Dutch. Reindeer? I don't think so. I may not know much, but I do know that there are no reindeer this far south."

"There's one not too far south from here in the shed," said Juniper. Another mistake.

Niko pounced on this. "So you do have him. He's not safe outside the forest, Duchess. I need him back."

Duchess had mediated many arguments between park sleepers, but never over something as exotic as a reindeer. Usually, in such disputes, she found herself leaning one way or the other, but this time she really had no idea who was right, if there even was a right. But there was a very obvious next step to take.

"It seems to me that since Niko says there's a missing deer, and Juniper says that the deer is outside in the garden shed, we should go and see it."

It was at this point that both Niko and Juniper realized that they had argued themselves into a corner. But before they could argue themselves out of it again Duchess took a last sip of her tea, then gathered her velvet cloak round her, and swept off toward the back door.

"Well done, genius," Niko muttered, then hurried after her.

"I'm not a genius," said Juniper. "You're a genius."

And she jumped up and followed Niko following Duchess.

* * *

The thing was, there was no deer in the shed. In fact, there was no shed in the garden, just a patch of flattened earth where the shed had definitely been until recently.

"Where's the shed, Junie?" Duchess asked. "How can an entire shed have disappeared?"

Juniper was immediately worried. "Skära! Skära! Are you here?"

But Skära wasn't there, and Juniper knew it. She could feel him not being there.

"He's gone," she said to Niko. "Someone took him."

Niko paced round the perimeter of the shed's footprint as though it might suddenly reappear.

"Who did you tell?"

"I didn't tell a soul."

"Well, who saw you then?"

Juniper started in on a denial. "No one . . ." Then she

remembered. There had been the boy and his mother. And maybe a few of the park sleepers. And of course . . .

"Trude Madden and her gang," she admitted. "But they just saw a flash, and I had a scarf pulled over my face."

Niko's face fell. "That scarf you're wearing now? The distinctive scarf like the one I've seen your mother wearing."

Juniper's hand flew to the knot of scarf at her throat.

"And Trude Madden," continued Niko. "Intrude Madden? Noted gang leader with the deadly bum bag? That's who saw you?"

Juniper nodded miserably. It sounded bad when Niko said it because it was bad.

"Poor Skära. He must be terrified."

"Terrified?" scoffed Niko. "Reindeer don't get terrified. He'll stomp that gang to pieces."

And now Duchess joined the conversation. "Reindeer, Niko?"

"Just a slip of the tongue," said Niko smoothly. "I meant red deer."

Duchess wasn't having any of it. "No more lies, Niko. You said reindeer, and you meant reindeer. What is going on here? And I mean really."

Niko didn't know when he was beaten and kept lying.

"Can't a fellow misspeak once in a while? Reindeer. Red deer. It's pretty close."

"No, Niko," said Juniper, frantic now. "This is too much. First Mum and now Skära. Stop lying. If you don't tell Duchess, I will."

Niko pointed a finger at her. "Don't do it, Juniper. We have a code."

"What code?" asked Duchess. "Who's we?"

"We are the Santas!" declared Juniper.

"Juniper!" said Niko, making the name sound like a swearword.

Duchess rubbed her brow as though a headache was brewing there. "You're the Santas? What kind of game is this? We're all very tired, sweetie. Maybe you need another lie-down."

Juniper went for broke, spilling all the very secret beans. "Santa is missing, and Niko's here looking for a reindeer. That's because he is Santa. And now I'm Santa too because he put me to sleep with magic, and then Skära and I connected, which I think kept the magic alive."

"The child is deluded," said Niko.

"No!" shouted Juniper. "Don't treat me like a baby. I'm a Santa now, and I know things. How to ride a reindeer and not just on the ground, in the sky."

Niko spread his hands. "This is lunacy."

Duchess took both of Juniper's hands in her own. "It does sound fanciful," she said gently.

"I'll prove it," said Juniper. "I can do Santa things. I

gave out gifts earlier, and every gift carried hope with it. Niko has forgotten that."

"People need more than gifts sometimes," Niko muttered.

Juniper held on to Duchess's hands. "You have to believe me. You met Santa years ago, remember?"

"I remember telling you that story," said Duchess. "But maybe I was dreaming."

"I know exactly what he said to you," said Juniper, "because Santas pass down memories."

"Don't do it," said Niko.

"He said, 'Some things should stay secret.' I'm right, aren't I?"

Duchess didn't speak right away, but it was clear from her expression that Juniper was indeed right. She somehow knew something that she could not have known.

"I've never told anyone that," she said, drawing away from Juniper. "It was a secret between me and Santa Claus."

"And now me," said Juniper.

Duchess turned slowly to Niko, and her expression was somewhere between dazed and confused. "Niko, my dear friend, I'm going to ask you once and, if you care anything for me, you will answer truthfully. Did you say those words to me long ago?"

Niko steeled himself, then answered. "That was me, Dutch. I said it."

"You said it?" said Duchess, making it a question. "You said those words to me?"

Niko nodded. "I did. In your brother's house."

Duchess couldn't take it in. "Is this a trick? Are you two playing some kind of game?"

"It's no game," said Juniper. "Niko was there that night. He remembers it so now I can remember it too."

Duchess rubbed her eyes. "I was a different person then. I don't like to think about that time."

"I'm sorry, Duchess," said Juniper. "We have to think about it if only for a second. Mum is missing and Skära too."

Duchess looked Niko in the eyes. "Skära the reindeer?"

Niko nodded again. "Skära the reindeer."

Duchess sank to her knees in the indentation where a shed used to be. "Santa Claus was gone. He was gone, and people had almost stopped believing. And somewhere inside me I was happy because he was the only one who saw how I used to be. And now you're telling me that the two people I'm closest to in this world are both Santa Claus. You are both Santas?"

Niko and Juniper shuffled side by side like guilty toddlers.

"Yes," they said in unison. "We are both Santas."

13

The Reindeer and the Sack

So the shed had completely disappeared. How had that happened?

It was simple, really. Once Dafydd Carnegie had revealed the identity of the girl in the green scarf, Lar and his boys were dispatched to stake out the Mews, only to find it empty apart from a middle-aged lady who, as Lar put it, "has too much hair on her head for one person."

This news was texted to Miss Trude back at base who replied: Hang back in the park, boys. We need the reindeer and the sack.

Shortly thereafter, the Trudettes were brought to the verge of panic by the arrival of a police car, but Lar was a veteran of police visits and calmed his men down by pointing out that there was only a single constable in the vehicle, which meant the police were not after a criminal. This was a public-service visit.

"Stay low" was Lar's instruction to his men.

It was a good call, and their patience was rewarded some minutes later when Juniper and her reindeer swooped down through the dawn sky and landed in the cottage's small garden on the park side of the cottage.

Irish people in general have great admiration for jockeys, and so the gang were very impressed by Juniper's handling of the reindeer. Lar himself was on the verge of giving Juniper and Skära a round of applause.

They watched as Juniper stuffed her boots and the sack into the creature's saddlebags and then hid the reindeer in the garden shed.

Five minutes later, Juniper and the bushy-haired lady climbed into the police car and drove away.

Lar called Miss Trude. "The reindeer's in the shed unguarded. The girl is off with the police—must be going to the station if they picked her up in the squaddie. What do you want us to do?"

There was silence for a moment while Miss Trude considered the options. Usually, she preferred a longer period of observation, but there was a lot at stake here. She also knew how ham-fisted her boys could be and did not want the reindeer injured.

"Right, son," she said, "send one of your lads to the police station to keep watch, so we'll have notice when they leave. I'll be along presently with the forklift."

There was no need to say any more. Lar knew exactly what his mother had in mind, and ten minutes later, Miss Trude drove a lorry through the park's main gate. At first glance, it seemed like the lorry was driving itself, but as it drew closer the top of Miss Trude's quiff was visible between the spokes of the steering wheel. If someone had been watching, they would assume there was some kind of park maintenance going on, which was exactly what Miss Trude wanted witnesses to think.

She was perfectly aware that they had a very small window to act, and so she reversed the lorry as far as she could up the path between the park itself and the cottage garden, careful not to crush the borders. Before Trude could even step down from the cab, Lar had dropped down the ramp, swung open the rear doors, and had turned on the forklift, which was a lot louder than the lorry.

"Get away from there, son," said Miss Trude when she came round the back. "No one drives that machine but me."

Lar added his own whine to the engine's. "Please, Mammy. I can do it. I'll make you proud."

Trude patted her bum bag. "You'd better," she said, stepping out of the way.

* * *

There is nothing worse than trying to impress your mammy when your friends are watching. Poor Lar made three runs at it before he managed to slot the forklift's forks underneath the garden shed.

But even with all Lar's nervous driving and Skära's ruckus from inside the shed they had the forklift reversed out and the truck sealed up in less than two minutes. Now the reindeer could demolish the shed if he wanted, but he still wasn't getting out of the steel container without an oxyacetylene torch.

Lar climbed out of the forklift, proud as punch, and Miss Trude tickled him under the chin.

"Well done, son. Now drive this rig to the Crumbly Lane stables and secure the beast. Then tell Carnegie we're holding our captive in the Kilburn yard."

Lar was puzzled. "But you just said take it to the stables."

"I did indeed," confirmed Trude. "But Carnegie is a big softy. If anyone asks him where their reindeer is, I don't want him to know. If he doesn't know, he can't tell."

Lar got the idea. "So, if Santa Claus does come looking, he'll find the Kilburn yard empty."

Miss Trude's eyes glittered in the morning light. "Not exactly empty, son, because you'll be waiting for him."

After all, Miss Trude thought, *I'd like to have a little chat with him about all those lumps of coal. There might also be a few secrets Santa Claus could share on the subject of taming a reindeer.*

She'd never tried to tame a reindeer before, magical or not.

But a beast is a beast, she told herself now. *And all a beast needs to know is who's boss.*

And Miss Trude had ways of showing a beast who was boss.

14

Shenanigans

So where was Dafydd Carnegie while all these shenanigans were going on? As it turned out, the head park-keeper of Cedar Park was having something of a personal crisis not too far away in the booth of a fancy coffee shop on the high street called Where U Bean.

Carnegie sat alone and stared down into the coffee art piped into the foam of his soy latte. Usually, he took time to admire the craftsmanship that went into the White Tree of Gondor picture that adorned each caffeinated creation, but not this morning. He had no headspace for *Lord of the Rings* fairy tales because he was thinking about Santa Claus.

I'm involved in a plot to steal from Santa Claus, he thought. *And there's no way to sugarcoat that.*

Dafydd Carnegie experienced a crisis like this approximately twice a year when he did something questionable to further his career. Usually, the feeling passed after a day or two, but Dafydd felt that this time was different because he was embroiled in the whole Miss Trude situation. Somehow he had gone from employer to employee and that was a dangerous place to be. He had just taken a call from the Irishwoman's son, who had gleefully informed him that all was proceeding according to plan, and that he was driving the reindeer to the Maddens' Kilburn yard.

Kidnapping reindeer, he thought glumly. *That's what it's come to.*

But the plan went much further than that.

Ever since Santa had gone AWOL, the entire world had been hoping for his return, but if Miss Trude had her way that would never happen.

It was all a far cry from Dafydd's childhood dream of starring in the West End. He couldn't even make himself go to shows anymore because it was too painful.

Remember when all you wanted to do was sing just for the sheer joy of it?

Drink your coffee, Daff, he told himself. *And forget about dreams.*

He had taken no more than a single sip when someone slid into the booth opposite him. Though perhaps *slid* was the wrong word because this person was so big he had to squeak himself along the velour seat cover, bumping the table with each sideways hop.

Dafydd looked up into the piercing blue eyes of the massive Viking-type stranger who had joined him in the booth.

"I'm having a think here, my man," said Carnegie, trying to sound authoritative. "And I would rather do that alone."

The large man's only response was to nudge Carnegie's coffee to one side with a massive finger and to place something on the table.

"Do you know what this is?"

Dafydd knew, of course, that it was a toy microphone. In fact, he'd wanted one like it for Christmas as a boy when he'd still been interested in singing.

He leaned in and squinted at the microphone. It wasn't just like the one he'd wanted. It was exactly the same model. The Singalonga Karaoke Mic Christmas Version, which had thirty seasonal classics programmed right into the chip.

"Singalonga," he whispered. "It's the Singalonga."

The Viking grunted. "And do you know who I am, Dafydd?"

Once again, Dafydd did know because Niko wanted him to.

"You're Santa Claus," he said. "And you know what I did."

Everything crashed down on Dafydd Carnegie then:

the emptiness of the life he'd built for himself in pursuit of a career that had led to him being alone in a café with nothing to look forward to.

"I should never have asked you to make sure I got the lead role in the Christmas show," he sobbed. "That poor boy got hurt. Cabby Bellows."

Niko chuckled. "Bellows. A good name for him. If I remember right, all he did was bellow."

"Nevertheless, it was a rotten thing to wish for," said Carnegie, wiping his nose.

"Wishing isn't doing," said Niko. "And Santa Claus certainly did not grant that wish. It wasn't me by the way, Dafydd. It was my father. But all the Santas can remember if we concentrate."

"Either way," said Carnegie, "even if I didn't exactly write it in my Santa letter, I wanted something to happen to that boy."

Niko felt a little bad for bringing the past back up like this. For Carnegie, it would be like ten years of therapy breakthroughs all at once over one cup of coffee.

"The thing is, Dafydd," he said, "you were a beautiful singer. The director didn't have a musical bone in his body. He didn't realize how good you were."

Carnegie sniffled. "So I deserved that part?"

"Yes, you did, and Cabby having his accident was just

that: an accident. You can think about that over time and see if it changes your view on things, but for now I need your help, so you have to decide which team you're on. Do you want to be a follower on Team Trude or a partner on Team Santa Claus?"

"I don't know," said Dafydd. "Miss Trude is very intimidating."

Niko nodded. "That's very true, and I'm not here to intimidate you. All I can tell you is that there will never be a better time to change your path."

Dafydd picked up the Singalonga and flicked the power switch. It came alive with a jingle of sleigh bells.

"It's even got batteries."

"Of course," said Niko. "That little gizmo is my first official delivery in ten years." His eyes widened as something occurred to him. "And you know what? It feels good to give a Christmas gift. I'd almost forgotten."

Carnegie stared hard at the karaoke microphone. "They're in Kilburn," he said finally. "I'll take you . . . partner."

Niko smiled broadly. "Thanks, partner. It feels good, doesn't it? Doing the right thing at Christmastime."

Santa Claus's smile was infectious, and Dafydd found himself smiling back.

"It does feel good," he said, realizing this was the best he'd felt in years.

★ ★ ★

Carnegie had a council vehicle of sorts. It was a forest-green three-wheeler micro-van with a tiny trailer cage for transporting tools and grass cuttings. Carnegie hadn't done any actual hard work in over a decade and so had fitted the trailer with panel walls, a tiny desk, and two sawn-off office chairs so that he could take meetings in the back.

Niko had folded himself into the rear compartment and watched the back of Dafydd Carnegie's head as he drove them both to Kilburn. Niko was reasonably certain that the man had not just sold him a pack of lies about the secret yard. It made sense that a career gangster like Miss Trude Madden would have hidey-holes where she could stash the reindeer so that it would be more difficult for Santa Claus to snatch him back. She couldn't be certain what Santa Claus's abilities were or even who he was, if he even was a he, so better safe than sorry.

Carnegie called back over his shoulder as he parked. "Here we are, Santa, sir. The yard is behind the old cinema. You know, it's ironic: I'm supposed to be chasing the fake Santas out of the park before the vigil tonight, and here I am helping the real one. Maybe it's not ironic. Maybe it's a coincidence. Those two have always confused me."

Niko unfolded himself in sections, and he could swear

he heard his joints creaking. It would seem that he was growing too old for shenanigans.

"Take care now, Mr. Santa, sir," Carnegie was saying. "And remember: From this moment on, you can count on Dafydd Carnegie, so long as there's no violence or indeed peril involved. Or confrontation."

Niko rubbed his neck. "Good to know, Dafydd. Thanks for the lift."

"Should I wait here, sir?"

"No. I'll take Skära home by the river. You could check on Duchess for me and then make sure nothing happens at the Santa Vigil. Perhaps you might sing a Christmas carol?"

If a person's face could be said to light up, then Carnegie's did like a streetlight.

"Oh, I couldn't, sir. It's been so long since I sang in public."

"Santa's orders," said Niko seriously.

"Well, in that case," said Carnegie, and was back in the micro-van before the echo of his words faded.

★ ★ ★

Santas have always had almost supernatural homing abilities, the broader strokes of which can be explained away by an expert knowledge of astronomy. But this did not explain how the Claus family could always find their way exactly where they needed to go, even if they'd never been there before.

Elf scientists theorized that the Santas were somehow connected to the earth's magnetic field, but if Niko was honest he'd never been much of a science buff and simply relied on the ability even though he wasn't exactly sure how it worked. Tomescu had done some blood work and informed him that the Claus family did, in fact, have an unusual concentration of iron particles in their bloodstream, and so it was possible that they could unconsciously surf the planet's invisible fields.

No need for surfing this evening, thought Niko now. *The Madden yard is behind the old cinema.*

In fact, Carnegie's directions were a little incomplete. Behind the dilapidated White Elephant Cinema, which still displayed a water-damaged poster from the first *Kung Fu Panda* movie, was a red-brick block of flats and behind that again was a basketball court. But once Niko had scaled the block wall on the north side of the court he did indeed find a shadowy, out-of-the-way yard dotted with rusting skips and lockups.

This looks exactly the sort of place where the Maddens would do their shady business, he thought, pulling up his hood in case there were security cameras hidden somewhere. Not that conventional cameras would capture any images of him while he was wearing the Santa suit, but he'd been out of the game for nearly a decade, and a lot can happen with technological advances in ten years.

Niko squatted down behind the cadaver of an old BMW that he suspected had been stolen and stripped for parts and concentrated. Now that Skära had been imprinted, he should be able to sense the calf if he was nearby.

He closed his eyes and gave it a minute, picturing the calf in his mind to help establish a link, but there was nothing.

That wasn't conclusive proof of anything, Niko knew. There could be running water nearby or maybe the reindeer was inside a steel box.

He would have to find Skära the old-fashioned way. Using his eyeballs. And he would have to be sneaky. Undoubtedly, Miss Trude would have people guarding her prize.

Fortunately, I have a lot of experience being sneaky.

Niko would have preferred to wait until midnight to creep into the yard, but he couldn't delay any longer in case Trude Madden stuck her hand into the sack and became Santa Claus by accident, which would be the greatest disaster to befall Christmas since the elfin warlocks manufactured the interdimensional sack all those centuries ago.

Niko groaned. Why had he even packed the sack in Skära's saddlebag?

Actually, he knew why: to punish Blixxen for eating the rhubarb. Blixxen was usually the one entrusted with the sack and the boots, but Niko had pointedly packed Skära's saddlebags with the tools of his trade.

The warm weather is melting your brain, Niko old boy, he told himself.

But it wasn't the warm weather, he knew. He was distracted by Duchess. Usually, when Niko Claus was on a job, he was all iron focus until that job was done, double-checked and dusted, but lately he found Duchess floating round his consciousness.

Josephine, he thought.

Jo.

I know who she really is.

I need to tell her.

And you can tell her, said his inner voice. *Later.*

And, when he told her, what would happen?

Would she think he was sorry for her?

Would it mean the end of his mission to help the people who needed him?

Would he have to explain why he had walked away from Christmas when Duchess was such a believer?

Would she feel about him the way he was beginning to realize that he felt about her?

Would she hate him?

So many big questions and he had no answers.

It was almost funny, but the best person to advise him as to how he felt about the new woman in his life was the last woman in his life.

I wish you were here, Sarika.

Niko tried again to focus on the mission: find Skära and the sack. The boots too, but mostly the sack.

But thinking about Skära led to thinking about Juniper, and it occurred to him that the girl must be beside herself with worry. She had already been at her wits' end searching for her mother, and now her new best friend was missing too.

I'll find Skära first and then Juniper's mother, Niko resolved.

After all, Duchess had asked him to help. And he could not say no to Duchess.

Niko shut all these thoughts away and tried to quiet his mind.

Find the calf, he told himself. *Forget the world.*

Now for rescuing reindeer, later for sorting out his relationship with Duchess.

Niko bent low and crept between the rows of skips toward the front of the yard, avoiding the puddles of water since people tended to notice any flickers in their peripheral vision.

He quickly made his way to the guard hut beside the gate. Niko could see half a dozen men inside arranged round a small table that was heaped with enough fried food to clog the Thames Barrier.

Keep eating your sausages, boys, he beamed at them. *No need to check the yard.*

So far as he could see, there was only one place Skära would be. There was a large truck parked just inside the gate with a reinforced trailer angled behind it.

"Kongegrabbe," Niko whispered to himself, which was the elvish-language version of bingo and came from an old Viking game called Capture the King or Kongegrabbe.

The Madden mob hadn't even posted a guard, and the trailer's door was facing away from their hut.

Those boys are living up to their reputation.

That reputation being that Miss Trude was the brains of the operation.

Niko chose a moment when it seemed that most of the men had their attention on the rapidly shrinking pile of chips on the table to carefully pick his way across an asphalt surface that was so cracked and warped it resembled a lake of frozen wavelets. In five seconds flat, he had his ear to the door of the container and could hear snuffling inside, which was all the evidence he needed.

There was a padlock on the door, but the keyhole was so large that had Tomescu been with him he could have reached in and unlocked it with his fingers. Niko's fingers, however, were fatter than the sausages on the table not twenty feet away. It didn't matter because Niko had a tool in the pocket of his work coat that looked a little like a stainless-steel egg whisk. He wound the business end into the keyhole and cranked the little handle, his pinkie raised as though he was taking tea with royalty. It took a dozen revolutions to wear down the gears, but then the big lock dropped open.

"Thanks, Tomescu," said Niko, and hauled open the heavy door.

It was dark inside, but that didn't bother Niko as he knew his night vision would adjust in seconds. Not that he could afford to wait seconds when the Trudettes might think to send out a sentry at any time. Better to hop inside, bundle Skära under one arm, and be out of here.

No harm done, he thought. *Things could have been a lot worse.*

Niko climbed into the truck and saw a deer-shaped lump at the back in the ruins of a garden shed. The deer-shaped thing barked at him, which was a surprise.

"Skära," he said. "Calm down. It's me."

He blinked half a dozen times to get his night vision going and saw that the deer-shaped thing was wearing one of those novelty antler headbands. He also saw that the deer-shaped thing was actually more dog-shaped. Labrador, to be specific.

"Ah," said Niko as the penny dropped. "It's a trap."

"Woof," said the Labrador, and the twinkling lights came on in its headband antlers.

Behind Niko, the door swung closed with a metallic thud that echoed off the steel walls, which were so thick that Niko could barely hear the men outside laughing.

What have I done? he wondered, and then answered his own question. *I have handed Christmas to Miss Trude, gift-wrapped.*

15

Jo to My Friends

It was now late afternoon on Red-Letter Day, and while Niko was walking into a trap in Kilburn, Juniper and Duchess were playing the waiting game in Cedar Mews. Duchess searched the internet for any news of a possible match for a Jennifer Lane who had been admitted to hospital and found nothing. Four injured women had been brought in overnight, but three were known to the police, and the other one had been identified by a family member. None of Duchess's contacts on Parklife had come up with any leads, and nobody had called the number on the missing-person posters.

It was very disheartening so Duchess distracted Juniper by quizzing her about all the goings-on of the previous few days. They sat in the cottage's little galley kitchen, which was so narrow that some years ago Briar had hinged one side of the table so it could fold down, and the Lanes had a little more room to pass by. When Juniper was finished with her breathless account, Duchess was understandably flabbergasted.

"It's all so hard to believe, sweetie," she said. "So now you're an apprentice Santa?"

Juniper nodded. "I don't even understand all of it myself."

"And you're magical?"

"Not like a wizard or anything, but I can do a few things. Like ride Skära. And the equipment works for me. The boots and the sack. Stuff like that."

"And Skära has this equipment, and Trude Madden has Skära?"

"That's right. It's all my fault. I got us both seen," said Juniper, and tears flowed freely down her cheeks. "Poor Skära. He must be terrified. I should be out there looking for him and Mum, not just sitting here."

Duchess took her hand. "No, sweetie. Niko said to stay here, and I'm sure he'll get in touch any minute with good news."

Juniper looked down at Duchess's fingers and squeezed them. She noticed that the veins running along the back of one hand were golden. Definitely golden.

How can Duchess's veins be golden, and how did I never

see that before? she wondered, but the answer came to her almost immediately. Duchess usually wore fingerless gloves or long frilly sleeves that covered her hands, and even when disguised as the duchess of Benbarty she'd been careful to cover one hand with the other.

"You have polar memories," said Duchess. "How much do you remember about me?"

Juniper thought about this. She could remember whatever previous Santas had seen during their tenure, in case it would help her deliveries when she was Santa, but the memories were not always there. She could see them in the corner of her mind's eye, but she had to concentrate on the person to bring them into focus.

"Nothing really," she said. "Unless you want me to."

Duchess sighed a sigh that reached two decades into the past.

"I don't want you to remember," she said, so softly that her words were little more than puffs of air. "You shouldn't have to because I should tell you."

Juniper wanted to say that she'd already remembered some of it, but that it didn't change anything. Instead, she said: "Whatever you want . . . Josephine."

Duchess frowned a little, but then rallied and said: "It's Jo to my friends."

★ ★ ★

The thing about Santa Claus is people want to tell him or her things. That instinct is still there to this day, which was why Dafydd Carnegie fell to pieces with Niko, and now Duchess decided to open her heart to Juniper, something she'd wanted to do for a long time.

Duchess closed her eyes as she told her own story, and Juniper took this as a sign not to interrupt. So she quickly wiped the fridge whiteboard with her sleeve and used the tethered marker pen to write down her questions for the end, though she didn't last till then without interrupting as it turned out.

Duchess confirmed what Juniper already knew thanks to her yuledrøm. She was, in fact, disgraced Irish scientist Josephine Spangles, the very person who somewhat arrogantly announced that the units for measuring Santa magic would be called Spangles, after herself.

"Oh, I was insufferable," said Duchess. "I told any colleague who would listen that Spangles were the answer to the world's energy crisis. All we had to do was believe in energy, and we would have it, and that I had found a way to turn bright ideas into brighter light."

Duchess rubbed the golden veins in her hand with one thumb.

"Not for a single moment did I think that I could be wrong. Not for a millisecond. So I built a generator that would be compatible with our neural pathways."

Juniper could not help interrupting.

"I saw a video of a scientist calling your generator a brain box," she said.

Duchess's smile was pained. "No, sweetie. That's what my fellow professors said to make me sound like a mad scientist. The generator was actually a very complicated vat of conductors and electrolytes. Over a thousand composite liquids and gels all measured down to the last drop. I organized a demonstration in Trinity College. Everyone was there in my field. People flew in from all over the world for the show, and it was a disaster."

Duchess covered her face with her hands. "There I was onstage in front of the community's best and brightest, wearing a ridiculous fishbowl helmet to draw out the neural sparks and gel gloves to interface with the generator, and then . . . nothing much happened. Oh, I got a couple of sparks into my helmet, but I just didn't believe it could work, not with all those people watching. And with Spangles, if you don't believe, then there is no magic."

Juniper was hooked by the story. She'd read articles about the conference, everybody in school had, but hearing about it from the infamous Josephine Spangles herself was fascinating and distracted her from her own problems for a minute.

"Nothing at all happened?"

"Nothing was generated, but something did happen. A spark burned the tip of my nose and startled me. I bumped the generator, sloshed some gel onto the stage, slipped in the puddle, and knocked over the whole thing, drenching the first three rows." Duchess laughed bitterly. "It was comical. Anyway, I'm sure you know all that."

Juniper nodded. "We read about you in a science magazine. The article was called 'Whatever Happened to Josephine Spangles?'"

"I can tell you that," said Duchess. "My funding was cut, and I was dismissed for unsafe practice."

"And that was the end of your experiments?"

Duchess bowed her head. "No. I wish. After I got myself fired, I became obsessed with the Spangle Generator. I reckoned that if I could see it working then I would believe it worked and could make it work myself, if that makes any sense."

Juniper was quick on the uptake. "So you needed Santa."

"Exactly. I had to get Santa Claus to activate my generator, even if he didn't know he was doing it."

"How did you persuade Niko to visit?"

"I tricked him," said Duchess miserably. "I tricked Santa Claus. What kind of person does that?"

"It's not so bad," said Juniper, mainly because she herself had tricked Niko by sabotaging the Armadillo.

"It is bad," Duchess insisted. "I knew Santa wouldn't be visiting me the following Christmas, but he would visit my niece. So I put a conductor pad beside her bed with the wire running to me in the next room where I was all set with my helmet and gel gloves."

Juniper immediately saw the problem with this. "You wanted to start up a new type of generator beside your niece's bedroom?"

Duchess started crying then, and it wasn't just a graceful sob. Her entire person was involved. Her face crumpled like a raisin, and floods of tears tracked the wrinkles under her eyes, her mouth opened in a despairing O, and she told the rest of the story in between hitching sobs.

"I did. I did exactly that. I tried to start up an experimental generator using a fuel I didn't really understand while my only niece was sleeping five feet away." Duchess wiped her eyes, which made a difference for about a second. "I still don't really understand what I was thinking. I was obsessed. I was so wrapped up in being the savior of humanity that I forgot about humans. So there I was in the next room, wait-ing for Santa Claus, and somehow I fell asleep."

"Niko likes to sing a little song coming in," said Juniper. "Very sneaky. He did it to me too."

"The next thing I know I wake up, and my helmet is full of golden light. But it's more than light, it's liquid too, and I didn't know what was going on because I was still half asleep. So I tried to take off the helmet, and some of the gold light gets on my gloves, and it shoots out of me and cuts right through the wall, right through to . . ."

Juniper was shocked. "Did your niece? Was she . . ."

"No," said Duchess. "It missed her but I could have . . . I nearly . . ."

And that was when Duchess laid her head on the table and let the sobs take over. "The next thing I knew, Santa, Niko, was in the room telling me that some things should stay secret. I must have passed out because I woke up out-side on the street with my brother's family. One hand was burned, and in time when the burn faded these golden veins were left as reminders of my foolish pride. I hated myself for what I'd done. I still do. My family haven't spo-ken to me since."

"Do they know where you are?"

Duchess found some tissues in a pocket and wiped her nose. "No. Not since the hospital. After the accident, I was sent to hospital. I wasn't in my right mind. Everything went round and round in my head. I'd developed this chest problem that the doctors thought was somehow stress-related adult asthma. I spent years in a special home, taking pills and trying to explain to counselors how Santa was angry with me for trying to capture his magic in a fishbowl."

"If you'd told me that yesterday, I probably wouldn't have believed it."

"So one day I just climbed through a window and left. I based the character of Duchess on a character from my favorite book growing up and decided to live her life away from universities and laboratories and family. Her life was easier to live than my own. I've had a new existence since then, the best part of which was meeting you." Duchess began crying again. "And now you know what I've done you can never look at me the same way again. I shouldn't even be allowed to take care of you."

Duchess's crying caused a coughing fit, and Juniper ran to fetch her a glass of water.

"But I know you," she said when Duchess's chest had calmed. "You would never put anyone in danger. It's just not Duchess."

"But maybe it's Josephine Spangles," said Duchess. "So I'll never go back to being her again."

Juniper was still puzzling over how someone so wise

and wonderful could have done something so irresponsible when there was a knock at the front door. She leaned back in her chair and saw, through the bubbled pane of glass, the distorted but still unmistakable shape of Dafydd Carnegie.

"It's Carnegie," she said. "We need the duchess of Benbarty."

"Oh my goodness," said Duchess, coughing nervously, "I'm a mess."

"We're both a mess," said Juniper. "That's how we're supposed to be. Mum is missing. If there's any chance that Carnegie knows something, anything, I have to listen to him. Even if it means going into the system."

Juniper raced to the end of the hall and yanked open the door. Dafydd Carnegie stood on the doorstep that Briar Lane had hewn from an old granite millstone (which was when Juniper had learned the word *hewn*).

"Mum?" said Juniper.

"No," said Carnegie, placing the spread fingers of one hand on his chest. "Dafydd."

"I meant was there news of my mum? You know, the future duchess of Benbarty?"

Carnegie swept into the cottage uninvited. "Let's dispense with that fiction, shall we? Things will go a lot more smoothly if we all tell the truth."

"So long as we're telling the truth, dear Dafydd," said Duchess, rising from the kitchen chair, "perhaps you might admit that you're up to your neck in all this with Miss Trude."

Carnegie bowed. "With shame, I do admit it, Duchess," he said. "But my icy heart has been thawed by our friend Niko. I have switched teams, and now fight for the angels."

Duchess was not convinced. "Just like that? Pardon me, Mr. Carnegie, but it sounds like you're quoting lines from a play."

"It's no play, madam," said Carnegie. "Our friend Niko can be quite persuasive, can he not? Santa Claus shone a light on some of the more unsavory events in my history and brought me up to speed on our little team. Unlike you both, I am very much on the naughty list, and I intend to remedy that starting this very moment."

"I'm on the naughty list too," said Duchess glumly.

"This could all be some kind of trap," said Juniper.

Carnegie steepled his fingers. "Speaking of traps, that's why I'm here. It occurs to me that I may have sent our mutual friend Santa Claus directly into one."

16

A Branding Exercise

Like a lot of Irish people, Miss Trude Madden came from a horsey family, but not the same kind of horsey family that many Irish people were proud to belong to. The Maddens dosed horses with steroids, ran ringers, stole horses, and transported them using their Junior Jockeys stables as a cover. Trude herself was particularly good at breaking wild horses, and she intended to use those skills on Skära now.

For all intents and purposes, Skära would be a horse.

"Why don't we see if you can be the golden goose for this family, little fella?" she said, entering the training pen, one hand behind her back, which is rarely a good sign.

Skära was tethered to a pole in the center of the ring, his eyes wild and close to panic. Imprinted reindeer are higher up the smarts chain than normal reindeer, and Skära was well aware that this human intended to do him harm, and so he bucked and tugged on the rope attached to the cruel bridle cinched round his head. It had taken two men to attach the bridle, and they had both been so battered by Skära's hooves in the process that they hadn't even managed to uncinch the reindeer's saddlebags.

Miss Trude smiled coldly. "Don't worry, boy. I won't hurt you too badly."

Skära cast his eyes about wildly.

"There's no escape," said Miss Trude. "I'm not taking any chances with you, my lad, because you are the future for the Maddens. Once I bend you to my will, then Christmas will be mine for the taking. And with it all the millions those idiot parents lavish on their children every year. The sky's the limit. Isn't that what they say, fella?"

The reindeer honked as though answering Trude when in fact he was warning her to stay back.

"The thing is," Trude continued, taking slow steps forward, "I have to show you who's boss. So the first lesson might be tough on you, but once we're over that hump it should be smooth sailing. Or in your case smooth flying."

Skära honked again, louder this time: a cry for help.

"No one knows where you are," Trude told him, stepping closer. "And even if Santa did know he's locked up in the same lorry where you were before Lar dropped you off."

Lar had indeed dropped Skära off, although "dropped off" didn't seem a dramatic enough term to cover the drama involved in lassoing the reindeer and dragging him from the ruined shed inside the container. Two of Lar's boys were currently out of commission with head wounds, but Trude considered that a small price to pay.

Skära reacted to her approach by whipping his head round in an effort to shake off the bridle.

Trude laughed. "You're not wriggling out of that, fella. Bigger animals than you have tried and smaller ones too. I stitched that bridle myself, and it's not for slipping."

Skära gave it one more try, this time lifting off into the air as far as he could, seeing if a little vertical pressure would either snap the tether or uproot the pole.

"That's a remarkable talent you have there, fella me lad," said Trude Madden. "The money you are going to rake in for me."

It was a no-go with the pole as it was set in concrete below the compacted clay surface, so Skära decided to use his cliff-goat-style abilities to gather his four hooves together to form one roughly circular hoof and perch on the head of the pole.

"Not bad," said Miss Trude with some admiration.

"And perhaps, if I was on my lonesome, that would be the end of it. But I'm not, am I?"

She reached into her bum bag and pulled out a referee's whistle. One sharp toot later and two burly types hurried over from the office, one holding a long-handled hook.

"Bring him down," commanded Trude. "For step one in his training."

Step one in the Trude Madden process was a training saddle. She planned to ride the reindeer until he was broken.

"Look lively, boys. And try not to get knocked unconscious."

Trude did not have much faith in these two lads' intellects, but they were both rugby players and so were marvelous at takedowns. She had once seen them tackle a shire horse that they were transporting to Sheffield, so a reindeer shouldn't be a problem, even a flying one.

"Let's see you get out of this, young buck."

Skära honked fiercely at the burly men, but, when that didn't scare them off, the reindeer acted. He flew upward to the limits of his tether, then swung down, circling the pole and wrapping both men in his own rope. Of course he still couldn't escape, but now the men were in no position to harm him for the moment at least.

Trude laughed. "Well, I never. Aren't you the clever one?"

And it wasn't over yet. Skära saw the tip of the hook a few centimeters from his nose and draped the rope over it and began to saw.

"I don't think so," said Trude, sliding the hook out from inside the rope and tossing it away.

Skära stabbed at the rope with his furry antlers, but it was no use. He had hogtied himself along with the two rugby players.

"Maybe I'll just leave you tied up there for the night," said Trude. "Until you forget your actual name and answer to the one I give you."

"His name," said a voice behind her, "is Skära."

Dafydd Carnegie was at the enclosure gate with Juniper Lane. He was holding Juniper's scarf in one fist. The green scarf that was wound tightly round the girl's middle, and it certainly seemed like she was his prisoner.

"I brought the girl, Miss Trude," he said, which was true. "She can help you tame this beast and get at whatever's in his saddlebags." This was not true, Carnegie was very firmly on Team Santa Claus now.

Trude squinted at him. "You brought the girl? A spineless jelly like you?"

Carnegie waved his free hand. "Look, the girl gave me vital information you need to have so I stuffed her in my little van."

Trude was understandably suspicious. "You stuffed her?"

Carnegie grimaced. "Perhaps *stuffed* is the wrong word."

"He lied to me!" blurted Juniper. "This beast told me the police had found my mother and he'd take me to the hospital." And then she started crying very real tears. Juniper found it easy to cry because her mother was still missing and if she was without shelter then Juniper did not want to think about what could have happened.

It was the tears that won Trude Madden over.

"Dafydd Carnegie, I am reluctantly and temporarily impressed."

"There's no need to hog-tie the reindeer now," said Carnegie. "Not when you hear what I have to tell you."

Trude folded her arms. "Well, out with it then."

Carnegie prodded Juniper farther into the small arena.

"I'm actually surprised we could just walk in here. No sentries?"

"Just these two idiots," said Trude, nodding at the trussed rugby players. "The rest are in Kilburn watching over the person who I presume is Santa Claus while I try to teach his calf here some manners." She frowned. "Am I the one answering questions, mister?"

"No," said Carnegie hurriedly. "Of course not."

"Because that's not how information flows in this relationship. Don't make me reach into my bum bag."

"Why don't I give you the information without any more dallying?"

"Why don't you do that?" said Trude, which sounded like a question, but was actually a command.

Carnegie composed himself for the big delivery. "Very well. Here it is. The key to this whole affair is the fact that nothing works without Juniper. Only she can control Skära and what's in his saddlebags. They have some kind of magical link. You can do whatever you want to this beast, and it won't make any difference. Eventually, it won't even be able to fly unless Juniper is close by."

Trude reached into her bum bag and drew out an apple, which seemed way too big to fit in the bag. She took a large bite and chewed thoughtfully.

"Is that the truth of it?" she asked Juniper. "You control the reindeer and the wonderful sack in his saddlebags?"

Juniper nodded, still teary. "Yes. The sack's magical and so is Skära. We're imprinted. A team. You need both of us."

It was Trude Madden's nature to be suspicious, so she

said: "Isn't that convenient now? I need you all of a sudden, just when I'm on the point of taming your beloved pet."

"I can prove it to you," said Juniper. "I can calm him down right now, and you can get your idiots out of there."

Miss Trude was not annoyed by this impudence. "It's true, they are idiots." She took another bite of the apple, which gave her ten seconds to think. "Very well, girleen. Calm the savage beast if you can do it from there."

"I can," said Juniper, and sang the Santa lullaby she'd heard Niko singing.

"It's growing late around the world . . ."

Juniper's voice was pure and somehow magical. It seemed like there was a whole choir singing instead of just one person.

"For every boy and every girl . . .
Goodbye to sun, hello to moon . . ."

Trude saw that Carnegie had his fingers in his ears and realized she'd been tricked.

"Treachery," she gasped. "Witchcraft."

"Santa Claus is coming soon."

Trude crumpled to the ground, and the apple rolled from her hand.

"Not witchcraft," said Juniper. "Magic."

✶ ✶ ✶

Of course, Skära didn't nod off. If reindeer fell asleep at Santa's lullaby, the Christmas Eve delivery would never end. Juniper released the calf from the tangle around the training pole, and they had an emotional reunion, hugging and nuzzling.

"I'm sorry, boy," Juniper sobbed into his ear. "It's my fault. I should have been more careful."

Skära licked Juniper's cheek, and it seemed she was forgiven.

"But we have more dangerous work to do," Juniper said. "There are people to find. My mother and Niko too. I got him locked up. I am so bad at being Santa."

She held on to the reindeer tightly for a long moment. She'd been so terrified that she'd delivered the power of Christmas to the Madden family that she was almost afraid to let him go.

"We need to get Niko back," she told Skära. "I need to put things right."

Carnegie coughed nervously. "Juniper, dear, do we have time for all this? Shouldn't we get a move on?"

Juniper wiped her eyes. "Yes, Mr. Carnegie. We should. The sleep spell won't last for long."

"In that case, we should most definitely hit the road," said Carnegie, thinking about how angry Trude Madden would be when she woke up.

Juniper climbed onto Skära's back smoothly, as if she'd been doing it for years. "Okay, you hit the road back to the Mews, Mr. Carnegie. Duchess will protect you until we get back. Miss Trude won't try anything on Santa Vigil night. Too many people in the park, and anyway I think she's probably learned her lesson."

"Maybe," said Carnegie, but wondered if a rockabilly lady who was prepared to kidnap Santa and his reindeer would ever learn her lesson.

"I'm going to rescue Niko," said Juniper, and then turned to Skära. "Can you find Niko, buddy?"

The reindeer snorted.

Can I find him? Do you even have to ask?

Juniper smiled. "That's what I thought."

17

Flying High

At this point, the main human characters in this festive tale are all flying solo so to speak. Juniper was literally on a solo flight. Carnegie was hurrying back to Cedar Mews in his three-wheeler, and Duchess was manning the cottage phone and monitoring @parklife for any news of Jennifer Lane, although her mind skipped from Juniper to Niko and back again.

It also occurred to her that if Juniper had Santa Claus memories then of course Niko's were even clearer as he was the actual Santa in question who'd saved her that night twenty years ago. And in that case the first man she had ever thought she could actually love in a romantic sense knew all about her shameful past and was lost to her forever.

The stress of this realization caused her chest to tighten and whistling coughs to force their way through the pinhole of her windpipe. It was as if the old adult asthma had returned with a vengeance. Duchess didn't panic, not at first, because she'd been through these attacks many times though not recently.

What could be causing the recent attacks? she wondered as she tried to breathe normally. Not the house. She'd stayed in the cottage a thousand times.

Not the park. It wasn't the season, and even if spring allergies were to blame they'd never bothered her before.

Think, Jo, she told herself. *You were a scientist once. There's a new variable at play here. What is it?*

As the stress-induced coughs grew in intensity, and Duchess found herself sliding to the floor, she realized that there was only one culprit she could think of. If she could have wryly chuckled, she would have.

It's a cruel irony, she thought, her mind oddly clear inside her spasming body. *I gave my life to magic, and now magic will kill me.*

Mr. Dafydd Carnegie skedaddled from the stables just as soon as Juniper and Skära disappeared into the London sky. He did think about securing Trude Madden and her goons with plastic ties so that he could gloat over them when they woke up, but it occurred to the regional director of parks that he had neither the plastic ties nor the backbone to follow this plan through. And so he scooted onto the road and climbed into his vehicle for the short journey back to Cedar Park, which would quite literally take him less time to walk.

In the van, he mused briefly on his life in general and where he wanted it to go. He realized with a small yelp that his life might not be going anywhere once Trude woke up, but even that thought couldn't dampen his mood for long.

I am on Team Santa Claus, he realized, and knew that his future, however brief that might turn out to be, would be a lot brighter than his past.

Juniper Lane was on a mission, a very serious mission, so she tried her best not to feel exhilarated by the moonlight trip to Kilburn. Yesterday she would not have even known the way to northwest London, but now she did. All she had to do was think about it a little and a detailed three-dimensional map sprang into her mind, and from her mind into Skära's.

In spite of everything, it was very tough not to enjoy the night flight, with the wind in her face and the rough feel of Skära's neck hairs between her fingers. The reindeer calf was ecstatic to be free and darted through the sky, hopping between currents to find the most efficient way to Niko. And if Juniper closed her eyes and concentrated she could see the night sky how the reindeer calf saw it: a swirling maelstrom of colored slipstreams that her partner ducked inside as it suited him so that his own energy expenditure was minimal.

Juniper remembered something that one of the previous Santa Clauses had said: *Let the sky do the work.* She liked that.

We're not flying through the sky, she realized, hugging Skära's neck tightly. *We're riding on it.*

She enjoyed the sensation for a minute or two, and then a thought intruded.

Niko probably won't be happy to see me since this is all my fault.

She found that didn't matter to her now. Whose fault things were could be worried about when Niko was free and the Lane girls were back together. And maybe Niko could help with that.

If not, I can do it myself, she thought. *I'm starting to get the hang of this magic stuff now, so surely I can find Mum this time.*

But first she had to find Niko.

Skära dipped his antlers and dropped down a hundred feet, then slalomed between a series of high-rise flats.

Juniper scratched behind the calf's left ear, which meant: *Nice move, pal.*

They were nearly there. Kilburn was lit up like a Christmas fair, all except one dark patch beside the cemetery.

That's where you are, thought Juniper. *You'd better watch out, Maddens. Santa Claus Lane is coming.*

★ ★ ★

Niko Claus was trapped in the back of a truck, and he couldn't see a way to escape. He'd tried to batter his way out, charging the door until his shoulder hurt, but all that had achieved was to make the men outside laugh even harder, plus it had scared the dog.

His next move was to feel his way round the walls, searching for a weakness. Even with his excellent night vision, it was tough to spot any fault in the container so he borrowed the dog's light-up antlers and stretched them over his own head and then made the rounds again, probing any dark spot or weld bubble for a possible exit route. Even with the antlers casting a weak glow on the metal walls, Niko's search was fruitless.

It was possible the ceiling might have yielded some results, but it was ten feet high, and he wasn't wearing his work boots. The only Santa equipment he had on him was the lock-whisk, which he couldn't see a use for, and so, for the first time since leaving the North Pole, Niko found himself wishing he had a mobile phone. He didn't like carrying around an electronic tracker, but it was better than being only the third Santa Claus to have ever been captured.

This thought stopped him in his tracks, and the antlers cast a pale glow on his surprised expression. That was the first time in a long time he'd thought of himself as a Santa.

Duchess is getting through to me, he realized. *And the kid too.*

"People have to do what they can do," Duchess had told him back in the Mews once he'd revealed that he was Santa. Scolded him in fact. "There are plenty of people who can fix up the park, but only one person who can bring hope to the world."

Niko snorted a little in the dark.

"Hope to the world. That's a little melodramatic, don't you think, pooch?"

The Labrador was delighted to be involved and yipped an affirmative. Niko wasn't sure which affirmative exactly, but most dog-speak was affirmative, unlike reindeer who had a moody side.

Niko walked to the end of the container and put his ear

to the door. He could hear the men outside chatting. It was hard to pick up the thread of the conversation, but he made out a few snatches:

"No texts. Mammy said radio silence."

And:

". . . up on the office roof."

Followed by:

". . . elf lands with a blowtorch . . ."

Niko rested his forehead against the cool metal and realized that not only had he been trapped, but the smartest member of the bunch who had trapped him was probably the Labrador.

"Who's a clever team member?" he called over his shoulder.

And a voice whispered back, "Me, that's who."

For a second, Niko thought the Labrador had answered him.

I've been on my own for too long, he thought. *Now the dogs are talking.*

But he had heard the words, and if the Labrador hadn't spoken them then who had?

Niko did another scan of the container and saw that there was a slot in the ceiling and in the glow of his battery-operated antlers made out an impish face beyond. A torch beam shone through the slot and illuminated a rectangle on the floor. Niko stepped into the light and smiled.

"Juniper," he said.

✳ ✳ ✳

Juniper and Skära had come in silently, which was not an easy move, but the reindeer was light on his hooves and managed to execute a treading-water-type movement over the truck so that he never actually touched down.

"Well done, partner," whispered Juniper, dismounting onto the top of the container.

Neither of them had any doubt that Niko was inside. Juniper could feel the polar magic shimmering through the roof, and Skära could actually recognize the big man's footsteps from inside.

Juniper had an idea. Something she could possibly try to get Niko out of there, but only if everything else failed because it was by no stretch of the imagination a good idea.

Skära drew his legs up and lowered himself soundlessly to the metal roof.

Juniper emptied the saddlebags and mouthed: *Stay there.*

She crawled on her belly to the rear of the truck and

peeked over the lip of the container to see Lar Madden and a few of his cronies gathered round the door.

"I want one of you on each corner of the vehicle," Lar was saying. "I'm going to park meself up on the office roof and keep an eye in case an elf lands with a blowtorch or something. You never know with this Santy crowd, am I right?"

Juniper withdrew her head like a tortoise going into its shell.

Lar was going to climb onto the office roof? That meant she had a couple of minutes to get Niko out of there.

Juniper swiveled on her belly and gazed along the container roof. There was only one irregularity. A small raised rectangle toward the center. She crawled back and found that the raised section was a small hatch, bolted from the outside.

She opened it just in time to hear Niko say: "Who's a clever team member?"

And she could not resist answering: "Me, that's who."

Juniper took out her phone and shone the torch into the belly of the truck, and Niko stepped into the beam.

"Ta-da," said Juniper. "We have about two minutes, Niko. Do you have any laser weapons or something like that?"

"No, Juniper. Nothing up my sleeve. Are you okay? Is Dutch okay?"

"She's coughing more than ever. It's getting worse, I think."

Niko's eyes glittered in the torch beam. "I need to get out of here, Juniper, and I can't fit through a ventilation hatch the size of a letterbox."

Juniper wiggled her hand into the hatch, and Niko saw that there was something wadded in her fist.

"I have an idea," she said.

"That is a terrible idea," said Niko.

"I know. I was hoping to think of something better, but time's running out."

Time was running out, and they both knew it. Jennifer Lane was still missing, Duchess's health was failing, and the park itself was in the mayor's sights. And, as if that wasn't enough, the sack would soon begin giving up letters and, for the first time in ten years, Niko thought that maybe he should draw one out.

He thought this for a couple of reasons. Firstly, if he didn't, then the interdimensional portal would close, and the sack would become just a sack, which would effectively spell the end of Christmas forever, and Niko was now feeling this would be an extremely bad idea. And secondly, following his brush with the Maddens, it had become imperative that no one apart from Santa himself take out a Christmas letter.

Niko shuddered. Imagine if Miss Trude had accidentally become Santa. Disaster.

He needed to make a list, check it twice, and cross all the above items off.

So even though Juniper's plan was risky there was no other way.

"Okay, Juniper. Go ahead."

Juniper pulled her hand out of the hole, tied the green scarf to the sack's drawstring, and lowered it down to Niko.

"Go on," she said. "Dive in."

And, against the advice of all the Santas who had gone before him, Niko Claus dived into the sack. And even though he was nearly massive and weighed in excess of a hundred kilograms he didn't even plump out the sides.

It took a few minutes for Juniper to wiggle the coarse sack back out through the vent, and in that time Lar made the climb onto the office roof by standing on a wheelie bin and scrabbling up on the felt roof from there. Normally, he would have taken another half a minute to take a selfie with the tall cranes of Kilburn looming behind him like *Star Wars* attack robots and then a further minute to compose a cool description to go with the pic. Today, however, he was mindful of his responsibility as his mammy's official number two and so decided just to glance across at the lorry on the off chance that something had happened in the hundred seconds or so since he'd given his boys their order. And lo and behold, wouldn't you know it, there was the girl jigging around on the container. And he couldn't be 100 percent sure, but in the city glow it seemed like there was either a very small horse or a reindeer beside her.

I don't want to shout "reindeer" if it's just a small horse, Lar thought. *The lads would laugh at me. Ha-ha, there's the eejit who can't tell the difference between a small horse and a reindeer.*

But then the shape moved its head, and Lar saw the boomerang antlers.

It is the reindeer! he realized, and was confident enough to shout: "On the roof! I'm 90 percent sure there's a reindeer up there and a girl. Get into the trailer and secure the big fella."

Lar's men did not hesitate because they knew what Miss Trude would do to them if they let their prisoner escape. It didn't matter what sort of magic was at play here, it would be their fault. It didn't even matter that it seemed like Miss Trude had let the reindeer escape herself because that would somehow be their fault too. So they followed Lar's order, opened the door, and piled into the back of the truck, ready to do battle. It was not the smartest move as they would shortly find out.

Even though the Santa sack was more of an interdimensional conduit than a regular sack, it was still difficult to get it out through the vent. Juniper had to twist and heave on the green scarf to move it bit by bit as the thick material clogged the opening. She attempted to do this quietly, but when Lar called from the office roof, she abandoned her stealth efforts and put her back into the job, planting her heels, grunting and groaning, and yanking the sack until it popped out of the hole. Juniper didn't even check to see if Niko was inside before stuffing it into Skära's saddlebag.

"Gotta go," she told the reindeer. "Upa-uda."

Skära did not need to be told twice. In fact, he didn't really need to be told once, and his hooves were pawing the air almost before Juniper was astride his back.

The reindeer ran off the container's edge but did not immediately climb to safety as might be expected. Instead, both girl and reindeer found themselves glaring, not altogether charitably, at Lar Madden.

"Can we buzz him?" Juniper asked her partner.

Skära honked. Of course they could.

A buzzing, as anybody who's ever seen a jet-fighter movie knows, is when a maverick pilot flies dangerously close to the control tower, giving everyone inside a bit of a fright. In this case, Lar was standing in for the flight tower. Skära lowered his antlers, snorted furiously, and dive-bombed Miss Trude's boy.

Unfortunately, both Juniper and the reindeer overestimated how frightened Lar would be, as in they thought he would be frightened whereas he wasn't in the least, because Lar was far more scared of his mother than he'd ever be of any other creature on the planet. When he saw Skära and Juniper speeding toward him, all Lar could think was that if he wanted to get this mission back on track, he had to grab the bull by the horns.

Or in this case grab the reindeer by the antlers.

That shouldn't have been possible as Skära had no intention of getting close enough to be grabbed, but Lar Madden was driven to perform a superhuman feat from fear of his mammy. Instead of backing away from Skära's flashing hooves, as any right-minded person would do, Lar raced along the office roof and launched himself into a space that was not currently occupied by a flying reindeer. Luckily for Lar, his timing was spot-on and, by the time Skära's antlers arrived, Lar's fingers were there to close round them.

"Gotcha!" shouted the man triumphantly.

The sudden increase in weight dragged Skära earthward. He was a strong calf, but this was one too many humans for any reindeer his size to carry, plus Lar was accidentally directing him by turning his antlers like a steering wheel as he hung on.

"Let go!" shouted Juniper, realizing that they should not have stuck around to buzz anybody, especially with so much at stake.

Skära struggled to gain altitude, but it was no use: the big Irishman hanging on to his boomerang antlers was just too heavy.

Juniper patted the reindeer's neck. "Don't fight," she said. "Go with it."

Skära glanced up and saw that they were headed straight for the open container and understood what Juniper had in mind. So, instead of trying to pull up, he used Lar's weight to drag them down faster and accelerated toward the lorry.

"Ha!" said Lar. "I've got them, Mammy."

But he didn't have them. Skära pulled as tight a curve

as he could manage under the circumstances and swung Lar into the container toward his men. Even the fear of Miss Trude couldn't stop Lar's fingers from letting go, and he tumbled into the depths of the container, knocking the Madden soldiers over like bowling pins.

Skära backpedaled in the air, pulling up short before he was trapped in the container too.

Juniper dropped to the ground and put her shoulder against the heavy door, pushing it closed, but not before the Labrador jumped out and extended his paw for a shake.

Juniper bolted the door and shook the dog's paw.

"Nice puppy," she said as Skära turned round to pick her up, and then she was up on the reindeer's back again, and they peeled away through the night sky so fast that from her perspective it seemed that London fell away below them into space.

18

Getting the Sack

There's an old elfin saying—*magic attracts magic*—that is even more true than the elves themselves realize because what hardly anyone knows, not even Duchess (yet), is that magic is much more than a science or a line of code; it is a living, benevolent parasite that will reach out for its own kind and bring the bearers together.

Bearers like Duchess with her golden veins that had lit up again after nearly twenty dormant years.

Bearers like Juniper who had the sparks baked into her by imprinting with Skära.

And, of course, the prime bearer, Niko himself, who was the one who interrupted Duchess's experiment back in Ireland.

And even would-be bearers like Trude Madden who have seen the glory of magic and covet it for themselves.

And witnesses like Dafydd Carnegie who have sat face-to-face with magic individuals and had their hearts opened.

Lar and his men would also eventually have entered the fray if they hadn't been locked in a steel box. Even magical attraction cannot break through steel.

And so it is at this point that our characters who went their separate ways for a short time begin their journey back to one another.

Niko Claus was in one sack, and Dafydd Carnegie was convinced that he was going to get a different kind of sack, i.e. fired by the mayor.

I was charged with putting an end to the Santa Vigil, he thought as he hurried through the park gate toward the Mews back door. *And the park is positively packed with Santa enthusiasts.*

It was true. There were so many people cosplaying not only Santa but various elves, snowmen, and even reindeer that it seemed that he was in the middle of a Christmas Con.

There were already more Christmas fans in the park than there had been the year before. The mayor had hoped the numbers would dwindle over time, but the opposite was true.

People need Christmas, Dafydd realized, and then he thought: *I need Christmas.*

And, while it might be true that he had failed the mayor, Dafydd suspected that for once he might have won at life. And what's more he intended to go on winning, even if he had to break some glass to do it.

The glass he might have to break was a pane in the Lanes' rear patio door because he could see through it that Duchess was clearly in some distress on the floor. In fact, she was so pale that if it wasn't for the fact that her leg was spasming, Carnegie would have believed her to be already dead.

"Duchess!" he cried, rapping on the window with his knuckle. "Duchess, Carnegie is coming!"

The door was locked and remained locked no matter how many times Dafydd jiggled the handle. He looked around for someone who could be ordered to break the glass, but there was no one, and so he told himself, "Do it, Daff. Break the window."

He selected a garden gnome and prodded the pane with the tip of the fellow's plaster hat. The glass tinged but did not break.

I need an incentive, Carnegie realized. *Who do I dislike most in the world?* The answer came to him quickly. It was the boy who stole his role in the Christmas show all those years ago.

He shouted at the top of his voice, "Cabby Bellows!" and shattered the glass to shards.

Seconds later, he was kneeling over Duchess, really quite alarmed by her alabaster pallor and whistling wheeze.

"Do you have an inhaler?" he asked.

Duchess's eyelids flickered, and for a second Carnegie came into focus.

"Spangles," she gasped. "Make Spangles. Kill or cure."

"Well," said Carnegie, "I didn't understand a single word of that, so we're going to the hospital."

Duchess's head shook possibly in agreement, disagreement, or it could have been an unconscious tremor. Whichever it was, Carnegie felt he had no option but to stick to his plan. He zapped Juniper a quick text, filling her in on the situation, to which she immediately replied.

See you there.

As he helped Duchess to her feet, Carnegie realized that he no longer felt any animosity toward Cabby Bellows.

I should break windows with gnomes more often, he thought.

✴ ✴ ✴

Miss Trude Madden awoke smiling until she realized she was not under the lace-frilled cover in her own single bed, but on the packed clay ground of the stable paddock.

What am I doing down here? she wondered briefly until the memory came to her.

The girleen sang me to sleep and has no doubt flown off with her little reindeer fella and the treasures in her saddlebags.

She had another thought.

"My own sweet boy Larceny!" she cried, and reached into her bum bag for her mobile.

One phone call later and Trude had changed her tune regarding her own sweet boy Larceny. In fact, her last words to him on that call had been: "Lar, you absolute excuse for a gormless gombeen."

Trude shook off her sleep fog and checked her bum bag for the sliotar sock. A sliotar, for those who might not know, is the rock-hard leather ball used in the Irish sport of hurling. To make a sliotar-sock cosh, a person simply stuffed the sliotar into a sock, in this case the purple-and-gold sock of the Wexford team where Miss Trude had actually been born.

Watch out, Juniper Lane, Trude thought, striding toward the paddock gate, audibly grinding her teeth. *Trude Madden does not give up on her Christmas dream so easily.*

✳ ✳ ✳

Juniper Lane's phone buzzed in her pocket so she asked Skära to tread air for a moment. After all, the message could be from her mother. But the text was from Dafydd Carnegie.

Duchess collapsed. Taking her to the hospital.

Juniper composed a quick reply with shaking fingers and scratched the back of Skära's head. "New plan," she said. "Full speed to the hospital."

Skära honked, and they were off.

When Niko went into the sack, he tried to hold on to his sense of space and time, but the sack had other ideas, and he found himself floating in a vast sparkly ocean of heavy orange gas, which was hopefully not toxic as he had no option but to breathe it in. He noticed that the orange gas had turned blue when he breathed it out.

My body is taking what it needs from the gas, he thought. *I hope Juniper escaped safely.*

"Look at you," said a familiar voice behind him. "Worrying about a child. It's almost as if you were Santa Claus again."

Niko recognized that voice instantly. He often dreamed about it.

"Niko, look at me," said the woman's voice.

"I can't," said Niko, shutting his eyes tightly. "I'm not strong enough."

"You are," said Sarika. "You're the strongest man I know."

Niko opened his eyes and turned like a swimmer out of his depth. And there was his beautiful bride Sarika glowing orange, sitting on the snow bench from where they'd often watched the northern lights. Her lustrous black hair swam round her face like an underwater halo.

"Oh, Sarika," he said, tears springing to his eyes, "I'm so sorry."

Sarika wiggled her feet, kicking up orange sparks. "I'm sorry too. That I can't kick up real snow. What are you sorry for?"

Niko took a deep breath, gathering his courage. "When I took you on the sleigh, I made you suffer for so long because I was selfish, because my heart was broken."

Sarika clasped her hands as though cocooning a ladybird, like she always had when delivering a lecture.

"Did you know, Niko, that a broken heart is actually a medical syndrome? Stress cardiomyopathy it's called, often caused by extreme grief. Symptoms include: disorientation and irrational behavior. You were not in your right mind when you took me on the sleigh or when you left the North Pole, but you are now."

"Still," said Niko, "I shouldn't have brought you along."

Sarika smiled. "There's no time on the sleigh. And I stayed on it. It was such a joy to watch Santa working. You'd told me about it, but I'd never seen it till that night. What a way to spend my last night on earth. That's why I'm here, Niko. To thank you."

Niko rubbed his nose. "You're just trying to make me feel better, Sari."

Sarika smiled, and Niko felt his heart skip. "I am trying to make you feel better, Niko. For a Santa, you certainly need a lot of boosting."

Niko had almost forgotten how much Sarika had teased him.

"Are you really here? Where is here?"

Sarika opened her arms wide and trawled through the orange dust with spread fingers.

"Here is a between place," she said. "After here and before there. And it's the only place we can meet."

Niko's head came up. "We can meet?"

"One time only," said Sarika. "That's all we're allowed."

"Allowed by who?"

"By this place," said Sarika. "If you stay here much longer, you'll never want to leave. You'll become dust and sparks."

Niko nodded because he understood why people were

not supposed to go in the sack. They would be very tempted never to leave, in spite of the consequences.

"So why did you come here, Sarika?"

"You tell me, Niko. You called out."

"I did?" said Niko, but he wasn't surprised.

"Your heart called out to me with a question. It's about Duchess, isn't it?"

Niko nodded. It must be about Duchess. "I suppose it is. I need to clear that with you."

Sarika laughed. "Typical man. I think you probably need to clear it with Duchess."

"You know what I mean. You were the love of my life."

"People can have more than one soulmate," said Sarika softly. "Most people never find one person; you found two."

Sarika rose from her spectral snow bench and floated over to Niko.

"The question you have to ask yourself is, would I want you to be happy?"

"Yes," said Niko. "Of course you would."

"And would Duchess make you happy?"

Here was a question Niko could answer without hesitation. "She already makes me happy. I'd like to make her happy."

Sarika began to fade in Niko's arms. "Speaking of Duchess, you do remember who she is, don't you?"

Niko flashed on the Christmas Eve he'd pulled Josephine Spangles out of an upstairs bedroom and away from a flaming homemade magic generator that she'd built in her brother's house.

"I do," said Niko. "What are the chances?"

The second to last thing Sarika said before disappearing was: "Remember it's okay to love two people."

"I'll remember," said Niko. "I promise."

The very last thing Sarika said was: "And it's time to go back to work, Niko. I never really understood the whole Santa Claus thing until I saw you working that night. You changed lives. Millions of them."

Niko might have argued that he was changing lives now, but Sarika was gone, and there was a disk of light opening far above Niko's head. He felt himself rising and thought: *This day could not get any stranger.*

Juniper was just about done in, physically and emotionally. She hadn't had nearly enough sleep for an eleven-year-old, and her meals had been far from regular since Mum disappeared, which accounted for most of the mental exhaustion. It was tough to fully focus on anything with no word from her mother. It seemed to her that the entire world had become unreal as though she was watching a movie about her own life playing out before her, and if she stopped to consider the facts it made the situation even more unbelievable.

She remembered asking her dad once how he'd managed to keep going through the nightmare of a Mediterranean crossing on a crowded cathedral boat only to be put into the system for ten years, and Briar had said: "I knew you'd come to save me."

Which puzzled Juniper because at that point she hadn't even been born, but Briar explained.

"I knew that one day I would meet my true love and that we'd have a family. And the joy in that family would wash away all my pain. And so, when you ask me how I kept going, I say that I kept going for you. You saved me."

Juniper hadn't understood at the time, but now she got it.

Love kept Dad going.

And it had been keeping her going too, until Duchess collapsed and her immediate response to this was despair.

I can't, she thought. *I just can't cope with anything else.*

And the way her luck had been going there would be something else. The sky would fall, or the sleigh would blow up, or the interdimensional sack would swallow them all.

Juniper felt beyond sad. She felt hollow, as though she'd been scooped out, without even salt and water left for tears.

Mum's missing.

Duchess is terribly ill.

In ten minutes, I could be alone.

But then she remembered her father, who had dreamed of loving her before she'd been born. And she remembered Skära, who would fly to the end of the world for her, and she thought: *I am Juniper Lane, daughter of Briar, apprentice to Santa and partner of the polar reindeer Skära, friend of Duchess, a scientist, and the daughter, too, of the best mother in the world: a mother who needs me.*

"Take us down," she said to Skära, spotting the emergency bay of Cedarwood Hospital below. "Back entrance."

19

Children of the World

Tomescu and co. were in Greater London, praying for another flash of orange on their monitors to bring them closer to Nicholas. Midnight was fast approaching, and if they didn't get their hands on the Santa sack by then Christmas was finished forever.

The Christmas squad's head elf was understandably in a foul mood.

"I can't believe this!" he shouted to no one in particular. "We're so close."

Nord cleared his throat. "I have an idea," he said.

Tomescu glared at him. "This better be a great idea because you have a lot to make up for."

Nord was shaking so much the bell on his hat jingled.

"I just thought that we should cross-reference this area

of London with Nicholas's past life. See if there was some place in the city that was particularly important to him."

"Why didn't I think of that?" said Tomescu with withering sarcasm. "Don't you think we've tried that? We've combed through every major city in the world. Let me guess: no matches."

"No matches," confirmed Nord. "Initially."

Tomescu pounced on the last word. "Initially? What do you mean, initially?"

"I ran a second scan on Sarika. And something popped up. She based a chapter of her university thesis on the people living in Cedar Park, which is inside the bloom."

Cedar Park.

Tomescu remembered talking about that place with Niko. What had their conversation been about?

Suddenly he remembered. "They met in Cedar Park. It's not in the file, but Niko told me about it."

Tomescu was excited now. This was a real clue. Something actionable.

"Show me this park right away," he ordered.

Nord tapped it in and brought up a live satellite feed of Cedar Park.

Tomescu prodded a wooded area beside the park. "What's that? Why is it showing up blue?"

"It's a forest area. New growth by the looks of it," said Nord. "Several degrees colder than the rest of the region."

"Polarization," said Tomescu, leaning in close to the screen. "Gotcha."

He hugged Nord tightly. "You are back in my good books," he said.

Vible spoke from behind the wheel. "Am I in the good books too, boss?"

"Maybe," said Tomescu. "If you can get us to Cedarwood before midnight."

The Cedarwood Accidents & Emergencies was completely jammers when Dafydd Carnegie showed up.

"This woman needs a doctor posthaste!" he shouted, rushing Duchess inside in a wheelchair.

In the movies, several doctors would have charged toward him, eager to help, but in a real-life London A & E no one even glanced his way.

The reception area was full to the gills, and even if Carnegie made it to the next room he would find dozens of sick and injured people on trolleys in the corridor, waiting to be seen, and he'd just have to wait his turn.

I can't wait, thought Dafydd.

He aimed the wheelchair at the double doors that separated admissions from the wards and bashed through to the corridor, hurtling past startled orderlies and picking up quite a following of security personnel.

Keep going, Daff, he told himself. *If you get deep enough into the bowels of this place, someone will have to see Duchess.*

It wasn't much of a plan, but in Carnegie's defense he wasn't used to helping people.

Juniper flew Skära round the back of the hospital and directed her reindeer partner to land behind a mini-skip piled high with medical-waste bags, which she did not want to think about, especially outside the hospital.

"Hide yourself," she told Skära. "Stick to the rooftops till I whistle."

The reindeer calf gave her a quick nuzzle and then did a vertical takeoff.

"Show-off," said Juniper fondly, then opened the sack mouth.

"Okay," she said, mostly to herself but also to the magic sack. "Time to give him back."

The sack, it seemed, was only too happy to get rid of Niko. The moment Juniper opened its mouth and wished for him, he was hawked up onto the paving stones and lay there covered in a blue gel that evaporated even as Juniper watched.

"Are you alive?" said Juniper, poking a spot on his shoulder where the gel had dried. "Tell me if you're alive."

Niko coughed a blue cloud. "I can hardly tell you if I'm not," he said grumpily, but then changed his tone. "But thanks for the rescue, I suppose," he said. "I was meant to be the one doing the rescuing."

"You seem fine," noted Juniper. "What was so risky about going in the sack?"

"I saw Sarika in there," said Niko. "I was loved. It was really tempting to stay, even if that meant fading away to nothing."

"Well, I'm glad you came back," said Juniper. "You're loved here too."

Niko climbed to his knees. "Okay. One thing at a time. Where's Skära?"

"Don't worry. I got him, and Mr. Carnegie helped."

Niko was impressed. "You're better at this than I was starting out. A little high-profile maybe."

Juniper was enjoying the compliments, but she didn't have time for any more chitchat.

"Duchess has collapsed," she said. "You need to heal her."

Niko was instantly on his feet. "Collapsed how? Tell me everything!"

It was always important, Juniper's mum had often told

her, to give as much information as possible to someone in the medical profession, which Niko was. Sort of.

"Duchess has asthma, and she's been coughing a lot since about the time I got myself imprinted. The worst for years. And her golden veins lit up again."

"Golden veins," said Niko thoughtfully. "Tomescu gave a lecture about them once, but I can't put my finger on what it was about."

Even though this was possibly vital info, it wouldn't come to him. It didn't matter; there was no time for anything now but a quick blanket healing for Duchess. If he even had enough juice left for that. He'd been a little careless with his polar power lately, and even the most basic healing took an awful lot of sparks, especially for a fellow who'd been away from the North Pole springs for a decade. Simply put, these were sparks that Niko wasn't sure he had anymore. And, even if he had the sparks, magic could not heal anything much more serious than a graze or a sniffle. If it could, Niko would have spent every last spark in the world saving Sarika.

Niko glared at his own hands. "I'll try a healing, of course. But I'm running out of juice. I need a recharge in the polar liveflud."

Magical healing was a tricky business. The effects could be augmented by a team of elfin paramedics and their magic-compatible trauma equipment, but Niko didn't have such a team on hand at the moment. He would have to see what he could do himself. And the sooner the better.

"Where are we?" he asked Juniper.

"The hospital," said Juniper. "Back door. Duchess is in there somewhere."

Niko pulled up his hood. "Stay close," he said. "My suit should cause enough interference for both of us."

★ ★ ★

They went in low and fast like special forces, which was, in effect, what Santas were trained to be. Juniper hadn't been trained, but she remembered some of it from her yule-drøm, and the rest came from being an eleven-year-old, the majority of whom are low and fast most of the time anyway.

The corridor was quiet apart from a nurse who was leaning against the wall, eating two fingers of a Twix at the same time.

"You can't come this way," she said through a mouthful of caramel and shortbread. "It's for staff only."

"It's okay," said Juniper, and then because she couldn't think of a decent excuse for being here said, "we're sneaking in for a surprise party."

"A surprise party?" said the nurse, then her eyes flicked

to a red emergency button on the wall. "We don't get surprise parties here."

This could have been a problem, but then the nurse noticed Niko's face and suddenly her eyes were brimming with tears, and she slid down the wall, dribbling half-chewed Twix goop onto her own chin and bawling into her hands.

"Sometimes sensitive people remember me," said Niko, "and everything about their youth comes flooding back. That right there is a happy cry."

Juniper might have said that it didn't look like a happy cry, but Niko was already advancing down the corridor.

"This way," he called over his shoulder. "I can sense Duchess."

✳ ✳ ✳

They emerged from a labyrinth of corridors into a circular ward with a nurses' station plonked in the center. The situation was dire, but Dafydd Carnegie, to give him his due, did not stop trying.

"Help!" he cried. "Assistance required! Is there a doctor in the house?"

Ironically perhaps, there did not seem to be an available doctor in the hospital. Plenty of nurses and patients, but no doctor. There were also plenty of security guards who all seemed to be on Carnegie's tail as he wheeled Duchess in rapid circles round the station, much to the amusement of the patients who cheered him on every revolution.

It took the security guards nearly a minute of running round the station to realize that they were quite literally chasing their own tails. And so two of them simply stood still and waited for the Carnegie train to come round again, which it did fifteen seconds later.

"Gentlemen, please," said Carnegie, "at least find me a doctor."

One of the more nasty-minded security guards said: "You're going to need a doctor, pal."

And perhaps Carnegie would indeed have needed a doctor had not Niko burst through a side door, his momentum carrying him into the middle of the nurses' station, and all attention was diverted from the small man in his tailored overalls to the enormous Viking-looking chap towering over the nurses.

The room went completely quiet as everyone waited to see what this giant would say. When Niko opened his mouth to speak, every other mouth in the ward dropped open in anticipation.

And what the big chap said was this:

"It's growing late around the world . . ."

It was just the first line of the Santa lullaby. One line wasn't enough to put people to sleep because it was not a good idea to do that in a hospital, especially to people with scalpels or lasers in their hands, but it was certainly enough to put people into a daze for a few seconds. And in that time a lot of emotions bobbed to the surface for a lot of people. Repressed memories were released. People let go of grudges they'd been holding on to for years. Friendships were formed inside those seconds just because of the shared magic experience. All in all, it was the most positive and creative moment many of those people would experience: a lifetime's empathy and joy squashed into a single instant.

Niko and Juniper kept operating inside the haze and ran to Duchess, who was desperately trying to breathe, but also smiling because of the lullaby.

Carnegie was also smiling while inside his dopey daze. "Santa," he said, tapping the side of his nose as if he was keeping a big secret instead of blurting it out in a hospital ward. "Two Santas." And then he burst into song:

"The hills are alive with the sound of Santas!"

Juniper couldn't help but smile. She liked this new Carnegie and hoped he'd stick around.

Niko lifted Duchess from the chair and laid her on the nurses' worktop between computer monitors.

"Oh, Dutch," he said, "please don't go anywhere."

Duchess found the energy to say a single word as her breath whistled out: "Spangles."

Niko stroked her cheek with such tenderness that Juniper thought she might cry.

"I know," he said, "you're Jo Spangles. We've met."

Duchess closed her eyes, and a single tear squeezed from the corner of one because Niko knew her secret shame: She'd endangered her own niece.

Niko took an instant to wipe away the tear with his thumb, then barked at Juniper, "Juniper, come here. I need your sparks."

Juniper knew that magic could be used to heal, but her knowledge was gleaned from yuledrøm and was patchy at best. She certainly didn't have any expertise because Santas had rarely performed healings on the road as it were.

"What should I do?"

"Hold her hand," said Niko. "I'll do the rest."

Juniper did as she was told. It was a one-way hand-holding as Duchess didn't squeeze back. She did not have the strength.

"Hold on, Dutch," said Niko, shaking his own hands like a pianist warming up. "Just a moment more."

"Watch this, everyone!" said Carnegie. "My pal Niko is about to blow your tiny minds."

Niko closed his eyes for a moment, and when he opened them the whites had turned golden, and if a person looked closely they might see tiny golden sparks swimming in there.

"Heal," he said, and placed his thumbs gently in Duchess's eye sockets. His thumbs lit up like two torches and the light traveled into Duchess, heading straight to her chest. Juniper felt her own magic being drawn out of her with a warm-water sensation, and her sparks joined Niko's swirling round Duchess's heart.

"It's going to be okay," said Juniper.

But it wasn't going to be okay. For a second, things were looking good, and Duchess's breathing seemed to improve, but then the magic retreated, repelled by the seriousness of her illness.

Niko tried to force the magic, but he had no more in him.

"I can't," he said, and the tears flowed freely into his beard. "I don't have enough sparks, Dutch."

Duchess opened her eyes and said what she had said before. "Spangles."

Niko nodded. "I know, darling." And then because he didn't know what else to do he said: "Professor Josephine Spangles."

Duchess tried again. "*Spangles.*"

Juniper got it. "She's saying you need more Spangles. And when she was a professor she said that they were generated by belief."

"Is that it?" Niko said to Duchess. "I need more Spangles, but where am I going to find a crowd of people who believe in me?"

The answer was blindingly obvious, but Carnegie got there first.

"Duh!" he said, which was a little rude, but Dafydd considered Niko a close friend who could take a ribbing. "The Santa Vigil. I can hear them singing from here."

Niko and Juniper shared a look.

The Santa Vigil, the look said. *Of course. Let's go.*

Niko swept Duchess up in his massive arms, kicked open the nearest fire doors and ran into the night, with Juniper close behind. She glanced toward the hospital rooftop and saw Skära's boomerang antlers bobbing along behind them.

Stay close, partner, she thought. *We might need a quick getaway.*

20

Santa Claus Lane

Trude Madden would never have even spotted Niko if she hadn't rented the electric scooter to get to the park. Her plan had been to go to the Mews and wait till Juniper showed up, but first she had to return the scooter to the nearest rank to Juniper's house, which the app told her was outside the hospital. And, even though she was in a fury, Miss Trude did not want a charge to appear on her credit card for not returning a scooter properly so she made the slight detour. She zipped along Cedarwood High Street, swearing at every car that passed her. In spite of all that had happened, she was still determined to have the magic sack. If she got that sack, all the trouble and strife of the past few hours would be worth it.

There was only a single unoccupied slot left at the scooter rank, and the struts were slightly bent, so Miss

Trude had to bash the scooter in several times before it fitted in.

Bashing that girleen Juniper Lane's head will make me feel a lot better, she thought, patting the lump in her bum bag where the sliotar sock rested.

Miss Trude found a nearby car with a biggish wing mirror so that she could check her quiff was perfect. There was no need really as it was held in place by half a tin of Rockabilly Girl Max-Hold Hi-Shine Wide-Nozzle Super Spray. In any event, she forgot all about her hair when she noticed two figures hurrying across the hospital car park reflected in the mirror.

Could that be?

It could be and it was.

Santa Claus and his irritating apprentice. Trude ducked behind the car, then peeped over for a closer look. The big man was carrying something, no . . . someone. That was a good thing, she realized. Let him worry about his patient while she socked Juniper Lane and located the sack. It would perhaps make sense to ask Juniper where the sack was before socking her, but she needed to beware of Juniper's magic lullaby.

"No one enchants Miss Trude Madden and gets away with it, girleen," Trude whispered to herself. Then she set off down the road running parallel to her prey, who climbed the car-park fence and took Crumbly Lane toward Cedar Park.

Niko was as close to frantic as he'd been since he'd taken Sarika on the Christmas Eve run. He was past caring about keeping a low profile or his decision to move on. All there was room for in his mind right now was Duchess. If people saw him, then they saw him. In fact, the more people that saw him, the better, because he needed all the Spangles he could get. He vaguely realized that Juniper was tagging along behind him, and he was glad to have her because even the girl's few sparks of wild magic might make the difference between life or death for Dutch.

And those were the options: life or death.

If he was honest with himself, then death seemed the most likely outcome because, even though the burst of healing magic in the hospital had revived Duchess momentarily, she had quickly dropped into what seemed like a coma, and it tore at his heart to hear her labored, irregular, whistling breath.

This can't happen again, he thought. *I can't bear it again*, and he held Duchess tight as if he could transfer the strength of his polar-bred lungs to her by osmosis.

★ ★ ★

Juniper tried hard to keep up with Niko but, even though he was decades older than her and carrying an entire human being in his arms, it was still a struggle.

I feel weird, she realized, following Niko's hulking figure down Crumbly Lane, which ran alongside Miss Trude's yard. The weird feeling, she suspected, was brought on by repeated use of magic. It wasn't a bad weird just new weird.

I'm feeling a way I never felt before.

She looked into her yuledrøm memories to see if she could find a reference for this feeling, but nothing presented itself. The closest she could come to describing it was a permanent version of that feeling that spreads through a person's chest at the exact moment they drink a cold fizzy drink on a warm day.

I hope it's permanent.

It was quite nice being magical.

And then she heard Duchess's breathing and stopped thinking about herself.

There was no direct route to the park from Crumbly Lane that Juniper could think of, and she was about to tell Niko that when he sidestepped and disappeared. Juniper realized that Niko had simply shouldered through a gap in the fence that brought him to a space between park and lane fences that she never knew was there. A little secret lane. As she passed through the gap, Juniper noticed twist ties on the fence links and realized this was a shortcut Niko had set up some time ago, and correctly figured he had these little routes dotted all over Cedarwood so he could come and go as he pleased. Usually, she was willing to bet, he would conceal the secret access after passing through, but on this occasion the stakes were too high for hiding his traces.

The lane ran in a gentle loop for several hundred meters. Niko stayed on the central grassy verge, out of the wheel ruts, and it was only when she saw those ruts that Juniper realized she'd been down this lane before. It was a service route for the park, and her dad had driven along it on his mini-digger when he was ferrying soil or saplings to different ends of Cedar Park.

"Dad," she whispered. "Still helping me."

Niko ran steadily, not even breathing hard, and called back over his shoulder.

"Where's the best spot to collect Spangles, do you think? Bandstand?"

"Yep," said Juniper. "There's always a gathering for a midnight singsong."

"Midnight," said Niko. "Not long from now."

Midnight on Red-Letter Day was very important this year. He had intended to pull out just one letter to keep the sack's magic active, but with Duchess failing it didn't seem important.

"Bandstand it is," he said.

"Got it," said Juniper. Then, for Skära's benefit, she called to the sky, "Bandstand. Bandstand."

She heard a distant honk of acknowledgment. The reindeer would be close by if he was needed.

They could hear it now: Christmas music was drifting over the treetops. A memory flashed into Juniper's mind. Her mum had coined a phrase for the sound of Christmas carolers singing their hearts out: *The angels are being heralded.*

This sudden thought of her mother sideswiped Juniper, and she actually stumbled off the central verge into one of the wheel ruts.

"You okay, partner?" asked Niko, who must have eyes in the back of his head.

"Fine," said Juniper, who had started crying for the umpteenth time that day. "Keep going."

I'll enjoy that later when no one is missing or dying, she thought. *Santa Claus calling me partner.*

Up ahead, Niko stopped at the first cedar in the line, which seemed black and impenetrable in the moonlight.

"Just a second," he said. "I'm trying to remember which tree this is."

Juniper knew that the fence would continue on inside the tree line, and it seemed impossible that a person, even a magical one, would know every tree in the line, but it appeared that Niko did because he laid Duchess ever so gently on the grass, reached one massive arm into the foliage and rooted around like he was hand-fishing for catfish.

"Nearly," he said. "It's around here somewhere."

While Niko was searching, Juniper smoothed Duchess's hair away from her brow. "Almost there now," she said. "The magic will save you. You were right about the Spangles."

"Got it," said Niko, then grunted and immediately after the grunt hauled back a section of tree and fence, his massive fingers threaded through chain links that he had apparently cut through sometime earlier.

Another secret door.

"Roll her through," he ordered Juniper. "Hurry."

Juniper doubted whether rolling patients was in any paramedic's handbook, but right now they were out of options, and if she had to give Duchess a firefighter's lift to get her to the bandstand then that was what she'd do. So Juniper rolled Duchess through the secret access, taking special care to cradle her head with each revolution, thinking: *She's so light. Too light.*

When Duchess was through, Juniper wriggled in after her and made room for Niko, who had developed a nifty horizontal shimmy technique so that he could pass through while holding the makeshift door open above himself.

"Okay," he said. "We get to the bandstand, and then it's time for me to reveal myself. When everyone is all *oooh and aaaaah, it's Santa*, then the Spangles should flow."

"Got it," said Juniper, thinking it might not be as simple as that.

People nowadays were not so easy to convince. She had been seen gallivanting around on a flying reindeer and still no one had really believed in flying reindeer except a villainous crime boss. Believing in Santa Claus was a little like believing in the lottery. Everybody believed that, in theory, they could win the big prize, but very few people truly believed it would happen to them.

But now was not the time for negative thoughts. It was time to stay positive.

Niko swept Duchess up in his arms once more, held her close, and ducked under the low branches into Cedar Park.

He waited to make sure Juniper was following him and said: "I've never done this before. Drawn attention to myself like this, been showy about things. Tomescu would lose his mind."

Juniper understood. She had a vague shared memory of Christmas's chief elf being quite the stickler for regulations.

"But it's for Duchess," she said.

"Yes," said Niko. "It's for my Dutch. Anything for her, right, partner?"

Juniper felt her heart literally swell as the magic coursed through her bloodstream. "Absolutely anything."

Niko nodded once and then took great strides down the natural amphitheater slope toward the Victorian band-stand backstage area.

And, in spite of everything, Juniper could not help but smile as she followed Niko. She knew that this was the kind of moment stories were built around.

People will talk about this.

It was one of those *where were you when . . . ?* situations.

Where were you when Santa Claus proved to the world once and for all that he absolutely did exist?

I was right in the thick of it, thought Juniper. *I am right in the thick of it.*

And she ran faster so she could be at Niko's shoulder. Duchess must have felt her there because she allowed her hand to trail down so that they could touch fingers.

* * *

There were more people in Cedar Park for the Santa Vigil than ever that night. And, while costumes had been the exception in previous years, this year they seemed to be

the rule. There were dozens of Santas, of course, male and
female, and hundreds of elves, quite a few dogs done up
as reindeer, several Gandalfs for some reason,

and everyone was holding a candle. The small duck pond shone with floating lamps, and someone had strung fairy lights round the edge of the bandstand roof. It

was a testament to how much people loved not only Santa Claus but Briar Lane too.

Juniper watched the action as she followed Niko along the line of barriers that separated the area behind the bandstand from the main park. This was an enclosure Briar had put together to stack benches, put tables under tarps, and set up a first-aid table for events.

"Look, Daddy," said Juniper, peering through the steel barrier. "Look what you inspired."

By the light of the moon, she could see that there were three stands for donations, and Juniper recognized workers from other parks at the stations who had made the trip on their own time to make sure the Cedar Park tradition did not die out. But Juniper knew now the vigil never would. It'd be impossible for anyone to stop this no matter how they tried or how many bags of donations they burned.

People needed love and hope in their lives, and the vigil was a powerful testament to that need.

Niko stepped over a rope at the back of the bandstand and mounted the steps, laying Duchess on the bandstand itself. This caused a murmur to spread through the vigilers because the bandstand was a protected structure with a red rope cordoning off the steps. This big fellow had simply stepped over the rope and climbed the three steps with his great clodhopping feet.

As word filtered back through the ranks of costumed Santas, elves, and snowmen, various opinions were voiced as to what might actually be going on here. The consensus was quickly reached that this must be a performance of some kind, and a smattering of applause spread through the park, amplified by the amphitheater's gentle slope.

However, many of Duchess's fellow park sleepers recognized her, and Niko too, and knew that something serious was happening.

Juniper tried her best to manage the crowd.

"Please give Santa Claus room for the present!" she shouted several times.

This was the worst thing she could have said because any children in the park gleefully misinterpreted hearing only three words—*Santa, Claus, present*—and they ran forward, squealing, followed by their parents.

★ ★ ★

It was chaos, which suited Miss Trude just fine. She had lost Niko and Juniper when they ducked out of Crumbly Lane, but reacquired them again by following the commotion in the park, and now decided that she would sneak up from behind while they were doing whatever they were doing. She stuck to the tree line, then climbed over the barrier to the left of the bandstand itself. Once over the fence, she was in the shadows, which was just the way Miss Trude liked it.

I have you now, girleen, she thought with grim satisfaction and reached into her bum bag for the sliotar sock.

This was not the controlled Miss Trude who did her business with calm efficiency; this was a Trude Madden who had, as her old daddy might have said, lost the run of herself.

Trude had only one child—Larceny Madden—and he had been controlled by her since the moment of his birth, and so she was not used to being defied or even bested by children. She might have been even more incensed if she'd known that Lar and his mates were being arrested at that very moment at the Kilburn yard following the discovery of nearly half a million pounds' worth of livestock and contraband.

Her blood pressure would have skyrocketed if she could have looked a couple of hours into the future and seen her own dear boy betraying her in the interview room and naming his mother as ringleader of the operation. But for now, Miss Trude was focusing all her anger on the girl standing twenty feet in front of her. That girl, of course, was Juniper Lane.

"There you are," she snarled. And it's not easy to snarl an entire sentence.

Trude twirled her sliotar sock like a slingshot and ran in for a strike. Somewhere in the back of her mind she knew that this was madness—to attack a child in a park during a vigil, especially with her distinctive quiff, which would mark her out in a lineup—but she had to have that magic sack. She also knew that to strike someone so small with the sliotar sock with the force she was building up would knock out half a dozen teeth, but it seemed like she couldn't stop herself now. Miss Trude also knew that she would not miss. There would be no glancing blow off the girl's jaw because Trude had spent thousands of hours practicing with the weapon and was a crack shot.

Juniper saw Miss Trude coming and knew she was in trouble. The Irishwoman was bearing down on her with murder in her eyes, and there was something twirling round her right fist, but Juniper couldn't tell what it might be.

Perhaps it's candyfloss, she thought, but knew it wasn't. It was a weapon of some kind being revved up to strike her.

Is that a sports sock? she wondered.

Juniper was rooted to the spot. It seemed so unfair that after everything she'd been through in the past few days she would be struck down by a sock.

There was only one thing to do. The old Santa lullaby trick. Juniper opened her mouth to sing and got three words out before Miss Trude let fly with her loaded sock.

★ ★ ★

Trude saw Juniper's mouth open and knew immediately what was about to happen.

That witch is going to mesmerize me!

It was so obvious the girl would try her siren-song trick again, and so Trude was forced to launch her sliotar sock a split second before planned. It whooshed across the distance between them and hit Juniper in the chest, knocking any air she'd intended to use for singing from her body. Juniper staggered backward and fell to the grass, one hand clutching her chest.

"Give me the sack, girleen," Trude ordered, looming over Juniper. "Then I won't have to hurt you too badly."

Never, Juniper might have declared if she'd been able to draw breath and speak. *And anyway I don't have it. Skära has it, and he's out of your reach.*

But Skära was not as out of reach as Juniper thought. From his holding spot in the city glow above Cedar Park, he saw his partner being attacked and swooped in to defend her, trumpeting the charge with a series of honks.

This would have caught most people by surprise, but Miss Trude was not most people; she was not even some people. Trude Madden had already been in a tangle with a flying reindeer, and Skära's trumpeting, which was supposed to scare Miss Trude, actually gave the Irishwoman the heads-up that trouble was on the way.

It might seem that the reindeer had the upper hand in this situation, but Miss Trude had been breaking horses for thirty years, and no beast had ever bested her. And in her opinion Skära was nothing but an airborne beast, and she knew all the butting, biting, kicking, and stomping tricks in a beast's arsenal.

Skära came in from behind, swooping down in a steep arc, honking all the way. Miss Trude never took her eyes off Juniper. When the girl took a sharp breath and grimaced, Trude knew impact was imminent. She pirouetted to one side like a bullfighter, allowing the reindeer to whoosh past, but not all the way. Trude grabbed on to whatever she could. And whatever she could turned out to be Skära's tuft of a tail and the corner of the sack that was poking out of the reindeer's saddlebag.

Miss Trude held the reindeer back, digging her heels in. What Skära should have done was to stop struggling, but he was young, and Trude's grip on his tail was painful, so he redoubled his efforts to break free. When Trude did suddenly let his tail go, he was catapulted into a nearby stack of benches, leaving her holding the magical Santa sack.

"Ha," said Trude. "That's us even, fella."

Her criminal instincts were screaming at her to leave immediately. She had what she came for, and everything had happened so fast that no two witnesses would tell the same story.

There's still a way out of this, Trude girl, she told herself. *It's dark, and you're in the shadows. No grandstanding now. Only a fool stays to gloat.*

But something gave Miss Trude pause. She felt an impulse to reach into the sack and pull out something.

Go, girl! Scram!

But first reach into the sack and draw out a letter.

A letter?

Is this sack asking me to pull out a Christmas letter?

In fact, that was precisely what was happening. Trude had managed to get hold of Santa's sack in that exact window where a non-magical person could gain control of it. Though she could not know it, the only way that Trude's plan to make Christmas her own moneymaking scheme could possibly work would be if she pulled a letter right now.

It would only take a second.

Trude reached into the sack, and the sensation reminded her of reaching her arm into a hot bath to pull out the plug.

Magic is warm, she realized. Her fingers began to tingle. *The letter is on its way.*

All around her, time slowed to a crawl, and Trude realized she was on the verge of great power. The sounds of Christmas carols were stretched and distorted. The brat Juniper Lane drew her first deep breath since being belted with the sliotar sock, and on the bandstand Santa Claus was kneeling over a woman.

None of that mattered because Miss Trude felt the edge of an envelope brush her fingertip.

"I own Christmas," she said to Juniper. "I am Christmas."

And Trude would indeed have been Christmas had she not broken her own rule and spared a moment to gloat.

"You thought you could beat me," she spat at Juniper, "you silly, foolish girleen. With all the power I have? Maybe I'll use some of my new power to take care of you."

And then something happened that surprised Miss Trude. She had attacked dozens of people in her time, and they all had one thing in common: Once they saw Trude Madden in attack mode, they were transfixed by her murderous glare like gerbils before a snake and could not take their eyes off her.

But this girl, Juniper Lane, did take her eyes off her

attacker. Her gaze quite clearly drifted over Miss Trude's shoulder, and her expression changed drastically from fear to puzzlement to unbridled love. Miss Trude knew the latter expression because, in spite of her own temperament, many men had fallen in love with her, the most recent being a prince of Saudi Arabia, and he had looked at her just like Juniper was looking at this mystery person behind her.

And then whoever that person was called out to her:

"Hey! Hey, Miss Trude!"

This person who is inspiring such love is calling me, thought Trude, and turned to check they weren't armed.

The caller was a blond lady with several tattoos on each arm, and she wasn't armed in the traditional sense, but her eyes were on fire, her fist cocked.

And Trude knew somehow. *That's the mama bear, and I have threatened her cub.*

"Now, missus," she said, "hold your horses there. I'm sure we can . . ."

But Jennifer Lane was not in a mood for holding her horses.

21

Wakey-Wakey

The Christmas elves arrived on the scene too late to do anything about the sack crisis. Vible parked the van as close as they could get to the park, and then Tomescu led the charge into Cedar Park itself just in time to see Niko emerge on the bandstand carrying an unconscious lady.

Tomescu tapped the arms of his smartglasses, activating a zoom function in the lenses.

"It's the boss!" he called to the other elves. "It's actually him, and he's right out there in front of everyone."

Tomescu was surprised to see Niko in the open like this. Usually, he was a very private Santa. Then again, the entire elf squad was in the open tonight. Desperate times called for desperate measures. Luckily, it seemed as though half the people in the crowd were dressed as elves so they should blend right in.

Nord was bobbing along at Tomescu's shoulder, weighed down by his equipment backpack.

"We're too late," he panted. "It's almost midnight."

"It's not too late," Tomescu snapped. "We can set up a time bubble. Any magic blooms?"

"Nothing from the sack. Not a peep." Then Nord checked the smartlenses in his goggles. "I take that back. We do have a peep. A major peep."

Tomescu climbed up on the park fence, straddling the cast-iron railings in a frankly dangerous fashion.

"There!" he said, pointing to a bizarre scene behind the bandstand.

He enhanced it with his glasses, and it seemed that behind the barriers one human female was looming over a younger female while the hindquarters of a reindeer stuck out of a nearby stack of furniture. The first human was the most important for the moment as she was reaching her hand into what was unmistakably the Christmas sack as evidenced by the orange glow, which Tomescu could clearly see on his smartspecs.

His heart sank into the curly toes of his boots.

We're too late, he realized. *That woman is about to draw a letter.*

Christmas was in human hands.

Disaster.

✳ ✳ ✳

So this sudden arrival needs a bit of explanation. How could Juniper's mum just show up out of nowhere, looking nothing at all like herself?

The woman who had distracted Miss Trude was undeniably a platinum blonde with tattoos, wearing a hoodie and sweatpants. That wasn't right surely. When Jennifer Lane had left the Mews, she'd had long dark auburn hair, not a single tattoo, and was wearing a scarf that was a bit scratchy, but Briar had bought it for her on a trip to Edinburgh for a festival so it was her favorite.

This was a very different Jennifer Lane.

So what had happened?

It might seem impossible, but what had actually taken place was not impossible. It was simply unlikely, which happens all the time when there's magic in the air.

Let's start at the beginning. When Jennifer left the Mews that fateful day, she was feeling good. Not great, but definitely better than she had in a couple of years. This was because she had remembered how amazing her daughter was, and made a promise that, from now on, she was going to appreciate and encourage Junie in every way possible. And part of that encouragement was to make Juniper happy by trying to be happy herself.

I need a change, Jennifer had decided. *I need to reboot.*

So, when Jennifer told Juniper she was going to Sandra's with some repairs, that wasn't the whole story. From Sandra's, she was going to Romina's salon to get her hair colored and then home to surprise Junie and Duchess.

This is what actually happened: Jennifer did indeed stop in at Sandra's with a bag of repairs, and Sandra commented that her friend's dress was literally hanging off her and needed to be taken in as Jennifer had lost several kilos in the past few years. Jennifer, who was determined to say yes more, agreed and handed over the dress, accepting the loan of sweatpants and a hoodie from Sandra.

From Sandra's, Jennifer crossed the main road roundabout to Romina's salon, which was not a high street salon exactly: It was a reclining chair in Romina's utility room. Jennifer requested quite a drastic cut to go with her color because she wanted a fresh look to match her fresh attitude. If she was being honest, Juniper's mum was already half regretting the decision when the hanks of hair began dropping onto the floor, but it was too late to turn back then.

While Romina was mixing Jennifer's color, she persuaded Jennifer to let her friend Taj give her a few sample henna tattoos that she was thinking of offering to customers for weddings and nights out. Jennifer thought it would be fun, and she couldn't wait to see the look on Juniper's face. Soon her arms were covered with intricate transfers. Unfortunately, during the process, some henna dripped onto Jennifer's scarf, and Romina insisted on getting it cleaned. The scarf was supposed to go in the dry-cleaning pile, but somehow it ended up in the recycling bag that went to the clothes bank the following morning.

When the tattoos dried, Romina applied Jennifer's color and warned her to wash it out in no more than two hours or she'd go bright blond, which wouldn't suit her complexion. Jennifer promised that she'd be sure to rinse her hair thoroughly at home. She set the timer on her watch, wrapped her head in a scarf, and set out for home.

While Jennifer waited to cross the road at Crumbly Lane, Lar, son of Miss Trude Madden, was driving his truck to the illegal incinerator yard, hauling a sneaky load of Santa Vigil donations collected by the Hamlets Garden Square parkkeeper. The truck's extended wing mirror was out, and, when Lar took his eyes off the road to glance at an incoming text from his wife, he took the turn a little bit tight. This would have been fine had not the illegally extended smuggler's wing mirror reached over the footpath and clanged Jennifer in the side of her skull. Juniper's mother was spun clear off her feet into the chain-link fence bordering the lane.

Lar felt the jolt of the wing mirror smashing into something and pulled in. He knew that he'd forgotten to fold the smuggler's glass in again and had hit something. But it was too soon for it to be another windowsill. A quick trot back along Crumbly Lane revealed a woman (who turned out to be Jennifer Lane) grotesquely suspended on the fence.

Lar's reaction to this was panic. His first thought was that she was badly hurt, and his second thought was that his mother would kill him for bringing the police this close to the yard.

But I can't leave her in the lane.

Lar realized that he had a very brief window of opportunity. The street was quiet right now, but Miss Trude's son knew the traffic-light timing and could hear vehicles massing at either end of the lane. Quickly, he disentangled the injured woman and gently lifted her into the cab, nearly crying with relief when he saw she was breathing.

Ten minutes and one nifty reverse later, and Jennifer Lane was slumped on a bench at a nearby bus stop, and Lar was making an anonymous phone call to A & E. By the time the ambulance came to pick her up, Jennifer's newly short hair was already turning blond and Lar was composing a fake text to her daughter.

Jennifer lay on a trolley for eight hours before a bed could be found, and even then it was not ideal. She was stashed in the juvenile ward for another day until a private room was found. And there she lay in a coma caused by anoxic brain injury until Niko tried to cure Duchess on the other side of the wall.

It was true that Niko's magic didn't work back in the hospital: He was way too pooped. That kind of magic needed mega-Spangles, and Niko only had a couple of kilo-Spangles in the tank and would eventually have to take a dip in the North Pole liveflud if he wanted to recharge. So, even with Juniper's few sparks added to the mix, it wasn't enough to do much more than open Duchess's eyes.

That's not to say that the polar magic was entirely wasted. Magic's a funny thing. At a molecular level, it behaves like an organism that codes itself to the DNA of the wielder. And so, when Juniper and Niko's combined blast of power was thrown off by Duchess's ailing lungs, it bounced around a little, looking for DNA matches that needed help.

It found one in a small private room that was only a single stud wall away from where Duchess lay sprawled on the nurses' station. In this room there lay a young platinum-blond, tattooed woman who had been brought in two days earlier in a coma.

As we now know, this woman was Juniper's mum.

The magic splurged out by Niko and his Santa apprentice was not enough to actually physically change Duchess's tissue, but it was just about enough to kickstart the brain of a coma victim, especially one who was desperate to wake up. Medical experts know quite a lot about comas. For example, they know that locusts shut down their neural and muscular systems until certain environmental stresses are removed, but there is little evidence that humans on the edge of nervous collapse can be tipped over into a comatose state by a physical trauma. Nevertheless, this was what happened to Jennifer.

Simply put: stress + wing mirror = coma.

But, when the polar magic settled over her mind in a shimmering gauze, it completed all the electrical circuits Jennifer's mind had been trying to make, and she shot up in her hospital bed screaming: "Juniper! Junie!"

No one heard her because outside the door was pandemonium.

A groggy Jennifer tumbled out of her bed, thinking: *Get home. I need to get home.*

Juniper's mum didn't know how she'd get home or even where she was exactly, but the answers would be outside the room: She was certain of it.

Jennifer found her borrowed clothes folded over a chair and tugged them on with clumsy fingers that weren't quite working as they should. She stumbled into the corridor where there seemed to be a pitched battle taking place with security guards shouting conflicting orders at the nurses and patients.

Nurses and patients, thought Jennifer. *I'm in a hospital.*

That realization actually relieved her because at least it explained a few things.

"Hey," said an old woman that Jennifer had accidentally bumped into. "Watch it, blondie."

Blondie? Jennifer thought. *Who's she talking to?*

Jennifer kept going, walking with one hand against the wall.

These sweatpants are so comfortable, she thought, because a bruised mind wanders. *I should wear them more often.*

The corridor opened to a nurses' station that seemed to be ground zero for the commotion, and through the throng of bodies Jennifer saw Juniper leaning over Duchess.

Her heart seemed to grow too large for her chest.

"Junie!" she wanted to cry, but nothing came out. "Junie, I'm here."

And Duchess was not well.

It's her chest. Jennifer just knew. *My poor dear friend has finally collapsed.*

There are many anecdotal tales of mothers displaying superhuman strength to help their children in troubled times, but none of these mothers had just woken from a coma. And so, even though Jennifer did her best to barge through the crowd, she couldn't reach her daughter before

Juniper followed the man carrying Duchess out through the fire doors.

It was all Jennifer could do to lean on her knees and croak, "*Junie. Where are you going?*" And then hot tears fell from her tired eyes directly onto the shoes of someone standing before her.

"I know where they're going," said a man's voice.

Jennifer looked up. It was Dafydd Carnegie.

"Not you," she said hoarsely. "Anyone but you."

"I know, madam," said Dafydd. "But it's not me. Not the me you know at any rate."

"What?" said Jennifer.

Dafydd slapped the arm of a wheelchair. "I'll explain on the way to Cedar Park!"

Cedar Park, thought Jennifer. *That's where they're going.* And she tumbled into the chair.

Dafydd Carnegie said a lot of things on the short wheel to the park. There were quite a few "madam"s and almost as many apologies. He did his best to catch Jennifer up on the events of the past few days. He also sang quite a decent version of "Reviewing the Situation" from *Oliver*.

Jennifer presumed she was delirious for most of the trip because it couldn't be true that Santa Claus had really been living in Cedar Forest. And surely the horrid Dafydd Carnegie wasn't actually a decent person with a lovely singing voice?

She forgot all about that when Carnegie went off-road into one of Briar's old lanes beside the park, and she saw Juniper just ahead, disappearing under a flap of foliage.

"Hurry, Mr. Carnegie," she said. "Please."

The flap of foliage was nearly their undoing because it was almost invisible in the dark. Eventually, Jennifer dropped to her hands and knees, fumbling at the hedge until her fingers touched the steel of chicken wire.

"Got it," she said, and rolled through. Mr. Carnegie would have to make his own way.

Jennifer Lane stumbled weakly down the incline toward the bandstand, and her spirits soared when she saw her daughter at the foot of the steps. However, her spirits sank almost immediately when she saw Trude Madden and heard her say: "Maybe I'll use some of my new power to take care of you."

Jennifer's pulse raced. Miss Trude was threatening her Juniper.

Threatening!!

Her heart pumped blood to her extremities, and

Jennifer felt instantly ready to climb a mountain or perhaps throw up.

She's threatening my Junie.

Jennifer had lost Briar and before that, her parents. She could not even contemplate something happening to Juniper.

"Hey!" called Jennifer, running stiff-legged toward the confrontation. "Hey, Miss Trude!"

And this is where the legendary determined-mother strength came into play. Minutes earlier, Jennifer hadn't been able to summon up the strength to speak because Juniper hadn't been in any immediate danger. But now her daughter was being threatened, and Jennifer's entire being seemed to pulse with the beat of her heart. She ran toward Miss Trude, and the mother in Trude Madden must have on some level connected with the look in her eyes because she turned, wearing an expression that Lar, had he been present, would never have seen on his mother's face before: fear.

"Now, missus," she said, "hold your horses there. I'm sure we can . . ."

And then Jennifer punched her so hard that she knocked Trude out cold.

22

Spangle Time

Tomescu had no idea why what had just happened had just happened, but humans were always punching one another, and he was prepared to take advantage of the scuffle.

"Take up positions round the circumference of the crowd in case we need to set up a bubble," he ordered his elves. "I'm going for the sack."

"It's too late," said Nord, and there were tears in his eyes. "You can't make it."

"I'll make it," barked Tomescu, swinging his leg over the fence.

But somewhere in the corner of his brain he knew that he couldn't.

* * *

Juniper ran to her mother and hugged her as tightly as she could. Jennifer hugged back and then they were both crying and laughing too. Juniper felt the heat of her mother's body and could hear her heart beating strong and steady, and it was the loveliest sound in the world.

"I thought you were gone," she said, allowing herself to admit it for the first time. "I thought you'd left."

"Never, Junie," said her mum. "I'll never leave."

"Jennifer Juniper," said Juniper, who was full-on bawling now.

"Jennifer Juniper," agreed Mum. "Forever and always."

And they stood like that, glued together, until Dafydd caught up with the wheelchair and said softly, "Juniper, put your mum down."

Juniper realized that her mum's legs had buckled, and she was basically holding her up.

"I'm sorry, Mum," she said, and lowered her into the chair with Carnegie's help.

"Dafydd is a good guy now," she explained.

"I know," said Mum weakly. "He's reviewing the situation."

Usually, Carnegie would have used that prompt to sing another verse or two, but on this occasion, there were more important things to do.

"Juniper," he said, "Duchess is in trouble."

"Go, sweetie," said Jennifer, who realized that everything Dafydd Carnegie had said about her girl's adventures was true. "Be magical. Fabulous!"

Juniper gave her mum's hands a squeeze, leaning in for one more hug.

"You're real, Mum."

"I'm real," said Jennifer.

Juniper went, pausing only to wiggle Skära out of the stack of benches.

★ ★ ★

A few people had seen what had happened with Miss Trude, Jennifer Lane, and the reindeer, but most of the vigilers were focused on the bandstand and what was going on there. The few who had seen the commotion weren't sure what they'd witnessed.

It had happened in a dark corner of the park in a shadow-dappled indent by the bushes, and was over in a matter of seconds. So, while it had seemed like a reindeer dive-bombed a woman and then crashed into some benches, and then that woman was punched by a second female, that couldn't have been what happened. Could it? More likely it was some sort of playacting, and the reindeer was a dog wearing strap-on antlers.

Some of those witnesses actually turned to their families or partners to ask: "Did you see that?"

But their families or partners were on tippy-toes, trying to get a better view of the bandstand, so the witnesses joined them on tippy-toes to look at the drama unfolding there.

Meanwhile, the glow emanating from the mouth of the sack began to fade.

Tomescu was fit for his age and did ten kilometers on the treadmill most days when he was at home so the distance to the sack from the park fence was no problem for him. The problem was not distance: It was time. The countdown on his smartlenses was ticking down to midnight, and it was not possible for him to make it before the elfin warlocks' spell took effect, and the sack became just a sack.

Twenty seconds left, he thought. *Nineteen . . .*

But he wouldn't give up. He was not that kind of elf. For ten years, Tomescu had kept the faith that he would find Nicholas Claus, and he couldn't believe that the universe would squash his dreams now that he was so close.

We need Christmas, he thought. *Every one of us.*

But, with every step, Tomescu's own spirit dimmed

until it seemed even to the indomitable, iron-willed chief Christmas elf that the season he had spent his entire adult life in service of would be lost forever.

He ran on with tears of frustration blown backward along his cheeks, swerving round the humans who were moving toward the bandstand.

Tomescu could see the sack on the ground on the other side of a divider; he could almost smell the burlap. It was half a minute away, which was twenty seconds too far.

A group of vigilers strayed into his path, and the elf found himself suddenly struggling through a knot of humans, all of whom were taller and heftier than him. Tomescu struggled to break free, but then the clock on his lenses ran out, and it was all over, so the elf allowed himself to go limp. He stopped struggling. Why bother? Midnight had passed, and the sack was dead. Without the warlocks' sack and its interdimensional qualities, there weren't enough sleighs in the world to transport all the Christmas gifts.

Christmas was over.

The vigilers swept Tomescu along to where he'd needed to be moments before—right in front of the fence—and he threaded his arms over the railings and slumped.

It didn't matter. None of it mattered because the sack had lost its magic. No one had drawn a letter, and the warlocks' spell would have shut it down.

Tomescu closed his eyes. He would rest for a moment, then help Nicholas. They'd think of something.

Think of what? his inner voice said. *No one pulled out a letter.*

But if the sack was dead what was that noise?

Tomescu opened his eyes to see an orange bloom buzzing on his smartlenses.

A magical bloom.

He shifted his focus to beyond the spectacles to see what was causing it, and what he saw was a reindeer calf with boomerang antlers and a Christmas letter half chewed in his mouth.

The calf had drawn a letter.

Magic attracts magic, thought Tomescu, relief flooding his brain.

Skära squinted at Tomescu as if he knew him from somewhere but couldn't quite place him.

"It's okay, fella," said Tomescu. "I don't know you, but you know me because of the yuledrøm."

Skära honked and then deftly snagged the magic sack with the tip of one antler and tossed it into his saddlebag.

Tomescu smiled. "It's okay, young calf. You did the right thing. You saved us all and Christmas too."

It could work, he supposed. For one year, the Gift Giver would be a reindeer calf.

But next year Nicholas will draw that letter himself, Tomescu vowed. *Even if I have to follow him until Red-Letter Day.*

Duchess was fading fast.

She lay in Niko's arms, and he could do little more than hold her gently so she wouldn't break.

"I met Sarika inside the interdimensional sack," he said. "And she told me to be happy with you."

Luckily for Niko, the only person who could actually understand this statement had climbed onto the bandstand and was now standing behind him.

"More . . . Spangles," said Duchess, wheezing between words.

There was a large tear forming on Niko's nose, and he turned to Juniper.

"I don't have anything, Juniper," he said. "I'm empty."

Juniper knew the theory. Anyone could generate Spangles for Santa to use. All they had to do was connect two particular parts of their brain across a dead section of the information superhighway. In other words, she needed the Santa Vigilers to believe.

I have to persuade these people that Niko is Santa Claus.

It was a big ask, she knew. Niko certainly didn't look

like any popular version of Santa. He looked like a Viking who'd escaped from a TV show.

The whole situation seemed so impossible. Actually, there was too much going on for it to qualify as a single situation. Mum was back, Skära was okay, but Duchess was not.

Juniper's brain was flooded with conflicting chemicals—happy endorphins that screamed: *Mum is back. Mum is back. Mum is back.*

But then adrenaline got in on the act because Duchess was so ill. And so Juniper felt like running in circles and falling asleep at the same time. Her heart beat like a bass drum in her rib cage. Her eyes and lips felt dry, and her fingers seemed extra-sensitive to the air.

You can do this, Juniper, she told herself. *You have to.*

She turned to the crowd, which seemed to have swelled considerably in the last few minutes. Even if the vigilers didn't know this big guy was Santa, he was still on the bandstand ministering to a sick woman, which, typically for this decade, everyone was videoing on their phones.

It doesn't matter, Juniper thought. *None of those videos will show anything more than interference.*

And, even if the phones captured every detail, it didn't seem important because Duchess was in trouble. She was trying to keep a brave smile going, but it was clear she couldn't hold on much longer.

Juniper climbed onto the railing, holding one of the bandstand columns.

"Hello, everyone!" she called over the hubbub. "I need you to listen."

Unsurprisingly, hardly anyone did. After all, there were more interesting things going on than a kid on a railing.

"Please," said Juniper, her voice strained, "Duchess needs you."

Still no one listened.

Juniper wept with frustration.

Carnegie tried to come to the rescue. He leaped nimbly onto the fence, flicked the switch on his Singalonga microphone, and sang the opening salutation from *The Lion King* where baby Simba gets presented on Pride Rock, which got everyone's attention sharpish.

The trouble was that now the people gathered for the Santa Vigil were convinced there was a play on.

"Oh, very good," said one lady.

"What a lovely voice!" said another.

"No, my friends," said Carnegie, his voice rising above the hubbub. "This is no show. I'm here to tell you that the one we have sung for these past years has returned." He swept a dramatic arm downward. "For this—is Santa Claus!"

No one was buying it.

"That's not Santa Claus," said a girl dressed as an angel. "This is a bad show."

"Give them a chance," said the girl's mother. "Maybe it'll get better."

Dafydd didn't know what else to do. "It's up to you, Juniper," he said. "Make them believe."

Juniper remembered something that Duchess had said to her in what seemed like another lifetime: "Most people only believe what they see."

And suddenly Juniper knew exactly what she had to do.

She stood on Dafydd's bent knee and used it to boost herself higher up the column. From there, she grabbed the gutter and dragged herself to the roof panels. Juniper was up high now. When the platform was added in, she was more than twelve feet off the ground, and it wasn't safe for anyone to be that high, especially a child, so every eye in the park was on her.

"That is Santa Claus," she shouted, "and I need you to believe it!"

"Get down from there, silly," called the angel girl.

Juniper climbed farther until she reached the ornate cupola and grabbed on to the spire, which she couldn't help noticing needed a coat of paint.

"Do you believe me?" she cried.

A lot of people said, "Yes, we do," but what they meant was: "No, we don't, but please get down from there."

There's nothing for it, Juniper thought, and then arranged her mouth in a pouting circle as though she was about to take a selfie. But instead she honked a bit like a goose, which was unexpected, especially to Niko, who tore his eyes away from Duchess.

"What are you doing, Juniper?" he asked.

"It's the only way," she replied, and Niko understood. He nodded because it was the only way, and some things are more important than secrecy.

Juniper let go of the spire and leaped into the air.

It was a good jump, perhaps three feet, and from the perspective of the crowd it looked twice that, but even as the people oohed they were all thinking the same thing.

What goes up must come down.

But she didn't come down because from behind the bandstand flew a brown blur with antlers.

Most people didn't see the brown blur until its hooves clipped the bandstand's roof plates and actually drew sparks from the spire.

"Is that a . . ." said the angel's mother.

"It's a reindeer!" squealed the angel herself, and promptly began to cry hot tears all over her costume.

"No, it's not. Don't be such a baby," said a small man

in a spandex elf costume who seemed more irritated than surprised.

But Spandex Man was wrong. It was a reindeer, but of course Nord knew that.

Skära had been summoned by his best friend's honk, and there was zero chance that he was going to let her down, which was literally the idea. So, in the twinkling of an eye it took for Juniper to jump, he was there to catch her.

Juniper's mum watched her darling girl fly into the air and thought she was imagining it. Perhaps she was still in the hospital, dreaming this impossible dream. She must be because it looked very much like there was a reindeer swooping up from below to cradle her daughter. Jennifer covered her eyes, and tears leaked between her fingers.

Meanwhile, up in the sky, Juniper Lane timed her mount expertly, relying on Santa dream memory. Dafydd Carnegie would have described the action as a dance move: the heel click. Her heels bounced off each other, flew wide and then came in again to grip Skära firmly round the flanks. Other jockeys might have reached under the reindeer's neck and grabbed a handful of mane, but this was more than a mount and its rider. This was a magical team that had no need for manes or reins: They had an intuitive balance that was genuinely magical.

And, even though Niko was sick with worry, he couldn't

help but acknowledge the move with the slightest twitch at one corner of his mouth.

"She's doing it, Duchess," he said. "Won't you wake up and watch?"

But Duchess could not wake up. Her lungs had been assaulted once too often and were in the process of shutting down, but that wasn't what would kill her. Duchess's heart would give out before that.

Niko knew now that he'd made the wrong tactical move staying with Duchess on the bandstand. He should have inspired these people somehow rather than just relying on their generation of spontaneous Spangles. But it was too late: Everything was in Juniper's hands now.

Twenty feet above, Juniper patted Skära's neck and said, "Don't be shy, fellow," she said. "Let's give them a look at you."

With a joyous bellow, Skära lifted his rump, dipped his triangular head, and dive-bombed the Santa Vigil.

He flew in dizzying circles, knocking off hats, chomping ice creams, honking in ears, touching down in clear patches, and basically making absolutely certain that he couldn't be mistaken for something else. This was exactly what Juniper wanted because most people would supply their own reasonable explanation for what was happening if it wasn't absolutely undeniable that there was a flying Christmas reindeer in Cedar Park.

"That's right, everyone," Juniper called as she whizzed by, "it's real! It's all real!"

Round and round they flew, drawing a whirlwind of delight from the crowd. It dawned on people one by one that they had stumbled into a genuine magical happening. There were still a few holdouts who suspected that maybe this was some elaborate theatrical show, but slowly the realization spread through the onlookers in Cedar Park as Skära flew close enough to touch.

Juniper did notice in passing that a small group of diminutive men dressed as elves didn't seem as thrilled as might be expected, but perhaps they were grumpy as a group.

I've seen them before, she realized. *In my yuledrøm.*

But she couldn't worry about what that meant right now. She had the most important job in the world to do.

Juniper tapped one of Skära's antlers. "Time to land," she said.

Skära was happy to oblige, but he knew instinctively that this was not the time for a mundane landing on the grass, which would make him instantly normal. The magic must be maintained. With this in mind, the calf trotted through the air to the bandstand, touching down on the slanted roof, his hooves clanging on the copper plates, maintaining his balance as easily as a cliff goat.

"Strut," Juniper told him. "I know you want to."

And Skära did strut, raising his hooves high with each step, circumnavigating the bandstand roof, each step sending a clang ringing across the park. The calf was undeniably magnificent.

Juniper looked out over the park, waving at her mother, who looked so weird with blond hair but had at least stopped crying, and then at the crowd who were focused on her with laser intensity. She felt their love and need. If there was ever any doubt in her mind that the magic of Christmas was food for the soul of the world, the waves of love coming off these people dispelled it.

I have them, she thought. *They'll listen now.*

"This is a Christmas reindeer," she shouted, "and that man is Santa! Do you believe me?"

People are often reluctant to answer questions as a group unless someone like Beyoncé is asking, but Juniper reckoned she got about 50 percent of the crowd.

"Do you believe me?" she asked again.

This time it was 75 percent.

"We need them all," said Niko.

Juniper wondered what more she could do. She'd given them a flying reindeer. Then it came to her.

What I have to do is give them Christmas.

She reached into Skära's saddlebag and pulled out the magical sack.

"Be Santa," she said to Niko, sending the sack fluttering down to him.

Niko reached out, and the sack responded by drifting into his hand.

He hated leaving Duchess even for a second, but not doing so might mean leaving her forever.

"Look," said Juniper. "Santa Claus brings gifts."

And to Niko she said: "Say the thing."

Niko peered into the sack. "I'm not that kind of Santa Claus."

Juniper mustered the courage to glare at Niko. "What kind of Santa Claus are you then?"

Niko rolled his eyes. "Oh, for goodness' sake." He reached into the sack and pulled out an impossibly large stuffed unicorn that defied the laws of physics by simply emerging from the much smaller sack.

"Ho-ho-ho!" he boomed, tossing the cuddly toy high over the people in Cedar Park where it floated comically. He dug into the sack again and again, tossing out dozens of gifts and donations, all the while shouting: "Ho-ho-ho!"

The crowd went wild. One hundred percent belief achieved.

And inside the stomachs of those assembled in Cedar Park, Spangle production went into overdrive. It may surprise people to learn that the stomach is where the magic happens. Perhaps the heart or brain would seem more appropriate, but the tummy is a little understood organ with a lot of complex shenanigans going on in its tubes and compartments. For example, it has a second brain that reacts chemically to external stimulation. We all know we feel fear in our tummies, and it produces certain gases. In the same way, a sudden surge of belief will release a puff of Spangle-infused gas, which generally makes its exit through the belly button.

And so, as Niko tossed out gifts, the tummies of the vigil attendees began to simultaneously gurgle, making a sound like a faraway drum solo, and though most couldn't see it, the Spangles generated by these gurgling tummies rose in sparkling mist strings. The strings spun themselves into a glittering funnel that aimed itself at Niko's heart, skewering him and infusing his every atom with Spangles, which reacted violently with his own polar magic. Niko felt himself rise to the tips of his toes and barely had time to grab hold of Duchess before they were both elevated by the power of a magical twister.

Juniper watched them rise in a beam of light. And it looked as though her friend and fellow Santa was being swept into space by an alien tractor beam.

"It's working," she told Skära, who reared up on his hind legs, honking after Niko. "She's going to be okay."

This was optimistic, to say the least, because healing

was a tricky proposition, and asthma
was a sneaky condition. So maybe
Duchess would be okay, and
maybe Niko would make
things worse.

Inside the sparkling
funnel, Niko and Duchess
revolved slowly. Niko had
one hand support-
ing her back and the
other on her cheek.
He could feel the full
weight of Duchess's
head on his palm, and he
knew she was beyond the
help of normal science. He also
knew that magic was science of
a sort, but the only human
who really understood that
was unconscious in his arms.

Niko sent the Spangles
into Duchess from both palms.

"Come on, Duchess," he said.
"Breathe."

Duchess may have moved her

head, or it may have just flopped with the spinning of the tunnel.

"Breathe, Duchess," said Niko again, and there were tears in his eyes while Duchess's own eyes shone golden as the magic searched her system for something that needed fixing. It seemed to Niko that he was too late. He felt utterly helpless and hopeless.

Not again, please, he begged the universe.

The gray in Duchess's hair turned red, strand by strand, as the magic worked its way into her body, spreading a soothing magical balm along the muscles surrounding her airways.

"I don't know what I'm doing," Niko said to Duchess, both of them spinning slow and weightless. "I've never done this before."

All along Duchess's windpipe, muscles loosened, and the merest wisp of breath snuck through to her lungs. Niko heard it whistle, and it sounded like hope.

"Come on, Duchess," he said. "Breathe."

Her windpipe relaxed another millimeter, and the whistle became a gasp, which Niko matched with a gasp of his own.

"You're doing it, Dutch. You're doing it."

Inside the golden nimbus, Duchess opened her eyes and said: "It's Jo."

The magical swell faded, and Niko sank down to the grass, still cradling Duchess, amid the people who didn't know exactly what was going on other than it was serious and magical. The little girl dressed as an angel began singing the song she'd been practicing for her vigil solo. And somehow, even though the song was totally inappropriate for the situation sentiment-wise, the little girl's unaccompanied warbling voice somehow made a sad situation tragic.

"*Here comes Santa Claus,*" she sang. "*Here comes Santa Claus. Right down Santa Claus Lane.*"

Some others joined in, but most watched events unfold before them as the man they now knew to be Santa Claus himself bent over someone who was obviously very special to him.

Niko laid Duchess on a pile of leaves and smoothed her rich red hair off her face. Then, without looking up, he said: "You make this permanent, Tomescu. If you don't, I'll never come back. Ever."

Niko knew his command of magic had eased Duchess's suffering this time, but he never wanted to see her like that again.

The grumpy elf stepped forward. "And if I do make it permanent, sir?"

Niko didn't promise anything, just shifted away so Tomescu would have room to work.

The elf tapped the arm of his spectacles to activate his communicator and said: "Okay, elves, shut it down."

The elves who had formed a pentangle at various points round the park moved their backpacks to the front of their bodies and twisted the bells on their hats so they glowed either green or red. Then, drawing on the Spangles that continued to flow from the crowd, they activated a Slow Time Bubble with themselves as the cornerstones.

It was both ridiculous and amazing to see. Onlookers didn't really know what was happening until it had already happened. The elves' eyes turned golden as the ambient magic was sucked into their hats, then projected in beams through their bells to meet at an apex overhead. At the contact point, the beams fizzled and spread to form a golden field that distorted the world outside, like a continuous crazy mirror.

The magic seemed to freeze everything outside the field, but if a person was to watch closely for five years or so they might see that the people outside the Slow Time Bubble were in fact moving with aching slowness. The humans inside it immediately fell asleep, and the sound of snoring rose like strange birdsong to bounce off the timboble's skin of surface tension caused by the interaction between magic and air pollution.

For some reason, Dafydd Carnegie kept on singing "Here Comes Santa Claus" even as he slept.

Tomescu, who was not part of the field-generation circuit, knelt beside Duchess.

"How long do we have?" Niko asked him.

"About five minutes in here," replied Tomescu, placing an ear to Duchess's chest, "which will pass in the blink of an eye out there. Even with all the magic you sucked out of these people and the battery packs we brought with us, I wasn't planning on bubbling an entire park."

Niko paced round the comatose Duchess. "Do it then," he said impatiently. "Do it."

Tomescu looked up. "I can't, sir. She's very ill. We need a hospital."

"You don't understand," Niko snapped. "The girl told me Duchess has golden veins."

Tomescu's head popped up. "Golden veins? You're sure?"

"I'm sure," said Niko. "And you're the one who told me what that signifies. I remember now." His head drooped. "I can't believe I missed it."

Tomescu actually tutted. "Please, sir, how could you have known? It was a billion to one against the first human to ever generate Spangles having a magic allergy."

"Just heal her, Tomescu," said Niko.

Tomescu hesitated. "If I do it now, sir," he said, "if I try, then she's magical. It's baked in."

"Baked, broiled, or barbecued," Niko snapped. "I don't care."

"Very well, Mr. Santa Claus," said Tomescu. "Stop breathing down my neck and let me do my job."

Niko took a step back, and the elf got to work.

"And you," Tomescu called, "get out of my light. You're distracting me with all the shadow-throwing."

The "you" in question was Skära, who had performed a standing takeoff from the bandstand and was prancing overhead with Juniper on board, who had been kept awake by her magic.

"Sorry," Juniper called, and brought the reindeer in to land beside Niko. "This is Tomescu, right? The one I see in my Santa memories?" she said, dismounting.

Niko nodded. "This is indeed Tomescu, who more or less runs the North Pole. You led him straight to me and Jo."

"Sorry," said Juniper, but she wasn't. Then she said: "Jo?"

And maybe it was the refracted time bubble light glittering in his eye, but Juniper could have sworn that the famously grumpy Niko Claus was a little teary.

"She told me to call her Jo. I'll need time to get used to that, so Tomescu has to cure her."

Juniper reached up and put a hand on Santa's shoulder, while Skära nuzzled his palm.

"You saved her today."

"Today is not enough," said Niko. "It has to be forever. And, when it comes to magic, I'm the sledgehammer, and Tomescu is the scalpel."

Tomescu, the scalpel of magic, pulled off his pointy hat.

"The damp is making her allergies worse," he said. "I'm not surprised. If the English had a few extra days in the year, they'd fill them with fog."

A bit harsh, Juniper thought, but kept that to herself because this was no time for interrupting.

Tomescu used his hat like a stethoscope, the point to his own ear. "My goodness, it's like Sleeping Beauty's brambles in there. Do you remember that place, sir?"

"Not personally," said Niko. "But I have a vague recollection of one of my predecessors trying to deliver in there. Yuledrøm, you know."

"I know," said Juniper. "I remember it too."

Tomescu froze. "You remember it too?"

Juniper felt guilty, as if she'd stolen her magic. "They're very fuzzy memories."

"We'll discuss this later," said Tomescu, and got back to his work.

He took a piece of what looked like gum from behind his ear and chewed it vigorously. When it was good and malleable, he spat it into one hand and rolled it out on Duchess's torso.

"I told you," Niko whispered. "Scalpel."

Juniper hoped so. She'd just have to trust that the elf had his own secret ways because it looked like he was making a tiny gum pizza on Duchess's chest.

The next step was just as mysterious. Tomescu positioned six candles in the gum and placed a finger on the wick of the largest.

"You, Santa Memories!" he said, snapping his fingers at Juniper. "Closer."

Niko elbowed Juniper. "Step up."

Juniper moved into Tomescu's range, and he placed his palm on her nose.

Juniper felt the magic shift in her tummy like a drowsy cat slowly turning in a sunny patch. It ran up her body, into her face, and through Tomescu's hand. From there, it traveled along the elf's limbs, turning his skin golden. Up one arm and down the other it fizzed, and from Tomescu into the candles, skipping from one wick to the next, lighting a golden flame at the tip of each.

This was surprising, but the most surprising thing was yet to come.

The pizza gum turned transparent. And the skin

inside the ring of candles became transparent too. Or at least this is what Juniper thought initially, but then, when Tomescu dipped his hand directly into Duchess's torso, she realized that Duchess's skin and rib cage had disappeared.

Juniper couldn't help but gasp. "He didn't even wash that hand."

"Magic is a powerful sanitizer right down to the molecular level," Niko assured her.

Tomescu smiled. "Apparently, someone was listening in class after all," he said, and gently began rolling Duchess's muscles between his fingers, coating each one in a golden dust.

"I have never seen lungs so inflamed," he said. "This should calm the tubes down, and that magic dust is in there for good now, sir."

"I know," said Niko. "Baked in—you keep saying—but is she going to be all right?"

Tomescu removed the candles and peeled off the gum.

"All right, sir?" he said. "I'd hardly go to all this trouble for just all right. She's going to be perfect."

"Perfect," said Niko. "Do you hear that, Juniper? Our Duchess is going to be perfect."

"Not unless her rib cage grows back," said Juniper.

"A cynic after your own heart, sir," said Tomescu, and nodded toward Duchess's chest where the skin and bones had already reappeared.

"Perfect," said Juniper, and, to her surprise, Niko smothered her in a hug. Even though his forest coat was extremely coarse and scratchy, Juniper didn't mind because sometimes even the biggest, grumpiest magical being needs a hug, and this was definitely one of those times.

Duchess woke up a few seconds later, and it was not the kind of slow, groggy awakening one might expect from a post-major-operation patient. She was immediately fully alert and lucid.

"It worked," she said. "You did it, Niko. I'm fine."

Niko helped her up from the cold ground. "More than fine," he said. "Perfect."

"I don't know about that," said Duchess, then hugged Niko tight and kissed him all over his face.

"Is Santa your boyfriend now?" asked Juniper.

Niko laughed. Actually laughed. And Juniper was pretty sure this was the first genuine laugh she had heard from his mouth.

"I should think I am. After all this. Not many boyfriends can stop time for their girl."

Tomescu stepped in. "Technically, sir, I, Tomescu, did the stopping and the healing. You provided the brute force, and I focused it. You were the mighty river, and I was the dam. You were the pot of thick, gloopy paint, and I was the artist. You were the bucket of manure, and I was the mechanical spreader."

Juniper giggled. "I like the manure one. Is that a metaphor, Duchess?"

"It's more like a thinly veiled insult," she said, turning to Tomescu. "I suppose I should thank you too, Tomescu."

Tomescu performed a traditional elfin greeting routine. He twiddled both ends of his pencil mustache, spread his arms wide, and bowed.

"It is a pleasure and an honor, Professor Josephine Spangles," he said. "You're the only person to ever get close to figuring out how the magic works. So I am delighted that you're joining our ranks."

Duchess thought about this. "If I'm joining your ranks, that means you baked the magic in."

"Exactly, Professor," said Tomescu.

"So you must have performed some sort of open-chest surgery, using concentrated Spangles to phase-shift my rib cage."

"That's exactly what I did," said Tomescu.

"And then injected concentrated Spangles to overcome my allergy. A bit like using venom to build up resistance to a snakebite."

The elf's eyes twinkled. "It's one of the few situations where magic can effect a major healing. It's so nice to have someone who understands the craft."

"Craft," said Duchess, grasping Tomescu's hand. "What you did is so much more than craft. It's miraculous. Thank you."

Niko pretended to be miffed. "Duchess. Jo. I'm your boyfriend, remember?"

Duchess smiled. "Let's leave labels out of it for now and just see where the love takes us."

"Love," said Niko. "Okay."

23

The Next Generation

Once everyone was safely inside the Mews cottage, Tomescu collapsed the Slow Time Bubble and shut the door behind him. Outside in the park, the vigilers did that kind of jerky, surprised wake-up that a person does if they fall asleep sitting on the sofa or in an airplane. They laughed or scowled, depending on their usual waking mood, and then got on with celebrating Santa Claus and wishing he'd go back to work. Little did they know that an elf called Tomescu fully intended to make sure this wish came true once he'd cleared up a few issues.

"It's like this," Tomescu told the packed sitting room. "Spangles, as Josephine christened them, are a finite resource, and even though there is a Spangle cycle that sees quite a lot of recycling, supplies are dwindling, and we need

Niko back in the saddle again, so to speak, if we're to boost the earth's supply. Simply put, the more belief and hope we have in the world, the more magic is generated, which is good for everyone, even Duchess now."

Duchess knew why. "Even me because I don't have Spangilitis anymore."

"Precisely," said Tomescu. "You were deathly allergic to magical particles. I never saw such inflammation. I think you were probably technically dead for a minute."

Juniper's mum was nodding along with this as if it wasn't at all unusual to have an elf taking about magic particles in her kitchen.

Duchess gathered her hair back in a ponytail. "My chest problems began after my big demonstration, and grew much worse when Niko came into my life and then Juniper was activated."

"That makes sense," said Tomescu. "Some human bodies are not compatible with magic. It's extremely rare, but it happens. Usually, it's no big deal. A couple of sneezes and at most swollen eyes, but Duchess found a way to generate pure magic, and her system couldn't take it."

"But now?" prompted Niko.

"But now Professor Spangles will be fine, providing she takes regular therapeutic dips in the polar springs."

"We can do that," said Niko. "Travel up in the sleigh a few times a year. It'll be nice to see everyone."

Duchess dried her eyes. "No, Niko. You have to go back."

"Also that's the North Pole sleigh," said Tomescu. "My boys are packing it up as we speak along with all of the reindeer including that scamp Skära."

"I can't go back," said Niko. "I made a promise, and I have work to do here."

Juniper piped up. "We can do that. Mum and me. We're already doing it. It would be easier if I had Skära."

Tomescu wouldn't hear of it. "Skära is the Gift Giver this year. He drew a letter. That calf saved the sack, which saved Christmas."

"I can help around here," said Dafydd Carnegie, who hadn't spoken till then, still a bit groggy after his time-bubble snooze. "The new me is up for all sorts of positive action."

Jennifer Lane shook her head. "I can*not* get used to this nice-guy bit."

"It's nothing, madam. I am reborn thanks to my best friend, Santa Claus."

Tomescu pointed at Juniper. "No helping with good works here for you, missy. You're coming to the North Pole.

I'm looking at the next generation's Santa right in front of me. You need proper training. I already have two elves scrubbing the internet because of you. Because of you, Niko was inside the sack."

That was so astonishing to Tomescu that he said it again, this time with more incredulity.

"*Inside the sack.* You could have ended up as dark matter, Niko, which cannot be observed directly, although it's no picnic observing you directly at the moment."

Duchess was the only one to get this science joke and laughed softly.

"That's another reason I left, Tomescu," said Niko. "Cracks like that."

Tomescu bowed. "I apologize," he said. "No more science jokes."

"Niko saw Sarika in the Santa sack," said Juniper.

Duchess took Niko's hand. "And what did Sarika say about all of this?"

"She said that I should go back to work," admitted Niko, "and that I should love you with all my heart."

"I think Sarika was a smart cookie," said Duchess.

Then Tomescu nearly ruined it by saying, "Of course, it more than likely wasn't actually Sarika. It was probably a rendering of her based on Niko's own projected memories and interpretations. In essence, Niko already knew what to do. He just needed someone he trusted to tell him."

Even Juniper realized that Tomescu was talking too much.

"Would anyone like some tea?" she asked. "Everyone says I make a good cup of tea."

It turned out that everyone would like tea. Especially when Jennifer revealed there was a tin of cake in the sweets cupboard.

The Lane girls huddled together in the galley kitchen, Juniper's arm round Jennifer's waist.

"I need to hear the story of your tattoos and blond hair," said Juniper, and giggled. The first giggle since realizing her mum was missing that reached all the way to her heart.

Jennifer turned the kettle off at the socket because the automatic switch was broken.

"We need to continue Niko's work, and Briar's too. From now on, this park becomes a haven for people in need. Agreed?"

"Agreed, Mum," said Juniper. "Does that mean I'm not going to the North Pole?"

"Over my . . ." began Jennifer, then switched to a gentler phrase. "Not right now, Junie. Let's at least get you through school. It will take me that long to process everything. And let me tell you something: If you're going anywhere before the age of a hundred, then I'm coming with you."

Juniper nestled tighter against her mother. "Definitely. We're the Lane girls."

Jennifer laughed.

"What's funny?" asked her daughter.

"If you take over Niko's job, then you'll be Santa Claus Lane."

Which was a good one and set Juniper singing:

"Here comes Santa Claus,
Here comes Santa Claus . . ."

And then her mother joined in:

"Right down Santa Claus Lane . . ."

They sang this a few times and then switched to another song when Jennifer bent over and presented her nose.

"Jennifer," sang Juniper, tweaking her mum's nose.

"Juniper," responded Jennifer, tapping her magical daughter's button nose.

Then they hugged and cried for a full minute, until Jennifer realized that there was not, in fact, any cherry cake in the tin, and that set her off crying again.

Epilogue the First

Niko and Duchess did go with Tomescu to the North Pole after the chief elf promised to adjust his snarky attitude a bit. It helped Tomescu's mood a lot that Duchess understood quite a lot of what he was talking about and even had a few ideas of her own. The elves started up an outreach program that focused on the world's housing problem and put the nodboks plans up on the internet so that the shelters could be clamped to trees all around the world. They could never solve the problem on their own, but at least they could highlight it to governments everywhere.

Niko returned to his old job as Santa Claus with Duchess on the sleigh bench beside him. Never again would he leave his beloved at home while he rode the tïmboble, and now that Duchess's Spangilitis was under control she proved to be his equal on the Christmas Eve run and designed a new route that shaved months off the flight time. They also included a donation box on the Christmas letter that could be ticked by children who felt they had enough stuff already and would like to donate their gift to a worthy cause. To Niko's surprise, this option proved hugely popular, and he had to rethink his opinion that modern first-world children were all totally self-absorbed and materialistic.

On their first Christmas Eve on the sleigh together, Niko produced a big ice-diamond ring and proposed to Duchess. She said she'd think about it and proceeded to do so for four seconds before saying yes.

Epilogue the Second

Dafydd Carnegie was as good as his word and launched himself and his new personality into helping to make Cedar Park, and indeed all the parks under his jurisdiction, into welcoming places for anyone and everyone who cared to visit. He became Jennifer Lane's right-hand man, even though technically he was her boss. Between them both, they raised enough funds to set up the Briar Lane Shelter, which could provide hot meals for over two hundred people a day and shelter for twenty.

When the mayor objected to this and attempted to fire Carnegie, Dafydd ran against him in the next election with the slogan: *Dafydd Carnegie Is Reviewing the Situation*, and won by a landslide. One of his first acts as mayor was to inaugurate the annual Mayor Carnegie Benefit Concert for People in Need, which featured a stellar lineup of West End stars, all of whom duetted with Dafydd himself.

Epilogue the Third

Miss Trude Madden was never caught by the Met police, though there has been a warrant out for her arrest since the day the press refer to as "the Sparks in the Park." Trude had woken up on the grass with a sore jaw to find that some weird combination of magic and dew had completely destroyed her quiff, and she could never quite get the same volume again, no matter how much product she used.

Trude mingled with the other dazed civilians wandering around and went straight to the tube station to retrieve a go bag that she always kept in a locker there. It didn't take more than a few phone calls to find out that Lar and his boys had been rounded up by the police in the Kilburn yard, which unfortunately had been brimful of stolen goods. She had no illusions that they would keep their mouths shut regarding her role in the gang, and so she decided to adopt one of the new identities in her go bag and start again in Edinburgh. Her boys should do no more than eighteen months in jail, and then she could put the gang back together. And when that happened their first job would be the same as the last job they'd tried to pull: steal Santy's sack.

Next time, she'd pack her bum bag with earplugs and weapons, and there would be no escape for the infuriating Juniper Lane.

The Fourth and Final Epilogue

Some days after the Sparks in the Park episode, Juniper was lying on her bed, working on a homework assignment, when she sat up straight for no particular reason.

What is it? she wondered. *Why am I so twitchy all of a sudden?*

This question was answered by a double honk from outside the room. Juniper was so eager to get onto the roof that it took her several seconds to fumble open the window.

Prancing around in excited circles on the flat roof was Skära.

The reindeer honked again, and Juniper was so glad to see her partner that she honked back.

They dance-hugged for a long moment before Juniper noticed a gift card tied to the reindeer's antlers, which were several centimeters longer than they had been.

The note read:

Take care of this fellow and stay off the radar.
Your friend,
NIKO
(The current Santa Claus—AT LEAST UNTIL
YOU ARE READY!)
PS: You can recruit one honorary elf.

I bet Tomescu doesn't know about this, Juniper thought, but there was such an overflow of happiness in her heart that she couldn't worry about the elf's reaction right now.

"Can we go for a night flight, partner?" she asked the reindeer. "I need to fly over to my friend Jade's house and recruit her as my honorary elf. Do you think we could do that?"

Skära's honk was affirmative.

Of course they could.

Acknowledgments

Eoin would like to thank the wonderful team at Macmillan for their warm welcome to the fold.

About the Author

Eoin Colfer is the bestselling author of the children's fantasy series Artemis Fowl. His other notable works include *The Dog Who Lost His Bark*, illustrated by P. J. Lynch, and the novels *Half Moon Investigations*, *Airman*, and *The Supernaturalist*. The recipient of many awards, he lives in Ireland.

eoincolfer.com